MAQ

MEN'S ADVENTURE QUARTERLY
ISSUE 8

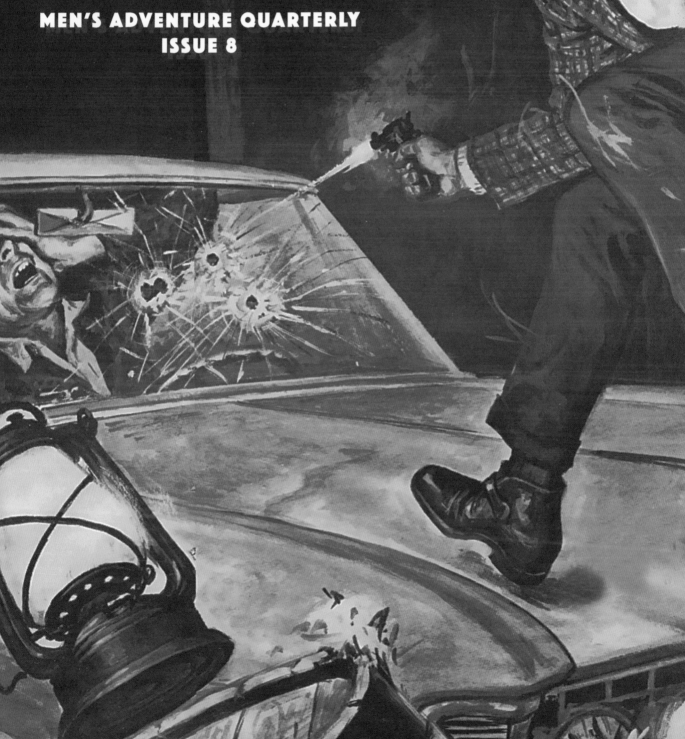

C000131373

INSIDE FRONT COVER: Art by Earl Norem from **MEN**, Jan 1972. for "Vegas Mad-Dog Heisters." a "Book Bonus" version of **LEMONS NEVER LIE** by Richard Stark (Donald Westlake). **THIS SPREAD:** Artwork by Bruce Minney from a "Book Bonus" version of **3 DAYS OF THE CONDOR** in **STAG** October 1975 that also shows still photos from the movie.

MEN'S ADVENTURE QUARTERLY is the only magazine dedicated to reprinting and discussing stories, artwork, articles, and photographs from men's adventure magazines published in the 1950s, 1960s and 1970s. All contents are either in the public domain to the best of our knowledge or included through reprint agreements made with the original creators or their heirs or estates.

If you have comments or questions about the content of the **MAQ**, or if you believe and can verify that something infringes on an existing copyright you hold, please email us at **MAQeditor@gmail.com.**

Editor & Publisher
Robert "Bob" Deis

Editor & Graphic Designer
Bill Cunningham

Contact Us:
MAQeditor@gmail.com

A Pulp 2.0 Design by Bill Cunningham
Twitter: @madpulpbastard
Facebook: Facebook.com/pulp2ohpress
www.pulp2ohpress.com

MEN'S ADVENTURE QUARTERLY No.8 is copyright © 2023 by Subtropic Productions, LLC. All rights reserved.

This issue of the **MEN'S ADVENTURE QUARTERLY** is a milestone of sorts.

My co-editor Bill Cunningham and I launched the **MAQ** a little over two years ago. We have now produced and published eight issues—two sets of four per year.

I admit I was being a little overly optimistic when I picked the word "quarterly" for the title. I've never published a magazine and didn't fully comprehend how much time would be involved in creating an issue. So, we haven't kept to a strict schedule, but we're not too far off from publishing an issue every three months.

This last few months have been especially busy for Bill and me. We both have our own separate publishing projects in addition to the **MAQ**.

For example, Bill recently published the first book in his **TOM CORBETT SPACE CADET** series. He also did cover designs for a number of cool publications, including great issues of fanzine Grandmaster Justin Marriott's **PAPERBACK FANATIC** and **BATTLING BRITONS** fanzines, and Steve Holland expert Michael Stradford's third book about the world's most recognizable illustration art model, **STEVE HOLLAND: PAPERBACK HERO.**

Meanwhile, Bill and I worked with the legendary illustration artist Ron Lesser and vintage paperback maven J. Kingston Pierce to produce and publish the lavishly illustrated book **THE ART**

OF RON LESSER, VOL. 1: DEADLY DAMES AND SEXY SIRENS. It's the first in a series of books we're doing about the paperback, movie poster and magazine artwork Ron has done during his six decade long career.

The hardcover edition of the Lesser book was released in late May. We plan to publish a paperback edition in this fall. The second and third volumes of our books showcasing Ron Lesser's artwork will be published in the Fall of 2024.

By coincidence, the same week the hardcover edition of Lesser Vol. 1 was listed on Amazon worldwide, another book I've been working on was released. That book, **THE NAKED AND THE DEADLY: LAWRENCE BLOCK IN MEN'S ADVENTURE MAGAZINES**, collects stories by the world famous author Lawrence Block that appeared in men's adventure magazines in the 1950s and 1960s. It's the 14th book in the Men's Adventure Library series I co-edit with Wyatt Doyle, head of the NewTexture.com indie publishing company.

The Block book comes in paperback and a deluxe, expanded, lushly illustrated hardcover editions. You can also get a copy signed by Block himself via www.BlockNaked.com.

In my "spare time" I'm working with Wyatt on a book of "Weird Tales" style stories from men's adventure mags that we'll debut at PulpFest 2023 in August.

I'm also working with Bill on **MEN'S ADVENTURE QUARTERLY** #9, the "Croc Attack" issue. Yep, MAQ #9 will feature classic MAM crocodile attack stories and artwork. That issue

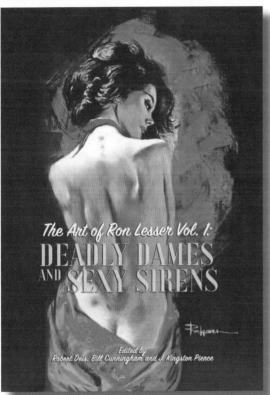

The Art of Ron Lesser Vol. 1:
DEADLY DAMES AND SEXY SIRENS

Edited by
Robert Deis, Bill Cunningham and J. Kingston Pierce

THE **NAKED** AND THE **DEADLY**

Lawrence BLOCK

in men's adventure magazines

EDITED BY **ROBERT DEIS & WYATT DOYLE**

ROBERT "BOB" DEIS

Co-Editor of the
MEN'S ADVENTURE QUARTERLY and
Co-Editor, with Wyatt Doyle, of the Men's Adventure Library book series. He owns one of the largest collections of vintage men's adventure magazine in the world and is an internationally recognized expert on the MAM genre. He's the Admin of the Men's Adventure Magazines & Books Facebook page and the MensPulpMags.com blog, where he keeps MAM fans updated about his forthcoming books and MAQ issues. He and Bill Cunningham also manage the Men's Adventure Quarterly Brigade Facebook group.

will also include an exclusive article about Australian men's adventure magazines by pulp culture historian Andrew Nette, whose latest books include **HORWITZ PUBLICATIONS: PULP FICTION AND THE RISE OF THE AUSTRALIAN PAPERBACK** and the crime thriller novel **ORPHAN ROAD.**

In addition, MAQ #9 will have an article about classic croc attack movies written by retromedia maven and author John Harrison. John is a regular contributor to the magazine **CINEMA OF THE '80s** and author of **HIP POCKET SLEAZE: THE LURID WORLD OF VINTAGE ADULT PAPERBACKS**, a must have book for fans of vintage PBs.

OPPOSITE, TOP TO BOTTOM: *TOM CORBETT SPACE CADET, PAPERBACK FANATIC 46, BATTLING BRITONS 5,* and *PAPERBACK HERO.* THIS PAGE: The just-released *THE ART OF RON LESSER VOL. 1* and the hardcover edition of *THE NAKED AND THE DEADLY,* an anthology of Lawrence Block's MAM fiction.

The *MAQ* issue you're reading now showcases some of my favorite stories about hit men and hit women from the men's adventure mags in my collection. I'd say it's our best issue yet, but I think that about every issue. I'm very proud of all of them. And, I'm stoked by the positive reviews we've received from many people Bill and I admire and respect. Here's are a few examples:

"I've run out of superlatives to describe just how good MEN'S ADVENTURE QUARTERLY is. If you're interested in the men's adventure magazines, beautiful art, and stories that are a real window into another era, I give this issue and all the previous ones my highest recommendation."
   - James Reasoner
   Award winning-novelist and founder of Rough Edges Press

"I was caught off-guard by the absolutely stunning quality of the magazine—from its striking visual layout, to its informative editorial content, to the stories themselves. This is top notch specialty publishing at its finest."
   - Paul Bishop
   Writer, pulp maven, and host of the Six-Gun Justice Podcast

"Bravo gentlemen, you're on a streak to the benefit of all pulp fans, old and new. Thank you so very, very much."
   - Ron Fortier
   Legendary comics writer, novelist, and founder of Airship 27 books

Those are just some of the glowing reviews we've received on the first eight issues of the MAQ. Feedback like that definitely encourages us to keep going.

If you want us to continue publishing the MAQ, you can help make sure that happens by writing your own reviews on Amazon or your favorite social media platforms—and by buying any back issues you haven't read yet. They're all available on Amazon worldwide.

If you're in the US, you can also get MAQ copies directly from me with free shipping via the online bookstore connected to my MensPulpMags.com website. Elsewhere in the world, using Amazon is your best bet, so the postage costs are reasonable.

If you have comments on questions about the MAQ, shoot us an email (MAQEditor@gmail.com) or join our Facebook group, the *Men's Adventure Quarterly Brigade* and post some comments there. We love hearing positive feedback, suggestions and well-intended constructive criticism.

If you have negative things to say, keep in mind that we've been studying stories about hit men.

• • •

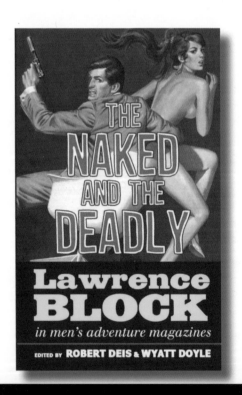

The paperback edition of *THE NAKED AND THE DEADLY: LAWRENCE BLOCK IN MEN'S ADVENTURE MAGAZINES* features cover art by Bruce Minney, used for one of the MAM stories in the book.

FROM THE CREATOR OF THE S. AMERICAN JAMES BOND 007 COMIC SERIES COMES A ROUGHER, TOUGHER SORT OF SPY WHO LIVES UP TO HIS CODENAME — *KILLER!*

IN ENGLISH FOR THE 1ST TIME!

PULP 2.0

KILLER

BASED ON THE HIT INTERNATIONAL COMIC BOOK SERIES CREATED BY Germàn Gabler

He aims
to please.

MGM presents "HIT MAN" Starring BERNIE CASEY · Co-starring PAMELA GRIER
Screenplay by GEORGE ARMITAGE · Based Upon the Novel "Jack's Return Home" by TED LEWIS
Produced by GENE CORMAN · Directed by GEORGE ARMITAGE
[R] RESTRICTED ⊖⊙⊖   METROCOLOR   MGM

SHARKY'S MACHINE, REVENGE OF THE NERDS), 70s superstar Pam Grier (*COFFY, JACKIE BROWN, FRIDAY FOSTER*) and TV's favorite chopper pilot Roger Moseley (*MAGNUM, P.I.*) went on to box office rentals of $1.19 million based on what was surely a much lower-budgeted production of just several hundred thousand dollars. This strategy is precisely what producer Gene Corman (brother of B-movie exploitation maestro Roger Corman) and studio MGM had intended from the start. Let's just say that if "imitation is the sincerest form of flattery" then *HIT MAN* is a double-barreled love letter to its English cousin… *GET CARTER*.

That story – how a low budgeted blaxploitation crime action picture partially set in Watts, California (the scene of the now infamous 1965 Watts Riots) came to be – is one that touches on our pulp culture, on the business practices of the movie studios, and has origins around the globe. What is *HIT MAN*'s relationship to *GET CARTER*, a British film that set the tone for many British gangster and crime films to come? The truth is always stranger than fiction, and to get to the truth we have to go back to the beginning – the book *JACK'S RETURN HOME* by Ted Lewis.

TIME: 1970
LOCATION: THE UNITED KINGDOM

Alfred Edward, "Ted" Lewis was born in

The blaxploitation motion picture *HITMAN* debuted in 1972 to a condemnation by the National Legion of Decency, which stated that its "dizzying spectacle of raw sex and supergraphic violence would horrify the Marquis de Sade". Despite this censure by the Catholic church (or perhaps because of it), the movie starring Bernie Casey (*GUNS OF THE MAGNIFICENT 7,*

TOP LEFT: The 1972 US release poster for MGM's HIT MAN, a movie designed to appeal to the burgeoning Black audience across the country. **RIGHT:** Star Bernie Casey as Tyrone Tackett, an enforcer visiting LA to discover who killed his brother. The story is based on the UK crime thriller GET CARTER starring Michael Caine.

BILL CUNNINGHAM

Author, graphic designer, and producer of "pulp media." Pulp 2.0, his graphic design and publishing company designs for publications including *BATTLING BRIT-ONS, PAPERBACK FANTASTIC, MEN OF VIOLENCE* and *STEVE HOLLAND: THE WORLD'S GREAT-EST ILLUSTRATION ART MODEL.* Besides co-editing the *MEN'S ADVENTURE QUARTERLY* with Bob Deis, he edits the *MEN'S ADVENTURE READER* and imports and translates international pulp comics for English-speaking audiences, and redesigns and republishes classics such as the *TOM CORBETT SPACE CADET* series of books.

THE BLAXPLOITATION REMAKE OF A BRITISH CRIME CLASSIC

Stretford, Manchester in 1940 to a strict, working-class upbringing. His parents didn't encourage any sort of creative endeavors such as art or writing, but a teacher early on recognized Ted's talents in this area. Eventually they were persuaded to allow Ted to attend the Hull Art School.

Working his way through school, Lewis graduated and moved to London where he worked in advertising and animation including The Beatles' movie *YELLOW SUBMARINE*. By 1965 he had completed his first novel *ALL THE WAY HOME AND ALL THE NIGHT THROUGH*. His follow up novel, *JACK'S RETURN HOME*, was published in 1970 and launched what has become known as the "Noir School of British Crime Writing." Gone were the larger-than-life charismatic characters of the British "Cozy" mystery or the outrageousness of the Ian Fleming 007 spy novels. Lewis replaced that with hard, working-class criminals just as explosive and ruthless as the weapons they employed. This radical perspective propelled Lewis to the best-seller list in the UK.

JACK'S RETURN HOME tells the story of Jack Carter, an amoral, pitiless London mob enforcer who returns to his hometown in the North to investigate the suspicious death of his estranged brother. Jack's arrival in his former home town causes unease among the local crime families, who don't want his prying to interfere with their criminal operations. Everything from not-so-subtle hints to outright violence is used to try to get Jack to leave, but he doggedly refuses, employing the same gangster bullying he's famous for to dig out the truth, all leading to a violent and ambiguous conclusion.

TIME: STILL 1970
LOCATION: STILL THE UNITED KINGDOM

The story was fresh, exciting, and amoral as hell. It was exactly what rotund, cigar-chomping Producer Michael Klinger was looking for and he optioned

TOP LEFT AND DOWN: Author Ted Lewis on set typing away. Michael Caine on the prowl for the men who killed his brother. Caine with actress Geraldine Moffat who eventually gets the boot. The 1st UK edition of JACK'S RETURN HOME which spawned three separate movies over as many decades.
OPPOSITE CENTER: UK Producer Michael Klinger who saw Lewis's novel and realized that it would make a terrific UK crime movie.

JACK'S RETURN HOME. He had been looking for a property to bring to cinemas following the conviction of the notorious British gangsters, The Kray Twins, and the late 60s relaxation of the very restrictive British film censorship laws. The public was immersed in the darkness of crime and Klinger wanted to be the producer to deliver on it. Author Andrew Spicer of *THE CREATIVE PRODUCER – THE MICHAEL KLINGER PAPERS* has written that *"he [Klinger] sensed its potential to imbue the British crime thriller with the realism and violence of its American counterparts."*

This underworld was not new territory for the veteran producer as Klinger began his career in cinema by his ownership of two Soho strip clubs, the *Nell Gwynn* and the *Gargoyle* – that were used for promotional events such as the Miss Cinema Competition and by film entrepreneurs such as James Carreras the founder of Hammer Films. Klinger used his status and contacts to form an alliance with a fellow Jewish East Ender Tony Tenser, who worked in publicity for a film distri-

bution company, Miracle Films. His partnership with Tenser under the banner, Tekli, led to producing such exploitation fare as including *THE YELLOW TEDDYBEARS* (1963)*, THE PLEASURE GIRLS* (1965) *LONDON IN THE RAW* (1964) and *PRIMITIVE LONDON* (1965). This later led to Klinger financing *REPULSION* (1965) when director Roman Polanski couldn't find financing.

Despite his cigar-chomping almost parody behavior as a producer, Klinger was sharp. He had a pho-

tographic memory, a focused intelligence and a drive to cultivate the same. All of this gave Klinger an ability to focus on markets and see opportunities to fill the needs of the populist movie-going public. This includes the low budget sexploitation film series *CONFESSIONS OF…* (five films between 1974-78), and challenging crime thrillers, *SOMETHING TO HIDE* (1972), *TOMORROW NEVER COMES* (1978) and *BLOOD RELATIVES* (1978). All while producing big-budget action-adventure films such as *GOLD* (1974) and *SHOUT AT THE DEVIL* (1976) – aimed at the international market with marquee name Roger Moore as the lead in both along with several American stars.

Klinger hired TV documentary director Mike Hodges to write and direct *GET CARTER.* Klinger secured financing from MGM Borehamwood which was a British subsidiary of MGM used to finance and more importantly take advantage of tax subsidies in the UK. MGM was getting out of the UK and *GET CARTER* would be the last project approved by the studio for production. Initially Hodges wanted for *THE AVENGERS* TV star Ian Hendry to play Carter but was surprised by Klinger that Michael Caine was going to play the British hitman. Caine came aboard acting as a co-producer and lending that same working-class attitude he had developed in *ALFIE* (1966) and *THE IPCRESS FILE* (1965). In a later interview Caine remarked, "One of the reasons I wanted to make that picture was my background. In English movies, gangsters were either stupid or funny. I wanted to show that they're neither. Gangsters are not stupid, and they're certainly not very funny."

The production took a hurried pace, going from optioned novel to finished film in 8 months. Director Hodges worked closely with Caine sharpening dialogue, scouting real locations around Newcastle upon Tyne, and developing the realistic look of the film with cinematographer Wolfgang Suschitzky who worked on documentaries with Hodges. MGM now had a gangster movie unlike any other British gangster movie.

Critics in the UK weren't kind – though they begrudgingly gave Hodges points for realism, and Caine points for acting - they couldn't see past the movie's violence and Carter's nihilistic approach. American critics embraced *GET CARTER* more warmly, but MGM, caught in the midst of a financial crisis, didn't go wide with the movie's release, and relegated it to grindhouses and drive-ins across the US and Canada. It seems they had another plan in mind. One that they had also put into place for another film in their library…

In 1949, W.R. "William Riley" Burnett wrote *THE ASPHALT JUNGLE*, a crime novel chronicling a jewel heist in a midwestern city. Hot on the novel's heels, Academy Award-winning director John Huston (*THE MALTESE FALCON, TREASURE OF THE SIERRA MADRE*) tackled the movie version. The 1950 film starred Sterling Hayden and Louis Calhern, and features Jean Hagen, James Whitmore, Sam Jaffe, and John McIntire. Marilyn Monroe also appears, in one of her earliest roles. The film was nominated for four Academy Awards.

But the studio's relationship with *THE ASPHALT JUNGLE* didn't stop there.

In 1958, the studio remade *ASPHALT* as *THE BADLANDERS*, replacing the midwestern modern setting with an 1898 western setting. Directed by Delmer Daves and starring Alan Ladd and Ernest Borgnine, the film was shot near Kingman, AZ and made a modest profit for the studio.

In 1971, In a true-to-form, let's-make-a profit style,

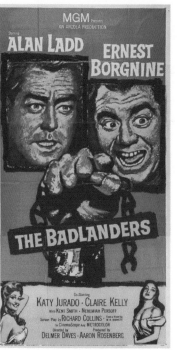

MGM decided to remake *ASPHALT JUNGLE* yet again utilizing the producing services of Gene Corman who had experience delivering "large" looking pictures on a reasonable budget. They contracted with him to remake *ASPHALT* under the new title *COOL BREEZE* aimed specifically at the burgeoning black, urban market and drive-ins. Apparently they were having success with *GET CARTER* at these theater syndicates. And that's what MGM needed most of all – low budget successes.

Now whether it was Corman who approached MGM, or vice-versa, Corman then got his hands on the *GET CARTER* script… and that's when and where *HIT MAN* was born.

Like its predecessor, *HIT MAN* was rushed into production. Corman engaged the services of director George Armitage (TV's *PEYTON PLACE, GAS-S-S-S, PRIVATE DUTY NURSES*) who had worked as a screenwriter, actor, and director for his brother Roger Corman. Gene and Roger had met Armitage previously on the 20th Century Fox studio lot while

they were producing **THE ST. VALENTINE'S DAY MASSACRE** (1967). In the April 2015 issue of **FILM COMMENT**, Armitage said,

> "The commissary was a place called the 'Gold Room' where the producers would go. They were all sort of mothballed, but they still had energy enough to snob the television people, who were making **HIGH NOON, LOST IN SPACE, BATMAN**. The movie producers would sit on

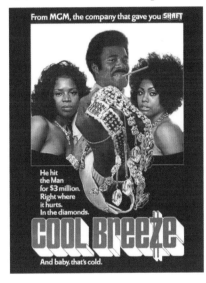

> the other side of the room from the TV people. This left the TV people with nobody else to snob, so they would snob Roger Corman... And that really pissed me off, because I was a fan of his. So I began to visit him on the set and the whole thing, and told him about the conflict that was going on, and he got a kick out of that."

Upon hearing what Corman wanted to do, Armitage was enthusiastic about rewriting the script, but felt that a black director should helm the movie and campaigned Corman for star Bernie Casey to direct,

feeling it would be more authentic. Corman said the studio wouldn't do it with a first-time director.

NOTE: this may or may not have been entirely accurate, and one must point out that **COOL BREEZE** was written and directed by white director Barry Pollack; a fact pointed out by **THE NEW YORK TIMES** in its review:

> "From MGM, the company that gave you **'GONE WITH THE WIND,'** there now comes **'COOL BREEZE,'** a mostly black remake of **'THE ASPHALT JUNGLE'**—also given you by MGM. Actually, the quality of blackness is somewhat strained, embracing as it does much of the cast, and most of the attitudes, and virtually all the ad campaign—but none of the major technical credits, including Gene Corman as producer and Barry Pollack, who directed and wrote the screenplay."

In any case, Armitage sat down to write the script, but worked with the African-American cast to make it all sound authentic to the location: South Central Los Angeles. After he turned in his draft to Corman, only then did Armitage learn the script he was given sans title was, in fact, **GET CARTER.**

In this case, **HIT MAN** is of course, enforcer Tyrone Tackett (Bernie Casey) who comes home to southern California from Oakland for the funeral of his brother Cornell. Cornell left behind his wild daughter Rochelle (Candy All), who rejects Tyrone's offer to live with him. Tyrone befriends his late brother's business partner, Sherwood Epps (Sam Laws), and stays in town to investigate his brother's death. He is threatened by

ABOVE: Actor Bernie Casey in the iconic pose that was used for the poster and many of the promotional images for the movie. When compared to Michael Caine's rather calm, staid imagery for *GET CARTER*, the differences between the two films are apparent despite their coming from the same source material, Ted Lewis's pulp novel *JACK RETURNS HOME*.

gangsters who tell him to leave town which spurs him on to discover the truth behind his brother's death.

The locations for **HIT MAN** are entirely dissimilar to **CARTER** in that Armitage and the production mixed in Sunset Boulevard nightlife utilizing the Colonial Motel on Sunset as a set piece for much of the action as well as a Porno theater/shop. South Central LA was filmed for the funeral home and Cornell's house, and downtown LA locations for the building site of the grand theater. The airport in the split screen opening sequence appears to be the Burbank airport with exteriors of LAX. All of these locations paint a decidedly different experience than the North of England. More colorful, filled with neon and sunshine – but nonetheless just as dangerous.

These locations are reinforced by the cinematographer, Andrew Davis, who went on to become the writer and director of several hit movies (sorry for the pun) including **CODE OF SILENCE, ABOVE THE LAW, UNDER SIEGE**, and **THE FUGITIVE**. His work here is not as "documentary" as **GET CARTER**, but shows the formation of a filmmaker at the beginning of his career, employing as much craft as the budget would allow.

In the opening title sequence, we find Tyrone Tackett amongst the crowds at the airport. His burgundy wine-colored suit and hat making himself a target for the gangsters who want him to head back home to Oakland and get back to the lady he's having an affair with – a pornstar who works for a "film producer" there in the Bay area. Since the SF Bay area was then known as a "capital" of the US porn industry (before it was moved down to the San Fernando Valley in Los Angeles). The implication is clear: go back North to your dirty business there and leave us characters alone. Armitage and music composer H.B. Barnum reinforce this theme with the timely signature opening song, *"Hitman, Hitman - what you gonna do about the sit-u-a-tion?"*

All of this reinforces the premise found in the original Lewis novel – *none of these people are untouched by crime.* Some revel in it. Some tolerate it. But everyone, especially the exceptional Pam Grier as Gozelda is affected by it. Crime colors their perceptions. It's only when Tyrone Tackett, a man who is also affected by crime, digs deep enough that he understands where the line between good and evil, between predator and prey, lies. That's when he explodes into action and brings the whole house down. It's a revelation that comes to him and the audience as a surprise occuring in a movie theater. Tyrone is suddenly aware he is surrounded by darkness – including Pam Grier – and it has cost him and his family dearly. (I'm not going to spoil it for you if you haven't seen **GET CARTER** or **HIT MAN**). When he drags Gozelda out into the light of day and gets the final details… it's on.

As one can imagine, Tyrone Tackett then orchestrates his revenge, which in light of everything we've seen is not revenge, but more like justice. He brings the entire criminal empire down around them by turning the factions against one another. He personalizes each "kill" he makes. As he takes his final revenge against the one that actually killed his brother, Tackett has his revenge turned back on himself:

FROM TOP:

Director **GEORGE ARMITAGE** didn't feel that he should be the one directing the movie. Bernie Casey should.

Producer **GENE CORMAN** told him however that MGM wouldn't do that.

Lead Actor **BERNIE CASEY** told Armitage to go ahead and direct and rallied the cast to add the proper black slang to the script.

Actress **CANDY ALL** was onscreen briefly but made a huge impact. The actress also appeared in **FRIDAY FOSTER** (1975) and **THE SWINGING CHEERLEADERS** (1974).

Nano Zito did!
(beat)
You know how mighty 'whitey' is...
he set me up!

They continue the exchange a bit then Shag echoes the Confucious proverb: "Seek revenge and you should dig two graves, one for yourself" However in this case, despite the near identical blood-soaked ending to **GET CARTER**, there is room for a sequel... which is probably exactly how MGM wanted it.
(I'm not going to spoil it for you so go watch the movie - It's on Amazon).

HIT MAN isn't a perfect film, but it is a slice of the time period, and the perfect sort of blood-soaked revenge tale that makes it a hit with MAM readers. In fact, MGM should have remade **HIT MAN** instead of producing the 2000 **GET CARTER** remake with Sylvester Stallone.

•••

SHAG:
What are you killing me for?! How many sixteen-year-olds did you pull for the Biggs Brothers? You know they had fathers and brothers too!

TYRONE:
You ain't dead for pullin' her motherfucka! You killed her! My brother too!

SHAG:
NO! NO! I didn't kill him!

A BLAXPLOITATION FILMOGRAPHY OF

PAM GRIER

BEYOND THE VALLEY OF THE DOLLS (1970)
THE BIG DOLL HOUSE (1971)
WOMEN IN CAGES (1971)
COOL BREEZE (1972)
THE BIG BIRD CAGE (1972)
HIT MAN (1972)
BLACK MAMA WHITE MAMA (1973)
COFFY (1973)
SCREAM BLACULA SCREAM (1973)
THE ARENA (1974)
FOXY BROWN (1974)
'SHEBA, BABY' (1975)
BUCKTOWN (1975)
FRIDAY FOSTER (1975)
DRUM (1976)

Steve Holland

THE [HIT] MAN OF [AT LEAST] A THOUSAND COVERS

During the boom of the paperback book from the fifties through say, the early nineties, one of the most critical selling points was the cover. The promise of the cover was often the tipping point for potential customers at the airport bookshop, neighborhood drugstore or corner newsstand. Before the domination of authors' names loomed larger than the book title, the illustration or photograph on the cover made promises that the books tried mightily to deliver. Sometimes the cover had literally nothing to do with the story inside, but if it was compelling enough, no one seemed to mind, unless the story wasn't engaging.

Many artists found fame as dependable deliverers of exciting, breathtaking artwork, often churning out several complete paintings a month. Some of the names are now among the most revered by fans of illustration art: *James Bama, Frank Frazetta, Stanley Borack, Robert Maguire, Frank McCarthy, Ron Lesser, Jack Faragasso, Mel Crair* and many more. While their styles varied wildly, they were all reliable, talented men who took their work seriously, regardless of the genre.

MICHAEL STRADFORD

is a multi-decade enter-
tainment executive. In
addition to successfully
program radio stations in
several major markets, includ-
ing Los Angeles, he was a senior exec- utive at
Quincy Jones's record label, **Qwest Records.** Strad-
ford enjoyed a long run as a content creator for **Sony
Pictures Home Entertainment**, Sony owned online
portal **Crackle.com** and most recently **Warner Bros.
Pictures.** He previously published *STEVE HOLLAND:
THE TORN SHIRT SESSIONS, STEVE HOLLAND:
THE WORLD'S GREATEST ILLUSTRATION ART
MODEL, STEVE HOLLAND: COWBOY* and the new
release, *STEVE HOLLAND: PAPERBACK HERO.*
Stradford has also written *MILESSTYLE: THE FASH-
ION OF MILES DAVIS* and *BLACK TO THE MOVIES
AND OTHER POP CULTURE MUSINGS.* He has
written reviews, profiles and interviews for several
magazines, as well as running his own pop culture
blog, **lookingforthecool.com**. Stradford lives in wed-
ded bliss in Southern California with his tolerant wife
Sybil and two equally tolerant dogs, Raj and Teddy.

Equally popular during the reign of paperbacks
were Men's Adventure Magazines (aka 'MAMs').
War stories, crime stories, heists, in short, all of the
popular themes that you find in each issue of *MEN'S
ADVENTURE QUARTERLY* found their origins in
MAMs. Paperbacks and MAMs used many of the
same artists, and often repurposed covers from one
format to the other and back again.

For both paperbacks and periodicals, one man
dominated the covers like no one before after. Even
more than thirty years since his passing. Steve Holland

was the favorite model for illustrators working on tight
timelines delivering memorable action packed covers
every month, often more than one at a time. Illustrator
Mort Künstler estimated that he did "maybe 1,000"
paintings featuring Steve Holland.

One would think that with the wide variety of
genres, publishing houses and artists that there would
be a deep pool of models for these illustrators to call
on to take reference photos to paint the covers from.
But former actor Holland had the classic profile
and physique combined with a solid work ethic

and a relaxed temperament that made it easy for the illustrators to trust that they were working with the best model in the business, so they used him over and over again. Artist Ron Lesser told me, "I probably used him maybe, 200 times? I don't remember any of his contemporaries, there was Holland and whoever. He was one of a kind."

Starting his modeling career in the mid-fifties when it became clear that his acting career was going nowhere, Holland quickly created a niche for himself as the man who could do it all in a camera studio. As a result, his schedule was always booked from morning to night, travelling all over New York

City, but posing at photographer Robert Osonitsch's Manhattan studio at 112 4th Avenue with regularity. Many classic covers originated there, but the bulk of the revered photographer's reference photos were lost to a fire and the rest of his photo archive was reportedly shredded by Osonitsch's widow shortly after he died in 2019. Literally millions of images lost to time.

Sol Korby is one of the few surviving illustrators to work with Steve Holland. He recalled, "His rugged good looks made him ideal to be a cowboy. But more than that was his acting ability. He didn't just place a hand here or tip his head there. He got into the role

and acted it. That transformed his modeling from mere poses to live action." There aren't a lot of guys who can look as comfortable in the saddle as in a business suit. Steve Holland was one of the few.

What follows is an example just how dominant Steve Holland was in the MAM category. At this writing, **MEN'S ADVENTURE QUARTERLY** has published seven issues featuring art and story from vintage MAMs coupled with new editorial content. Of the seven issues, Steve Holland has been on the cover of three and has at least one illustration or photo (often more) in every issue.

In the interview *MAQ* editor/founder Bob Deis did for my book **STEVE HOLLAND: THE WORLD'S GREATEST ILLUSTRATION ART MODEL**, Bob said; "It's mind boggling. I've counted over a thousand MAM covers with artwork that Holland modeled for and guesstimate that he appeared in at least several thousand MAM interior illustrations."

Steve's frequent 'co-star' on MAM covers and interiors was the gorgeous and blonde Eva Lynd. Bob Deis and Wyatt Doyle produced a beautiful book on her life and career, **EVA: MEN'S ADVENTURE SUPERMODEL** with her participation. Through that collaboration Bob connected me with Eva who also lives in Los Angeles, and she was kind enough to give me an interview about her time working with Steve.

She remembered Holland as someone she didn't know outside the studio but was very professional and friendly whenever they worked together. "Steve was one of these people who knew what he was doing, there was no question about it. I remember he was incredibly business-like, but we clicked very quickly because we worked well together and both of us appreciated that very much. We didn't have to discuss and 'you're going to do this, and I'll do that'. When Al (illustrator Rossi) told us what he wanted we just went into the pose, and it worked well. We liked working with each other."

While they were never more than working colleagues,

Eva had a clear idea of what made Steve Holland so successful as a model. "Well, for one thing he had the look. He had that fabulous look: very masculine, everybody falls in love with the way he looks because that's the first thing that strikes you. He knew exactly of the emotion to put into his pictures, whether it be stalwart, strong, and marvelous, even vulnerable."

One of my favorite bits of business with Steve Holland and MAMs is counting how many Hollands would be featured on one cover. As a versatile performer with complete command of his body and facial expressions (in addition to the illustrator saving money) it wasn't uncommon to see Steve Holland escaping a POW camp, fighting Nazi Steve Holland as German military officer Steve Holland calls for

Artist reference photos of Steve Holland. LEFT TO RIGHT: Ron Lesser's photo of Holland used for the cover painting he did for *THE CROSSROADS* by John D. MacDonald (1960); Lesser's photo of Holland for *MAFIA WIPE-OUT* by Frank Scarpetta (1973); a reference photo by artist Sam Levine for an unknown use; and, artist Robert Maguire's reference photo used for the cover of *THE BACK-UP MEN* by Ross Thomas (1976).

more troops, while resistance fighter(s) Steve Holland is on the other side of the fence waiting to complete the escape as driver or pilot Steve Holland revs up the engine!

In his interview Bob highlights a memorable painting by Bruce Minney in the November 1961 issue of *MALE* to illustrate the wonder of multiple Steve Hollands. On the cover there are nine figures, including a dead Japanese soldier. Holland was all nine. Minney was effusive in his praise for Holland. In a conversation with Bob in 2011 Minney said, ""He was great to work with. I'd show him a sketch or say give me a guy dying falling backwards and he would just know what to do."

Bob explains, "the Illustration artists usually didn't get reimbursed for the fees they paid to models they used for MAM artwork, so when they had a model like Steve in the studio to shoot reference photos, they often had him do poses for multiple characters. And, because they usually had to work fast to meet short deadlines, they often didn't bother to try to change his face for every character. Some MAM artists I've talked to, like Samson Pollen, said that by the '60s, due to Steve's heavy exposure, art directors did sometimes ask them to change his face."

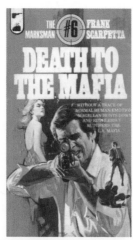

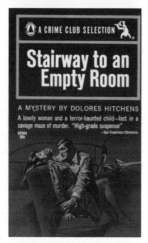

Holland went back and forth from MAMs to paperback covers for more than thirty years. He's arguably best known as the face and physique of pulp hero *DOC SAVAGE, THE MAN OF BRONZE.* Originally created in 1933 as a companion magazine to the greatest pulp hero of all time, *THE SHADOW*, the bronze crimefighter was resurrected in paperback form by Bantam Books in 1964. Master photo realistic illustrator James Bama brought him to life using good friend Steve Holland as the subject of 62 covers. Bama's covers with Holland along with Frank Frazetta's legendary *CONAN THE BARBARIAN* covers signaled a new approach to paperback illustration art that changed the industry for good.

After Bama left Doc and moved to Wyoming to paint western art, the illustrators who replaced him, Bob Larkin and Joe DeVito, continued to use Holland as Doc, even as he entered his sixties. DeVito initially thought he would use a younger model, but quickly saw

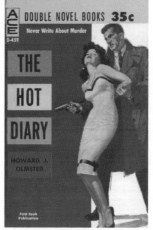

the error in his ways. "All the coaching in the world could not help the other models even come close to what came naturally to Steve. He would just go into a pose, and virtually every one was brilliant. He had such an innate body language, such a sense of balance. He would just go into a pose that for him was nothing, one after the other and then I would try to get the other guys to imitate him. After looking right at him the whole time, no one could do it!! It taught me the difference between an intuitive talent, somebody who's just got 'It' and someone who doesn't. You may think it's a simple process, but it's not."

Bob Larkin, who painted Holland on over thirty *DOC SAVAGE* covers and everything from *CONAN* to nearly all of the Marvel superheroes and beyond, remembered Steve Holland's prep work for a Doc Savage shoot: "He'd get dressed up and put the baby oil on to look sweaty. He'd go from one pose to another. We used to call him 'MOM: Man of Motion'. Steve would give me every pose possible and (then) extras just in case I changed my mind when I was working on the job."

Holland typically nailed what the illustrator wanted in 15-20 minutes. Then he would give the artist some other ideas to chew on. Following that they'd use the rest of the hour to stockpile poses for future use. "I'd book him for three hours sometimes and try to get five or six jobs out of that", Larkin recalled. "I was working for National Lampoon, Avon books, Bantam, a whole slew of companies. When I needed a figure, any action stuff, Steve was my man. I couldn't trust any of the other male models to do anything right."

As he aged, Holland's features grew more severe, the lines in his face and around his eyes showed a man who had endured the ups and downs of life but was still fighting the good fight. His more 'seasoned' visage was ideal for cowboys, hitmen and leaders of men.

His modeling career had wound down in the early nineties, but he discovered that he surprisingly had built a modest but enthusiastic fan base. Recognized for his work as *DOC SAVAGE* and other characters Holland was a guest at several comic book conventions and was shocked when fans would ask for his autograph or to take a photo with him. His daughter Nicole remarked, "it was quite phenomenal how little attention he paid to his fame on book covers, posters, *FLASH GORDON* TV series, etc. He was an incredibly 'salt-of-the-earth' man. And he was a true minimalist, long before such things were in the popular vernacular". I mentioned to Nicole that from my research he might be a bit uneasy with the new spotlight being generated by the interest in his career. She said, "Yes, he probably would feel somewhat uncomfortable with the attention, but I think he would also get satisfaction simply for a

job well done."

He stayed fit all of his life. "He was in great shape" said Joe DeVito, "even still had all the hair and everything else and he had that look in the eye. When you're working with a guy like that, there's a certain presence that they have and you either have it or you don't. Steve had it coming out of his ears. He just had 'it'".

But as time went on, he put modeling out to pasture as he began to focus on one of his true loves, painting. Steve Holland painted a few covers that made it to publication, but in late middle age following his third divorce, Holland was restless and unsettled. While none of the illustrators that I interviewed had anything bad to say about him, in his final years' friends noticed that the easy going, relaxed Steve Holland that they knew was in some kind of personal transition. Illustrator and friend Peter Caras recalled seeing him the year before he died. "He wasn't himself. A bit more reserved. He wasn't as energetic as I remembered him to be. It was very sad actually, I hadn't used him for a while, but he was still in great physical looking shape. But he wasn't the happy go lucky, screwing around, that kind of thing with me."

Famed western illustrator Carl Hantman was an artist that Steve Holland held in high regard. In his final interview about six months before his death, Holland reflected on Hantman's skill. "Carl Hantman

OPPOSITE CLOCKWISE: *DEATH TO THE MAFIA* by Frank Scarpetta, *I'LL KILL YOU NEXT!* by Adam Knight, *THE HOT DIARY* by Howard J. Olmstead, *STAIRWAY TO AN EMPTY ROOM* by Dolores Hitchens.
THIS PAGE CLOCKWISE: *THE KILLING MACHINE* by Bruno Rossi, *WOMAN ON THE ROOF* by Mignon G. Eberhart, *MAFIA WIPE-OUT* by Frank Scarpetta, and *THE MAFIA* by Noel Clad.

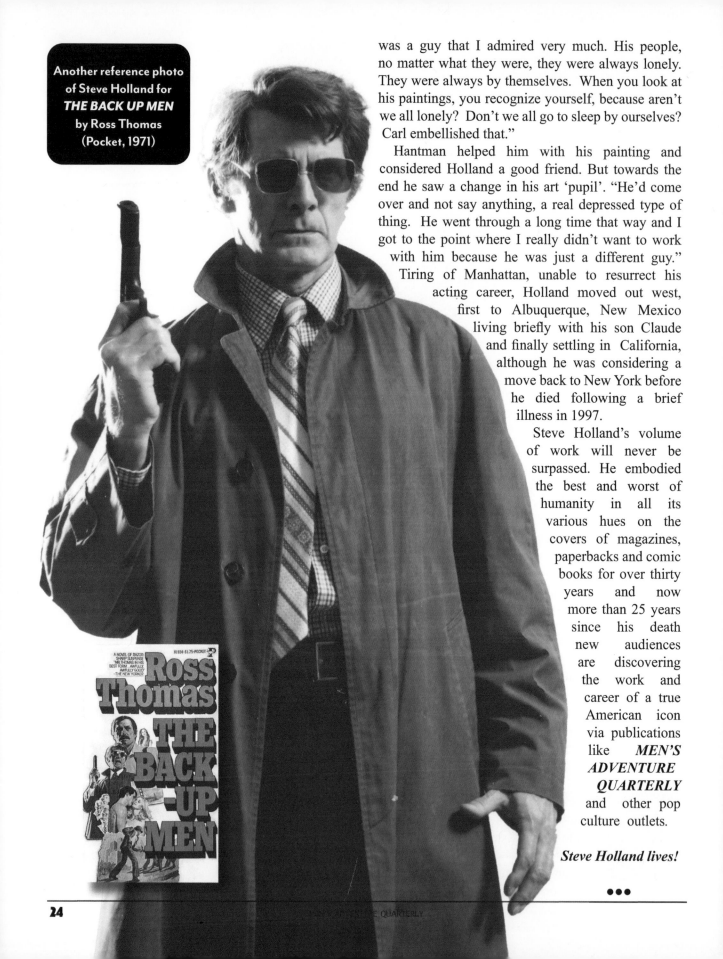

Another reference photo
of Steve Holland for
THE BACK UP MEN
by Ross Thomas
(Pocket, 1971)

was a guy that I admired very much. His people, no matter what they were, they were always lonely. They were always by themselves. When you look at his paintings, you recognize yourself, because aren't we all lonely? Don't we all go to sleep by ourselves? Carl embellished that."

Hantman helped him with his painting and considered Holland a good friend. But towards the end he saw a change in his art 'pupil'. "He'd come over and not say anything, a real depressed type of thing. He went through a long time that way and I got to the point where I really didn't want to work with him because he was just a different guy."

Tiring of Manhattan, unable to resurrect his acting career, Holland moved out west, first to Albuquerque, New Mexico living briefly with his son Claude and finally settling in California, although he was considering a move back to New York before he died following a brief illness in 1997.

Steve Holland's volume of work will never be surpassed. He embodied the best and worst of humanity in all its various hues on the covers of magazines, paperbacks and comic books for over thirty years and now more than 25 years since his death new audiences are discovering the work and career of a true American icon via publications like *MEN'S ADVENTURE QUARTERLY* and other pop culture outlets.

Steve Holland lives!

•••

GET IN ON THE
ACTION!
WITH

THE Steve Holland ACTION LIBRARY
BY MICHAEL STRADFORD

AVAILABLE NOW ON AMAZON AND IN FINER SPECIALTY BOOKSELLERS

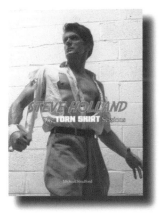

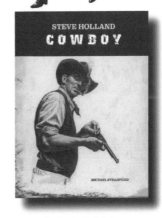

WWW.STEVEHOLLANDBOOK.COM

HITTERS
HITMEN AND HITWOMEN

H itters" or hit men perform murder for hire. They are also sometimes called 'button men' by the Mob – the Mafia. They "push a button on a guy" to make him dead. The following is an overview of the hit man genre in fact, fiction, and film.

Hit men are usually guys. They are often a member of, or affiliated with, organized crime – the police, or involved in some way with the political process. Hired killers have a certain appeal and therefore appear in a multitude of vintage paperback crime novels, and in men's adventure magazines – and of course, in popular movies. Hit men are often portrayed prominently in true crime tales. They're tough and brutal, deadly and workmanlike in fiction and in fact.

Hired killers have always been useful. In the long-ago Wild West, Tom Horn, was basically a hired gun for the railroad to terrorize settlers. Fact, not fiction. John Wesley Hardin was a killer who just seemed to like to kill – he is reputed to have killed a man just for snoring!

In *FLINT* by Gil Dodge (Signet, 1957) in fiction, we have a western novel based on a Jim Thompson crime story. Flint is a cold-blooded hired killer, and Dodge is a pseudonym for Thompson's editor at Lion Books, Arnold Hano. So there is a connection between these two books and authors.

Some other Westerns in this genre include *HIRED GUNS* by Max Brand (Pocket Books, 1950), where they gave him a job to end a nine year feud, using murder. *HIRED GUN* by Archie Jocelyn (Avon Books) is another Old West hit man type of novel.

However, it wasn't only cowboy killers who took contracts. As early as 1880, and ending in 1906 – the year of the great San Francisco Earthquake – the San Francisco Chinatown tong wars were

FLINT by Gil Dodge (Signet, 1957), a western novel based on a Jim Thompson crime story.

raging full time. It was an era when Chinese were killing Chinese with bloody axes, or hatchets. The *boo how doy* were professional soldiers for the Chinese tongs and killers who used hatchets. In **THE HATCHET MEN** by Richard H. Dillon (Ballantine Comstock, 1972) the true story of these Chinese hatchet men killers will haunt you. It is a world gone today, but it existed in fact, and even made it's way into the movies. In one famous film of the 1930s, acclaimed Jewish actor Edward G. Robinson played a Chinese killer, in *HATCHETMAN*. Films explore the hit man story from books and magazines – taking it from crime fiction books and magazines – and from true crime facts.

In fact, many of the actual killers in fiction are based on men from real life – mob enforcers and 'button men' like the guys that made up Murder Incorporated, or who did work for Al Capone, or *MURDER MACHINE* killer Roy DeMeo; or 'Iceman' Richard Kuklinski – each of these men will put the ice cold hand of fear down the spine of anyone who ever met them -- or even reads about their deadly deeds in books about them.

In the 1920s and 30s Al Capone and his mob, aka 'The Outfit' or 'The Chicago Outfit' put out contacts on various Chicago gangs during the Prohibition booze wars. *SCARFACE* by Armitage Trail (Dell, 1959, cover art by Victor Kalin), shows Scarface Al on the cover and details Capone's life, and his greatest hit, the wipeout of the Bugs Moran gang in the *Saint Valentine's Day Massacre* on Friday, February 14, 1929. Capone's contract killers deleted seven of Moran's guys in a vicious bloodbath –

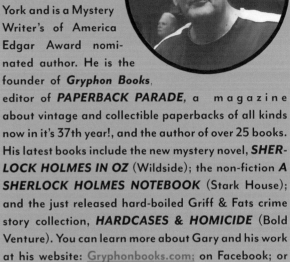

GARY LOVISI

lives in Brooklyn, New York and is a Mystery Writer's of America Edgar Award nominated author. He is the founder of **Gryphon Books**, editor of **PAPERBACK PARADE**, a magazine about vintage and collectible paperbacks of all kinds now in it's 37th year!, and the author of over 25 books. His latest books include the new mystery novel, **SHERLOCK HOLMES IN OZ** (Wildside); the non-fiction **A SHERLOCK HOLMES NOTEBOOK** (Stark House); and the just released hard-boiled Griff & Fats crime story collection, **HARDCASES & HOMICIDE** (Bold Venture). You can learn more about Gary and his work at his website: Gryphonbooks.com; on Facebook; or on his YouTube books channel.

Photo by Laura Cali.

TOP LEFT: *THE HATCHET MEN* by Richard Hilton (Ballantine, 1972) ABOVE: SCARFACE by Armitage Trail (Dell, 1959) and THE SAINT VALENTINE'S DAY MASSACRE by Boris O'Hara (Dell, 1967)

but they missed Moran himself. It was a murder for hire hit that shocked Chicago to it's very core and is still unsolved. Capone sent Moran the most famous Valentine of all time!

Another version of this atrocity is the book, **THE ST. VALENTINE'S DAY MASSACRE** by Boris O'Hara (Dell, 1967). This is a novel based upon the film of the same title, which was based on a screenplay by top crime fiction author, Howard Browne.

In **MURDER INC.** by Sid Fedder and Burton B. Turkus (a Brooklyn, NY, D.A who was involved with solving these murders at the time) we delve into a vicious mob murder gang who enforced the Mafia's edicts nationwide – usually from candy stores in

Lounge, which he turned into a house of horrors where victims were taken to an upstairs apartment and shot or strangled to death. Then the body was trussed up in the bathroom over a bathtub, cut open and drained of blood, and then the guys sawed apart the corpse and bagged the parts. Afterwards they all sat down together and ate pizza. The bags were later thrown into various garbage dumpsters and ended up buried in the Flatlands landfill, where they were never seen again. It is assumed the DeMeo crew killed over 200 victims – most of the bodies were never discovered, most of the cases were never solved. Actually, these guys were in essence, a Mafia serial killer murder crew. In fact, sometimes DeMeo would order his guys to go into the

Brooklyn's Flatbush section. They killed hundreds of men, in often brutal and sometimes innovative ways. They were masters of death in the 1930s and 40s. Their top man who gave out the 'contracts' for each kill was Mafia capo, or captain, Albert Anastasia, aka 'The Mad Hatter' because he was prone to extreme rage and violence. He was uncontrollable. Anastasia not only ran this murder gang – he often went out and did hits himself – *just for the fun of it!*

In **MURDER MACHINE** by Gene Mustain and Jerry Capeci they tell the story of Mafia Gambino Family soldier Roy DeMeo, and his crew of killers based in Brooklyn. They did hits for the Gambino crime family throughout New York in the 1960s to 1980s. DeMeo operated out of his bar called The Gemini

bar and pick out a lone guy to bring upstairs to kill. He said the boys needed practice…*to keep up their skills!*

One of the most brutal murder for hire guys was Richard Kuklinski. He was a six and half foot giant with a bad temper and no remorse. He was known as 'The Iceman' because he was so heartless. He killed over 200 people. He was affiliated with the Gambino crime family, through Roy DeMeo, and did hits for them, but he was also a freelancer. He enjoyed killing his victims in ever innovative ways. He learned poisoning from a hit man friend – who incredibly was a neighborhood Mr. Softee ice cream truck driver. Kuklinski later killed him too. In fact, later on when Kuklinski was in prison and asked about his friends, he told the interviewer they were all dead -- *he had killed most of them.*

These are some of the templates for the fictional hit men and hit women we read about in vintage paperback crime and in the pages of men's adventure magazines, and that we see in the movies. It is amazing, powerful stuff!

In 1936 Graham Greene, wrote **THIS GUN FOR HIRE**, about Raven, an ice cold killer. A literary author, Greene also wrote pulp crime that he called 'his entertainments'. The book was made into a hit film with a young Alan Ladd as the cold-hearted killer.

Not intrigued by 'gun men'? Well then, maybe the ladies can grab your attention!

There are plenty of women killers in fact and

example of this. It shows a blonde pointing a gun at a brunette, all set to drill her in the back. It gives an idea of how deadly a woman with a gun might just be. Many vintage crime fiction paperbacks show such images in their cover art. Of course, most of these images come from stories about true crime characters and events. In **KISS HER GOODBYE** by Allan Guthrie (Hard Case Crime, 2005, with cover art by Chuck Pyle) we have a terrific hard-boiled crime novel about a tough Scottish gal who enjoys using a baseball bat to make troublesome problems go away.

True life female assassins are even more brutal. These include Idoia Lopez Riano, aka 'The Tigress', who killed more than 20 in the 1980s for ETA, a group

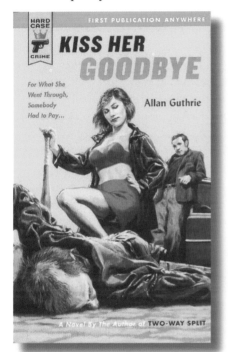

LEFT TO RIGHT:
MURDER INC. by Sid Feder and Burton B. Turkus (Perma Books)
MURDER MACHINE by Gene Mustain and Jerry Capecki
THIS GUN FOR HIRE by Graham Greene (Superior),
KISS HER GOODBYE By Allan Guthrie (Hard Case Crime, 2005)
BADGE OF THE ASSASSIN by Robert K. Tanenbaum and Philip Rosenberg (Signet, 1990).
BOTTOM:
DARK THREAT by Patricia Wentworth (Popular Library 1951)

fiction. In real life, or fiction, most of these women use their sexual attraction to lure their victim. This sexual attraction is shown, and even avidly displayed, on the covers of many vintage paperbacks and men's adventure magazines. While not all female killers are hit women, per se, these women seem to do quite well murdering men – or when necessary – taking out anther women. The cover art of **DARK THREAT** by Patricia Wentworth (Popular Library, 1951, cover art by the great Rudolph Belarski) is one

seeking political independence of the Basque region from Spain. Then there is Maria Jimenez, aka 'La Tora' who worked for the Zetas drug cartel in Mexico and killed 20 people on their behalf. One of the most notorious was Jeanette Van Nessen, a true gun for hire, a freelance killer from The Netherlands. She charged 80,000 British pounds per hit and was involved with the Black September Movement and killed an Israeli Mossad agent – she in turn was terminated by another Mossad agent.

There are also an endless amount of super spies – like James Bond – or private eyes – like Mike Hammer – fighting against Castro, the KGB, neo-Nazi groups, or the Mafia, or other organized crime outfits, or super criminals. Some of these hitters fit into the hit man or hit woman genre because of their activities. Donald Hamilton's Matt Helm begins by avenging the murder of his wife by enemy agents, who are after him – as he is after them! He is brutal and very tough -- not at all the man Dean Martin played in that silly Matt Helm movie. James Bond himself, could be said to be a hitter, after all, he had a license to kill. And he used it most effectively.

Police are another group that are often the subject of hit men in fact and fiction.

BADGE OF THE ASSASSIN by Robert K.

Tanenbaum and Philip Rosenberg (Signet Book, 1990), is the true story of a hit squad that was formed in 1971 in the Bronx, with the purpose to kill cops. This paramilitary hit squad ended up murdering two innocent cops. Just because they were cops.

In fiction, ***DEATH SQUAD*** by Herbert Kastle (Dell, 1977) is a hard brutal novel. These cops were tired of playing a legal tug-of-war with corrupt officials. They were cops by day – but by night they were vigilantes. They became more deadly than the criminals they hunted.

Hitters also manifest themselves in the political area. In true crime this can be a dirty business and can shock a nation to it's very core. The murders of President John F. Kennedy, Senator Robert F. Kennedy and Civil Rights leader the Reverend Doctor Martin Luther King were organized hits. Hit men performed the murders. Oswald was a 'patsy' or the actual killer of the president, but he had ties to Cuba, the CIA, the FBI and the Mafia. He himself was hit, live on national TV by Jack Ruby, a Mafia and CIA connected thug. Kinda makes you think.

True professional hit men, like Mafia killers, do have a code, of sorts. No kids, no women, no police, judges or 'citizens' (regular working people not involved with the Mob) – it just brings too much heat. However these rules can also be somewhat elastic. Sometimes these rules can melt away when necessary. In the Mob, when you get the order to do a hit – you do it. If not, you're the next one to be done!

There are a lot of hit men movies where a hired killer is a major part of the story. In ***NO COUNTRY FOR OLD MEN***, the book by Cormac McCarthy (from 2005), and in the film from 2007, we are introduced to Anton Chigurth (played by Javier Bardem), a relentless and chilling killer out on a job that looks more like a rampage. He is a coin tossing death merchant, because he flips a coin when he confronts his victims – heads you live – tails you die.

In ***THE PROFESSIONAL*** (1994) we have Mathilda (a 12 year old Natalie Portman in her first movie role), who meets up with hit man Leon (Jean Reno). Leon saves her from being killed by corrupt murdering DEA agents (led by an over-the-top drugged up psycho Gary Oldman). Leon, who calls himself 'a cleaner' works for local Mafia boss Tony, but he has a code, and tries to keep to it. This is an over-the-top film, but it shows much of the manner in which a mob hit man does his work -- at least as far as the movies are concerned.

Two movies set during the Cold War highlight dangerous women spies with guns and are peripheral to the hit man genre. These include ***SALT*** (2010) where Angelina Jolie, as Evelyn Salt, is a CIA agent suspected of being a Russian Spy and fights to prove her innocence. In the 2017 film ***ATOMIC BLONDE***, we have Lorraine Broughton as a tough and sensual MI6 agent in a tale set during the time of the Berlin Wall.

HITMAN (2007) with Timothy Olyphant as Agent 47, works for a secret group of assassins who do hits worldwide. It is a riveting film and Olyphant is a fearsome and relentless killer. There was a sequel ***HITMAN: AGENT 47*** from 2015.

Another film in the genre is ***PROUD MARY*** (2018, starring Taraji P. Henson) who is an African-American hit women. She works for a ruthless gangster and in an

almost mirror image of *THE PROFESSIONAL*, the story here is about her fight to save a young boy from being killed by mobsters. It is over-the-top, brutal and violent, but shows the hit man – a woman in this case – as Hollywood makes her out to be.

To say that these films are not exactly realistic, is stretching it more than a bit, but they do offer terrific action, adventure and excitement. Much as do the paperback books and men's adventure magazines that deal with secret agents, spies, private eyes, detectives, cops and others who seek revenge and justice against the Mob or other evil-doers.

Popular series heroes that we see in famous paperback series like *THE DESTROYER* and *THE EXECUTIONER* burn with righteous anger and revenge for terrible injustices received, or dark bloody betrayal. These paperback books, and men's adventure magazines – like many Hollywood films – are exciting, amazing and riveting for readers and viewers. Their popularity is legend, and the hit man saga is vastly enjoyable, and even glamorized – but it should be remembered that there is a very wide chasm between the fictional hit man – *and the reality of blood and murder meted out wholesale by his vicious deadly cousin in real life.*

•••

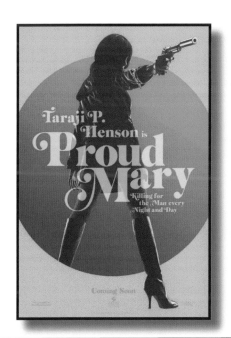

OPPOSITE:
DEATH SQUAD by Herbert Kastle (Dell, 1977) chronicles cops turned assassin-vigilantes.

THIS PAGE:
PROUD MARY (Screen Gems, 2018) models itself after films like *THE PROFESSIONAL* and *GLORIA*.

In *NO COUNTRY FOR OLD MEN* (Paramount Vantage, 2007) , Javier Bardem uses an air-powered cow "knocker" to eliminate his victims. His unusual weapon makes his kills hard to trace. The movie is based on the book by Cormac McCarthy.

SPECIAL BOOK BONUS

Lily Brazil: WEEK-END GIRL
(SHE WAS A PICKUP WITH NO FUTURE)

stag

FEB.

25c

HOW COMPANY'S
BLOODIEST MISSION

*FASTEST GUN
SOUTH OF BODIE*

FEMALES
ON PAROLE
THE TRAGIC TRUTH
ABOUT DESPERATE WOMEN

This story, "Setup for the Kid" is a noir-flavored tale of two professional hitmen who meet in Florida and travel together to carry out a contract they were assigned to work on together. One—named Gregson—is a young, up-and-coming shooter who uses a high-powered rifle with a SniperScope and silencer. The other—Lonnie—is an older, jaded pro tasked with getting Gregson to the spot where he can assassinate his target.

On the way to the victim's location, they discuss various things; some relevant to the job, some as inane as how hot Florida's weather is. Their conversations remind me of several spoken by Samuel L. Jackson and John Travolta in Quentin Tarantino's film *PULP FICTION*. The dark humor in the story, especially in the ending, is also Tarantino-esque.

The writer, Bill H. Hunter, had stories in a few men's bachelor and adventure mags in the late 1950s and at least one in the *MYSTERY TALES* crime story digest.

MYSTERY TALES was published by Atlas Magazines. Atlas was part of publisher Martin Goodman's diverse Magazine Management empire, which included comics (like Marvel), paperback books, and various types of magazines. Among Goodman's periodicals are many of the best known men's adventure magazines,

INTRODUCTION
BY BOB **DEIS**

By Bill H. Hunter
From *STAG*, February 1957
Cover artwork by Bob Stanley
Interior illustration by Robert E. Schulz

such as *STAG*, the mag "Setup for the Kid" appeared in.

Goodman's MAMs were initially published under the Atlas name. In the mid-'50s, the Mag Mgt. MAMs were dubbed "the Diamond line" and identified by the "Sign of the Diamond" logo. (This is why they are often referred to as the "Atlas/Diamond" MAMS.)

In 1942, Goodman tried publishing an Esquire-style men's magazine titled *STAG: THE MAN'S HOME COMPANION*, but it bombed and was discontinued after two issues. He revived the name STAG in 1949 and used it for what would be his first real men's adventure mag.

Vol. 1, No. 1 of the new *STAG*, with the subhead "*TRUE ADVENTURE • PERSONALITIES • HUNTING and FISHING • SPORTS*" on the cover, was launched in December 1949. The cover painting, by Albert Fisher, shows a bombshell blonde surrounded by men in the bleachers at a baseball game.

LEFT: Publisher Martin Goodman (1908-1992) in 1952.

NEAR LEFT: The 1st issue of *STAG*, December 1949. Cover art by Albert Fisher.

Goodman premiered his second MAM, *MALE.*, in 1950. *STAG* and *MALE* both sold well. So, in 1952, he created a third MAM, *MEN*. He launched *FOR MEN ONLY* in 1954. Every year or so during the '50s, he tried publishing new variations on the MAM format. Goodman's first four flagship MAMs ran for more than three decades. Others that had shorter lifespans include *ACTION FOR MEN, ACTION LIFE, ADVENTURE LIFE, ADVENTURE TRAILS, BATTLEFIELD, COMPLETE MAN, HUNTING ADVENTURES, KEN FOR MEN, MAN'S WORLD, MEN IN ACTION, SPORT LIFE, SPORTSMAN*, and *TRUE ACTION*. The artist who did the cover painting for *STAG*, February 1957 was Robert C. Stanley (1918-1996). The interior illustration for "Setup for the Kid" story was done by Robert E. Schulz (1928–1978). Both are among the great mid-20th Century paperback and MAM illustration artists.

Bob Stanley had no formal art school training, but he did have a lot of talent and ambition. In 1939 he started contacting pulp magazines and got his first cover art assignments. His career was temporarily sidelined by his military service in World War II. During the war, he met and married Rhoda Rosenzweig, the red-haired beauty who became the main female model for his later paperback and magazine artwork.

After WWII, Stanley got more cover assignments from pulp mags, but that genre was rapidly fading. In the '50s, he began doing cover paintings for the burgeoning paperback and men's

adventure mag markets and soon became one of the most sought after artists in those realms.

From the '50s to the '70s, Stanley created hundreds of paperback cover paintings for Dell, Bantam, Beacon, Lancer Books, Lion Books, Popular Library, Pyramid and other publishers. He also created hundreds of cover and interior illustrations for MAMs published by Magazine Management and other companies. He even illustrated the original cover art that we used for the first issue of *MEN'S ADVENTURE QUARTERLY.*

His wife Rhoda was his usual female model. He typically used himself as the model for male figures. They're often the gal and guy featured in his cover art. Bob and Rhoda divorced around 1970. He remarried and moved to Big Pine Key, Florida, where he seems to have retired from being a professional illustration artist and died in 1996.

Like Bob Stanley, Bob Schulz did scores of paperback covers and MAM cover and interior paintings in the '50s, '60s and '70s. Unlike Stanley, Schulz had formal art training. He studied at the Art Students League in New York in the early '50s under the legendary teacher Frank J. Reilly. After Reilly died in 1967, Schulz served as an ASL teacher himself.

Most people who are aware of Schulz today know him from his paperback and MAM work. However, he also painted award-winning portraits and landscapes and did advertising art. In fact, one ad image he created is known to millions of people—his portrait of the handsome lumberjack

FOR THE GREATEST IN ADVENTURE READING, LOOK FOR THE FOLLOWING SYMBOL ON THE COVERS OF YOUR FAVORITE MEN'S MAGAZINES:

Sportsman TRUE ACTION
Ken FOR MEN FOR MEN ONLY
MAN'S WORLD MEN
MALE stag
ACTION for MEN BATTLEFIELD

ABOVE: Bob Stanley and his wife and favorite female model Rhoda. ABOVE CENTER: The 1959 version of the "Diamond" logo used in MAMs published by Martin Goodman's Magazine Management company.

in the red plaid shirt used on the packaging and ads for Georgia-Pacific's Brawny paper towels.

Schulz created the first "Brawny Man" portrait in 1974. Although his image has been updated several times, a Brawny Man image has been used for the product's packaging and ads ever since.

Schulz's family created a Facebook page for him a while back. One post there is an interesting anecdote about the original Brawny Man model. It says: "The model used was a gas station attendant from Stockholm, NJ. He was offered a big contract to appear in TV ads for a national advertisement campaign, but turned it down because he would not venture the 55 miles to NYC for any amount of money."

•••

LEFT: The first issue of *MAQ* featured art by Robert Stanley.
BELOW: One of Bob Stanley's covers for Dell: *A TASTE FOR VIOLENCE* by Brett Halliday (Dell, 1950). Stanley and his wife Rhoda were the models for the painting.
BELOW LEFT: Robert E. Schulz's most famous image: the "Brawny Man" used for Georgia-Pacific's Brawny paper towels.

NORTHERN'S NEW BRAWNY TOWEL HAS SCRUB STRENGTH

To help you scrub up grime, crayon marks, even baked-on foods.

To make household clean-ups easier on you, we've added scrub strength to Northern's new Brawny Towels. Brawny's scrub strength will help you scrub up: grime, baked-on foods, crayon marks... you name it. We take tough, absorbent fibers and bond them together. Tighter...for scrub strength. Try new Brawny. New Brawny is one of the strongest towels made... we guarantee it. See package for details.

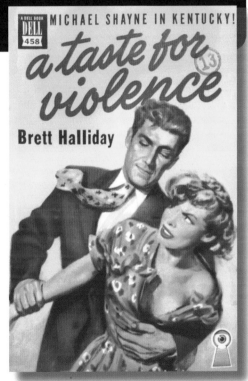

Setup for the Kid

Gregson was an expert, a pro who took pride
in his work and his tools—especially the SniperScope.   And no
one was going to tell him how to do his job—no one.

by Bill H. Hunter
ILLUSTRATED BY ROBERT SCHULZ

STAG FICTION

WHEN the guy came up the steps and through the gate marked Track Five, Lonnie moved away from the post and walked toward the row of lockers by the men's room. He stopped at locker 34 and pretended to search his pockets for change while he listened to the man's approaching footsteps. Lonnie heard him stop at number 30 and then Lonnie turned toward the man.

"You come in on the Mainliner?" Lonnie asked.

"Yeah," the man answered. "The long way, too. Through Laredo." Both men relaxed and some of the strain left Lonnie's face. They appraised each other for a minute and, while the other guy eased his bags to the floor, Lonnie took in his lanky build and blond hair. When he straightened, Lonnie was staring at him.

"What's the matter?" the guy asked.

"You're awfully young."

"I'm old enough," he said quietly.

"I don't doubt that, friend. What I meant was that most of the men on this kind of assignment are old-timers."

"I've got a new method."

"So I heard. What's it like?"

"Can we talk here?" the man asked.

"No, let's shove. This all your gear?"

"Yeah."

"The car's parked outside. I'll give you a hand." Lonnie picked up one of the bags.

"What's your name?" the thin guy asked as he followed Lonnie toward the door.

"Code or real?"

"Hell, I know your code. I mean real."

"Lombardi."

"Mine's Gregson."

Inside the car, both men were silent as Lonnie steered through the late afternoon traffic. When the traffic thinned on the outskirts of town, Gregson turned and inspected the car's interior.

"Is this the car we'll use?" he asked.

"I'm not sure yet, but I think so."

"What's it got?"

"You mean engine?"

"Yeah."

"From zero to 130 in 10 flat."

Gregson grunted, "Doesn't look it, either."

"Whattaya mean?"

"I mean you can't tell it. Doesn't look like a rod."

Lonnie laughed. "You know why it doesn't look like a rod?"

"The green, I guess."

"Yeah—a big bundle, too."

"Anything else?"

"All the glass is BP. Plates in your door there and mine here. Individual switches for tail and brake lights. Radio for police network."

"Nice," said Gregson.

"It's all right. How does it look for your style?"

"O.K., I guess."

"Whattaya mean, guess?" exclaimed Lonnie. "Don't you know your own setup?"

"Hell, yes, I know my setup. Look, Lombardi, don't let my age get you upset. So, I'm younger than most guys you work with. That doesn't mean I don't know my job."

"I didn't mean that, kid. Let's put it like this: I don't know a damn thing about you. You're good, I know that, or else you would've never pulled this assignment. They tell me to meet you, and find out if you need any special equipment. That's all I'm trying to do."

"Well, jeez, how the hell do I know if I'm going to need anything? I don't even know what kind of hit we're making. Is it here in the city?"

"No, it's in Florida. About 35 miles outside Tampa."

"Open country?"

"I guess so. It's a small town."

"I thought so."

"Why?"

"That's my road game."

"Will you need anything?"

"Is that back window removable?"

"Nope."

"Well, get it fixed so I can take it out and put it back in a hurry."

"Anything else?"

"That's all. I've got my stuff in the bags."

AFTER a few minutes of silence. Lonnie turned the car into a drive leading to the Ace-Hi Motel. He stopped the car alongside cabin 12 and the two men carried the bags inside.

Gregson looked around at the room. An unmade bed stood in a corner under two high windows, and a table littered with full ash trays and magazines leaned against the wall. The door leading to the bathroom was open and Gregson saw the empty beer cans under the lavatory.

"You been here long?" he asked.

"Two days. Been reading mostly."

"So I see. You mean there's no dames—" He stopped at Lonnie's reproachful stare.

"Forget it, man. Forget it. Look, I'm going out for a while. I'll be back in something like two hours. You sit tight."

"I'll freeze."

Gregson picked up a magazine from the table and sprawled across the bed. After a while he arose and took off his coat. While lighting a cigarette, he looked toward the bathroom. He went inside and then came out with a can of beer. He was sitting in the chair asleep when Lonnie let himself in. Gregson jerked and came out of the chair at the sound of the door closing.

"What's the matter, kid? Tired?"

"A little," said Gregson, rubbing his palms over his face. "Never could sleep on a damn train."

"Me neither."

"Well, whatcha find out?"

"Everything's set," answered Lonnie, as he pulled off his coat. "Any beer left?"

"Yeah, I only had one."

Lonnie opened two cans and then pulled a chair up alongside the bed. He sat down heavily and kicked off his shoes.

"Everything's set, huh?" Gregson asked.

"Yeah, I left the car downtown. It'll be ready in two days. I'm flying down in the morning. You leave in three days with the car."

"Where do I pick it up?"

"You don't. It'll be parked outside that door when you get up Saturday morning."

"Well, what in hell do I do for three days?"

"Nothing."

"Nothing? Whattaya mean, nothing?"

"That's it, kid. You eat at the restaurant across the street. Reading material and beer you get from room service. Read, drink beer and play the radio. That's all you do. No whisky; no dames. Got it?"

"Yeah, but..."

"No buts, Gregson," and Lonnie's voice was hard. "That's the way it is, and that's the way it's gonna be."

"Yeah, I know. Hell, I can stand it. What's three days, anyway?"

"Now you're talking, man. Now, here's the deal: I'll call you Friday night from Tampa to let you know where to pick me up. I'll get all the info I can on our boy, and when you get down there we'll go over it together and work out something..." Lonnie's voice droned on and on, and it was past midnight when the lights went out in cabin 12.

Gregson was shaving on Friday night when the call came in. The old guy with the twisted foot who handled room service knocked on the door and said that he had a call from Tampa. Gregson slapped at the lather on his face with a towel, and hurried to the phone booth.

"Hello, hello. This is Gregson." Nobody answered. Gregson knew the connection was still made: he could detect the soft hum. His heart skipped slightly and he looked wildly around the motel yard. *What the hell is this?* he thought.

"Hello, is that you, Lombardi?"

"Did you come in on the Mainliner?"

"Hell, yes. The long way. Through Laredo. What is this, a gag?"

Lonnie's soft laugh trickled over the wire. "No gag, kid. Just wanted to be sure."

"Well, you scared hell out of me."

"You did all right."

"I know, I know. We're both good. We oughtta get on TV with that routine." Both men laughed, and Gregson's shoulders dropped with a long expulsion of breath.

"How's it going, kid?" asked Lonnie.

"O.K., I guess, but I'm ready to move. How about it?"

"I'm all set. You can leave any time you want."

"I'll have to wait for the car."

"That won't be long. They'll probably drop it some time after midnight."

"I'll be ready."

"O.K., kid. Take it easy on the way down. Don't pick up any fuzz."

"I'll make it," answered Gregson. "Where you staying?"

"Cabin 24, Whitworth Motel."

IT WAS 17 hours later when Gregson pulled into the chute alongside Cabin 24 at the Whitworth Motel. Lonnie came out without a shirt and helped him with the bags. Inside the cabin, Gregson threw off his coat and shirt.

"Hell almighty, man, Florida's hot."

"You'll get used to it."

"Like hell. I don't want to get used to it. Let's hit, and then get the hell out of here."

"Will you be ready by tomorrow night?"

"Man, I'm ready now."

"No, we'll wait till tomorrow night. That's our best chance anyway."

"What's his habits?"

"He'll be at a club meeting tomorrow night. Get home between 10:30 and 12."

"We take him then?"

"Yeah. It's ideal for your style. Residential area. No patrol cars. Quiet neighborhood; everybody's in the sack by 10 o'clock."

"Sounds O.K."

"It *is* O.K., man."

The next night, at a little past 10, Lonnie was at the wheel as they drove slowly past a low, flat house with gray shingles and a cut stone chimney.

"Is that it?" asked Gregson.

"That's it. No garage or driveway, which means he parks in the street."

"That's O.K. That shrubbery isn't tall enough to get in the way."

"How close you want to be?"

"Anything under 100 yards."

"What about right here at this tree?"

"That'll be fine."

After Lonnie had stopped the car, Gregson climbed into the back seat and opened one of the bags. He took out a canvas-wrapped bundle and put it down on the floor. He worked with the package a couple of minutes and then turned toward Lonnie.

"O.K., get it out of the trunk." Lonnie climbed out, raised the trunk lid, took out the rifle and shut the lid as quietly as possible. He opened a back door, handed the rifle to Gregson, and then climbed back under the wheel.

He watched Gregson connect the package to the rifle, and then asked, "What did you call that thing?"

"SniperScope " replied Gregson, as he continued his work.

"And you can see in the dark with it?"

"Yep " grunted Gregson.

"What makes it work?"

"Batteries "

"That all?"

"Hell, no; *that's* not all. The goddamn Army spent a fortune developing this thing."

"You sure it doesn't make any noise?"

"This silencer cost somebody close to 1,500 bucks."

"Where'd you learn about it?"

"What are you—writing a book or something?"

"Now take it easy, kid I'm just talking. Hell, I gotta do something."

"You just let me worry about my end of it, and you take care of yours. O.K.?"

"I have already, kid. I have."

"If you want to talk about something, talk about when that son-of-a-bitch is gonna show up."

"Are you ready?"

"I will be as soon as I get the window out."

"You need any help?"

"*No, no—hell, no.* I've pulled this thing 15 times already. I know how it's done."

"All right, all right. Don't get sore."

"I'm not sore," said Gregson, tugging at the window.

"See, there it is, all fixed."

"You all set?"

"All set. What time is it?"

"Ten forty-five."

"O.K., light me a cigarette, will ya? I don't want to blind myself."

"O.K. Here you go."

BOTH men smoked in silence. The night was quiet and breathless. Somewhere off toward the west a boat engine started and then died when the screws were put into motion.

"Man, it's hot," said Gregson.

"I never seen nothing like it. This shirt is soaking wet."

"It's rough, all right."

"Hey, Lombardi."

"What's this guy getting bounced for?"

"Hell, I don't know."

"Maybe he's pushing somebody around,

"Man, what difference does it make? Now if you ask me *why* he's getting bit, I could tell you."

"The green, huh?"

"Now you're getting to the point."

"It's funny we don't ever know a damn thing about the guys."

"Better that way."

"Did you ever…"

"Hold it, hold it!" whispered Lonnie shrilly. "A car just made the turn at the corner. Duck down till we see who it is."

"He's stopping," said Gregson, his voice muffled by the cushions in the back seat.

"There went the lights."

"Raise up and check."

"That's his car. That must be him. Come on, kid, get on 'im.'

"Man, I'm on 'im."

"What's he look like?"

"About 58. One-twenty pounds. Little guy. No hat."

"Is he wearing horn-rim glasses?"

"Yeah."

"That's him. Bang 'im, kid, bang 'im."

"Here goes."

Across the soft stillness of the warm night came the sound of a clipped, desperate grunt. A quiet thud followed, and then silence—a taut, pregnant silence. Lonnie listened to the sound of Gregson's breathing for a second and then asked, "What about it?"

"He's down."

"For good?"

"I don't know."

"*Goddammit*, whattaya mean, you don't know? Ain't you looking at 'im?"

"Yeah, I'm looking I've got the scope right on 'im."

"Well, whattaya think?"

"He's still flopping."

"Flopping? *For chrissake!* Don't they all flop? Have you ever seen one of them that didn't kick around a little?"

"I can't tell yet."

A long 30 seconds passed. Across the bay a horn sounded. A frog croaked.

"His legs are still jerking."

"Well, pop 'im again."

"Wait a sec, will you? I don't want to waste a round."

"Waste, hell. Hit him again, so we can get out of here."

"Wait…wait…Just a minute. There…There, he went. OK. It's all right."

"He's dead?"

"I'll bet on it."

"O.K. Fix the window and we'll drag."

They were across town before either of them spoke.

"Well, what about it, kid?"

"It was all right. Everything went fine."

"No complaints?"

"Naw, but I tell you one thing : I hope I draw Alaska next. I can't stand this goddam heat."

•••

TATTOO REMOVING
WITH THE **TATEX METHOD** — WITHOUT PAIN, NEEDLES OR UGLY SCARS
The Chemical "Do-It-Yourself" Kit

The **TATEX METHOD** will remove any tattoo, regardless of age! Use safely in your home. **ASK FOR FREE FOLDER NO. C.**

ATLANTA COMPANY
907 BEACHPOINT PROMENADE
FAIRPORT BEACH-PICKERING, ONTARIO

TREMENDOUS PROFITS
with Hagen's **EXCLUSIVE TEAR-GAS PENCIL!**
100% PROTECTION

SELL EASY TO SERVICE STATIONS, BAR-CAFE WORKERS, SHOPS, STORES, LOAN OFFICES, BANKS, HOMES! Discharges smothering clouds of tear-gas to instantly stop, stun and incapacitate the most vicious man or beast. Effective substitute for firearms; leaves no permanent injury. No selling experience needed. Handle as profitable sideline, soon you'll sell it full time. Start now! Send $5.95 for complete demonstration kit of Automatic Tear-Gas Pencil, 10 Demonstrators & 3 Tear-Gas Cartridges. Not sold to minors. **HAGEN SUPPLY CORP., Dept. C128,** Saint Paul 4, Minnesota.

IMPORTED KNIVES

Free Catalog
DAGGERS, STILETTOS, SWORDS, HUNTING KNIVES, POCKET & PEN KNIVES, FENCING EQUIPMENT, BOWIES, THROWING KNIVES etc. *From Germany, England, Italy, Spain, Mexico, Sweden, & others.*
WRITE FOR YOUR FREE CATALOG

J.D. CLINTON
MT. CLEMENS 43   MICH.

Want to Cuddle Up to Me?

YOU CAN! I'm on the exciting new
Cuddle-Up
☐ Blonde
☐ Brunette
☐ Redhead
Please check
PILLOWCASE
Washable
I'm in full color and can be all YOURS!
You won't want to miss this sensational new item.

only $1 95 Each postpaid
or 2 for $3.50
Send now to CUDDLE-UP INC
Dept. C.S. 550 Fifth Ave., New York, N.Y.

EXPLODING **ARMY HAND GRENADE**
EXACT REPLICA   only $1.00

Here's real battle authenticity. This menacing hand grenade looks and works just like a real one. All you do is pull the pin, wait 4 seconds, throw the grenade, and watch the fun as it explodes automatically. It's completely harmless, but the explosion it makes can be heard for a block. Really scatters the gang when you throw this baby in their midst. It sure looks and sounds real. Can't break. Can be exploded over and over again. Heavy gauge steel firing mechanism. Only $1 plus 25¢ shipping charges.

10 DAY FREE TRIAL
Don't delay! Order now! If not 100% delighted simply return for prompt refund of full purchase price

— MONEY BACK GUARANTEE —
HONOR HOUSE PRODUCTS CORP   DEPT.
LYNBROOK, NEW YORK   HG-39
Rush me my exploding Hand Grenade at once. If I am not 100% delighted I may return after 10 Day Free Trial for prompt refund of purchase price.
☐ I enclosed $1 plus 25¢ shipping charges.
☐ Send C.O.D. I will pay postman on delivery & C.O.D. & shipping.
Name
Address

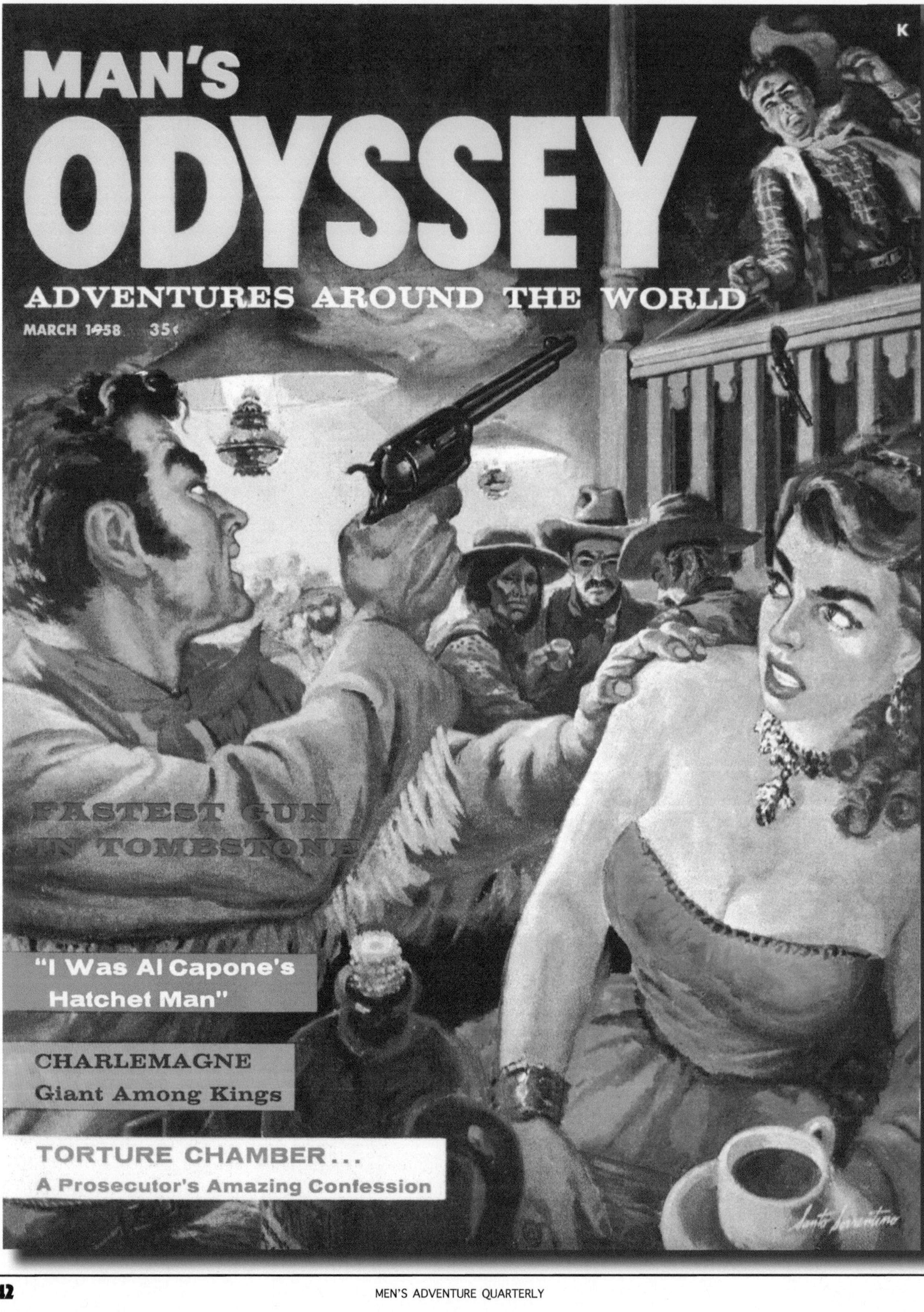

MAN'S ODYSSEY
ADVENTURES AROUND THE WORLD
MARCH 1958   35¢

FASTEST GUN IN TOMBSTONE

"I Was Al Capone's Hatchet Man"

CHARLEMAGNE
Giant Among Kings

TORTURE CHAMBER...
A Prosecutor's Amazing Confession

Many people who've been convicted of crimes and served time in prison have written books and short stories that reflect their experiences as criminals. But to my knowledge only Dave Mazroff, the author of this next story, went on to become an extremely prolific writer for mystery and crime digest magazines and men's magazines.

Mazroff was a very interesting guy. From the mid-1930s to the mid-1950s, he was basically a professional criminal who worked for some of the biggest gangsters in Detroit and Chicago. He was involved in many crimes and did time in prison for several, including robbery, extortion, assault with a deadly weapon, and arson.

In 1945, he was one of several suspects in the murder of Michigan State Senator Warren G. Hooper. Sen. Hooper was shot to death shortly before he was scheduled to testify in a grand jury about taking a bribe from mobsters in return for changing language in a horse-racing bill that threatened their illegal gambling operations.

Mazroff denied any involvement in Hooper's murder and denied ever being used as a hit man. He and every other suspect evaded conviction. Of course, ironically, in the story "I Was Al Capone's Hatchet Man," he admits being a hitter for Capone.

He was definitely a bad dude in his younger days. In 1950, he was convicted of getting a woman to falsely accuse Detroit Lions football player Lou Creekmur of rape in an effort to extort $10,000 from him. That landed Mazroff in Jackson Prison for two-and-a-half years. He served more years after that for shooting a man in a restaurant and for being involved in an arson scheme.

In the late 1950s, after his last stint in prison, Mazroff began submitting fictional and fact-based crime and mystery stories to digest magazines and men's mags. He soon became a fairly successful writer, ultimately selling hundreds of stories and articles.

Most were published in *MIKE SHAYNE MYSTERY MAGAZINE* between 1968 and 1977. He also sold stories to other crime digest mags, including *ELLERY QUEEN'S MYSTERY MAGAZINE,*

By Dave Mazroff
From *MAN'S ODYSSEY*, March 1958
Cover artwork by Santo Sorrentino

David "Dave" Mazroff

ALFRED HITCHCOCK'S MYSTERY MAGAZINE, CHARLIE CHAN MAGAZINE, and *GUILTY DETECTIVE STORY*, and to MAMs like *ARGOSY, ADVENTURE, SEE,* and *MAN'S ODYSSEY*.

Mazroff's stories were generally well-written and especially popular with readers of the Mike Shayne digest. Stories with his byline were often touted on the covers of issues they appeared in. He even won a Shamus Award for "Best Short Story" for the story **"The Death Merchants, Bonnie and Clyde,"** published in the March 1968 issue.

INTRODUCTION BY BOB DEIS

Mike Shayne, the tough, Miami-based Private Detective character, was created by Davis Dresser in his 1939 novel *DIVIDEND ON DEATH*. It was credited to the pseudonym Dresser became known by—Brett Halliday.

Dresser followed *DIVIDEND ON DEATH* with *THE PRIVATE PRACTICE OF MICHAEL SHAYNE* in 1940. Later that same year, elements of both books were adapted into the film *MICHAEL SHAYNE, PRIVATE DETECTIVE*, with Lloyd Nolan starring as Shayne.

Thus was launched what became a multi-decade multimedia empire that went on to include: over 70 novels and 300 stories written by Dresser and other writers using the Brett Halliday pen name; a dozen movies; a television series; a radio series; a comic book; and, the *MIKE SHAYNE MYSTERY MAGAZINE*, which ran from 1956 to 1985.

Brett Halliday became the house name for *MSMM* and a number of writers penned Michael Shayne stories under it early in their careers. One of the best and most notable was my friend James Reasoner, who went on to become an award-winning Western and action/adventure novelist and head of Rough Edges Press. Another was Dave Mazroff.

Mazroff claimed to have written many Mike Shayne stories for *MSMM*. That's hard to verify, but he definitely did write many fiction and non-fiction stories

for the magazine under his own name.

Mazroff sometimes mentioned his criminal past in his stories, like the one in *MAN'S ODYSSEY*. But after he became a stringer for *MSMM* he was less forthcoming.

In 1973, an Associated Press reporter interviewed Mazroff in Miami, where he lived at the time. That reporter, Kay Metzcher, apparently didn't do any research on Mazroff's background. She just blithely reported what he said about himself.

He told her he started out as a police and court reporter in Chicago. He suggested that was how he learned about the world of professional criminals and "got to be friends with Al Capone." Mazroff's rap sheet and his *MAN'S ODYSSEY* story show otherwise, but Metzcher swallowed it whole.

Mazroff told her about a new character he had created for the short stories and novellas he wrote for *MSMM*—Rick Harper. He describes Harper as an MIT graduate turned private detective who "pursues

virtuous causes, such as seeking revenge against the mob for killing a little old lady."

Mazroff seems to have expected Rick Harper to become as popular as Mike Shayne. "I want to get into TV and motion pictures," Mazroff said. "And Mike Shayne's kinda dead."

Mazroff kept writing for another decade, but his Rick Harper character wasn't a big hit and he didn't break into TV or movies. He died in Los Angeles in 1982 at age 75.

The cover painting for *MAN'S ODYSSEY*,

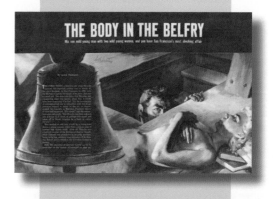

Springfield (O.) NEWS-SUN, Sunday, July 1, 1973

Writer Weaves Experiences, Fact Into Stories

POMPANO BEACH, Fla. (AP) — As long as readers thrill to scenes where detectives by brain and brawn overcome muggers and thugs, writer David Mazroff will continue to churn out mystery stories.

For over 40 years Mazroff has woven experiences and facts from courthouse digs into fiction and nonfiction pieces that have sold in the millions.

His main character is private detective Mike Shayne, who from his Miami office is featured in novelties and short stories in the monthly Mike Shayne Mystery Magazines.

Mazroff, also known as Brett Halliday, describes the shamus as a guy of average education and intelligence who gets knocked down but bounces back to logically solve case after case.

"The formula for this kind of writing is to get the guy into a whole lot of trouble and then get him out," says Mazroff, who lives in Sunrise, Fla.

The author of over 500 stories and novelties is an easygoing, always-thinking man nearing retirement age. After years of pulling Shayne through scrapes, Mazroff has created a new character, Rick Harper. This young, sophisticated MIT graduate is a roving private detective, who pursues virtuous causes, such as seeking revenge against the mob for killing a little old lady.

"I want to get into TV and motion pictures," Mazroff said. "And Mike Shayne's kinda dead." By this he means the stereotype, rough-and-tumble detective character is dead.

"Rick Harper has an encyclopedic mind. He's been with the FBI, the CIA and in military service. He's an expert in karate and judo. And the ladies chase him but he doesn't chase them."

Despite cramming of the tube with detective series, Mazroff foresees no saturation point. And he definitely objects to complicating plots with new-fangled electronic bugging devices.

DAVID MAZROFF

March 1958 was done by the little-known artist Santo Sorrentino. Between 1957 and 1962, Sorrentino did cover and interior artwork the men's adventure mags *ACTION, ADVENTURE, MAN'S CONQUEST, MAN'S ILLUSTRATED, REAL ADVENTURES,* and *TRUE ADVENTURES* and a for few men's bachelor magazines. He also tried his hand at "fine art" paintings of landscapes and nudes.

Sadly, his career was cut short in 1962 when he drowned while swimming in the Hudson River.

•••

OPPOSITE: One of Dav Mazroff's many stories in *MIKE SHAYNE MYSTERY MAGAZINE* was the cover story for the November 1969 issue, which reuses Mort Engle's cover art for *PRIVATE EYEFUL* by Henry Kane (Pyramid, 1962). That same art was reused for Lawrence Block's story "Twin Call Girls" in *MAN'S MAGAZINE*, August 1963, one of the men's adventure mag stories reprinted in the book *THE NAKED AND THE DEADLY: LAWRENCE BLOCK IN MEN'S ADVENTURE MAGAZINES*, co-edited by MAQ editor Bob Deis with Wyatt Doyle. Below the "Twin Call Girls" are two MAM stories featuring illustrations by Santo Sorrentino, from *ACTION*, March 1958 and *REAL ADVENTURE*, July 1957.

ABOVE: The 1973, AP news about Dave Mazroff. BACKGROUND: Mort Engel's artwork for *PRIVATE EYEFUL* by Henry Kane (1962), later reused by *MIKE SHAYNE MYSTERY MAGAZINE* and *MAN'S MAGAZINE*.

" I WAS AL CAPONE'S HATCHET MAN"

AL CAPONE, notorious gangland chief, sent Mazroff to cut down the competition

Wide World Photo

BIG TIM MURPHY HAD TO BE RUBBED OUT, AND IT WAS MY TURN TO PLAY EXECUTIONER

EVERYBODY around Chicago during the early days of Prohibition was a big guy. Big Jim Colosimo, Al Capone, who was called the Big Guy, and Big Tim Murphy, who stood six feet four inches and was a big guy in the Windy City's underworld. Colosimo had imported Johnny Torrio from New York and Torrio brought in Frankie Yale and Al Capone. I was already living in Chicago and my hot, eager hands were dipping into the crime pot before Al showed up. Capone moved fast. Colosimo hired him as a bodyguard. On a nice clear morning Capone shot Colosimo in the head and took over. But not entirely. Standing in his way was Big Tim Murphy, who couldn't be pushed around or scared off. But Big Tim had to go and I was the boy elected to send him. It was a real cozy task.

I put a .38 snub nose in a shoulder-holster and drifted over to the Frolics Cafe, Denny Cooney's nightclub on 22nd between Wabash and State.

Before I left Capone said to me, "Maybe Frenchy Mader and Con Shea will be with Murphy. It ain't gonna make me mad if they go, too. But if they don't leave together then forget about them two. If Murphy is out of the way them guys will probably blow town."

I said, "Okay, Al. Either way is all right with me."

He said, "You sure you don't want anybody with you? You can handle this by yourself? Huh? You won't make any mistakes?"

"I won't make any mistakes," I replied, too surely.

But I did.

Big Tim Murphy threw away a brilliant career because he was a crook and an outlaw at heart, a guy who loved the bright lights and the flashy dames. Had I had his opportunities I would never have picked up a gun or turned a shady trick.

Murphy was born in the stock yards district of Chicago where you either had to fight or run, and if you ran you were caught and beat up anyway. Murphy never ran. He also never lost a fight, and each kid he whipped later became his friend. He has that kind of personality. He somehow was appointed as a page boy in Congress and there he learned his politics and politicians. He returned to Chicago while still in his teens but a man in his appetites. Before he was twenty he was arrested on charges of assault to rape. He beat the rap. He then was arrested on charges of assault to kill. He beat that rap too. With the effrontery of a fox in a hen-house he ran for the Illinois legislature and was elected.

From the outset he sought ways to use his position for graft. He was forever searching for the gimmick, for the twist and the curve, the angle and the loophole that would afford him a profit because he constantly needed money. Night life and women. The pleasures of self-indulgence. These were his meat and drink. He did everything with the self-same impudence. He accepted bribes, even for things he couldn't deliver, he lied to his constituents and to his colleagues, and it spelled the end of his political career. He shrugged it off as a matter of little concern.

Standing six feet four, Murphy had a ready smile on his handsome Irish face and a way with words. He affected ten gallon hats and a bold swagger and he walked around Chicago as if he owned it. For a time he did.

After leaving the legislature Murphy met Frenchy Mader and Con Shea, two of the toughest and shrewdest racketeers around Chicago at the time. It was Shea, a heistman and vice lord, who set off the turbulent teamsters' strike a few years earlier, organizing the strategy and operation from one of his brothels. Murphy, Mader and Shea, after they merged, became known as "The Unholy Three." They got in Al Capone's way. It was their big mistake. Capone had a rule for that sort of thing.

After Capone knocked off Jim Colosimo he took over the beer and

"If they got in our way they were put out of business . . ."

alky business on the South Side, as well as the brothels and the other rackets. Big Tim Murphy threw Capone's beer into the street and put in his own. When that happened Al would send some of us around to throw Murphy's beer into the street. The poor tavern owners were going nuts and broke in their efforts to keep up with the constantly changing power. We caught some of Murphy's hired hands and beat them up, sent several of them to hospitals, scared others off. But not Big Tim or Mader or Shea.

In the meantime The Unholy Three set out to organize the city's gas workers, and Capone sat back and watched and waited.

"Let them guys do the front work," Al said to us. "When they get it organized we'll take it over, eh?"

Everyone agreed. Why disagree? It sounded good.

IT WAS at this time that the big era of crime began in Chicago, the era that was never to lessen, which hasn't diminished to this date and which may never end because Chicago is constructed politically so that the precinct captains and the ward heelers, who work under the Big Combination, control the votes and thus the power.

The lawlessness spread and touched everyone in the city. Since no racket can operate without due and proper protection from authorities, politicians were getting as rich as the hoods. That's how organized crime breeds. You take in the police and the city officials as partners, silent partners but nonetheless partners.

After Murphy organized the gas workers he was arrested for the crime of receiving stolen autos. This was one of his sidelines. He would alter the serial numbers or transfer parts from one car to another and then sell the cars. The police had been tipped to this racket and with the help of the tipster had built up a strong case against Murphy. But Murphy had been around a little while and knew the score.

"Look, you guys," Murphy told the detectives, "I know who told you about this deal, and I know why. I'll take care of that guy later but right now I'm telling you to lay off me. I'm not a two-bit punk. If you take me to court on this rap I promise you the city will be out of gas tomorrow. I'm the boss of the gas workers' union and I'll call a strike inside of four hours unless I'm out of here and free."

He was turned loose.

Satisfied that he now had the key to powerful influence, that he could strangle the city's utilities, take away their gas and light, stop deliveries of bread and milk, he moved ahead to organizing other city workers and succeeded in taking over the Street Cleaners' union. An ex-con labor leader named Maurice "Mossy" Enright was rash enough to attempt to stop him. Enright was killed in front of his home.

Murphy was promptly arrested for the murder, and the street cleaners were as promptly called out on strike. Murphy dickered for his liberty, and for wage advances and other considerations for the street cleaners from his cell in the County Jail. He talked long and loud to newspaper reporters and presented himself as a martyred labor leader, and as such went to trial.

He was acquitted.

Capone smiled and shrugged his shoulders. He could wait. The die was cast for Big Tim Murphy. He was newspaper copy as a hoodlum and racketeer. He was getting into more peoples hair. He was becoming a nuisance. The friendly smile had changed now to one of arrogance. Murphy, like most hoods who win several cases in court, believed he was immune to any type of prosecution. He swaggered through the city's night life spots. With him were Con Shea and Frenchy Mader and a bevy of beautiful women. He was riding high, throwing money around like it was confetti. He had his followers, the leeches, and free-loaders, the fawners. I saw him several times in various places. He hailed me from across the room and usually made some wise crack. Once I ran into him at the Blackhawk. I was with Frankie Yale. We were both rodded. Murphy jumped up from his chair.

"Hey, there! You—Frankie. Dave."

We ignored him.

We kept on going toward the back of the restaurant. Murphy's raucous laughter was the only sound in the room. He said, "That's right, boys," he said, "keep right on going. You'll find your aprons and dishes in the back." He laughed louder and the others at his table laughed with him.

Frankie made a move for his gun but I touched his arm. "Slow it down, Frankie," I cautioned him. "Let him have his fun."

We reported the incident to Capone the next day and Al shrugged it off again with that same smile.

Murphy, Shea and Mader now went after the construction workers. By threats and promises they gained control of that union, too. They were really coining money, playing it both ends to the middle.

As soon as a job was well under way one of the three would approach the contractor and sell him protection. If the contractor refused he was told the union would pull off the workers. The work stoppage would mean costly impairments. The contractor paid off. The amounts varied from as low as $25,000 to as high as $100,000! Those who refused to pay were punished. In 1924, Murphy's men bombed about twenty buildings, set innumerable incendiary fires, slugged foremen and superintendents, and knocked off several rival hoods.

How far Murphy, Mader and Shea would have gone is anybody's guess, and my guess at the time was that they were going farther than Al Capone. I couldn't understand why Al was waiting, why he didn't order the executions. But now the incident Al was waiting for occurred.

MURPHY HAD many of the city's and state's politicians on his payroll. He also had a lot of the cops in Chicago on his payroll. Two of the cops, Terrence Lyons and Thomas Clark, welshed on some kind of deal, according to the information we got, and they were assassinated.

Big Tim Murphy and about twenty-five others were arrested. The newspapers made a great to-do about the crimes, about Murphy's hold on the city, and demanded action against him. Al was elated. All the heat was on Murphy and so long as it stayed there Capone could operate smoothly and without trouble. But—although it was widely known that Tim Murphy had ordered the executions of the two cops—it was also known that he, himself, had not done the shooting and there was no one who came forward to accuse him of setting up the kills. He was subsequently released for lack of evidence. One minor hood was convicted of the crimes and received a sentence of 14 years. That settled the murder rap. It also settled the Unholy Three. They were so hot in Chicago they could melt hatchets.

And now Al said, "Go get 'em."

So I put the .38 snub nose in a shoulder holster and another inside my belt and drifted over to the Frolics Cafe. And in the Cafe were Big Tim Murphy, Con Shea and Frenchy Mader. They had a table near the entrance. There were three women with them and they were all having a real gay time. I took a table across the room, ordered a drink and waited. I could see that Big Tim was getting drunk and that was okay with me. About two o'clock in the morning the party began to break up. I paid my tab and walked out to wait. There was a light rain falling and the sky was dark. I hurried across the street to my car and got in. Murphy's party came out. Mader and Shea said something to Murphy and then they each took their girl, got into cabs and drove away. That left Murphy and his girl standing in front of the Frolics. There were the usual hangers-on around, cabbies, the all-night boys, the gamblers trying to round up a game. Murphy hailed a cab. He and the girl got in and the cab made a U turn, drove past me, turned left onto Wabash and headed north. I followed.

The rain now began to fall harder. I trailed the cab to Addison Avenue. I turned right, went one block and turned right again then stopped on the corner of Brompton. Murphy and the girl got out. The cab drove off and I got out of my car, gun in hand. Murphy and the girl were walking west toward a hotel. I was about fifteen feet behind them.

I said, "Murphy!"

He wheeled around. His gun was in his hand and he fired. I felt a hot shock flash through me and then I shot. There were more shots but I couldn't tell whether they were coming from my gun or Murphy's. The girl was screaming. Suddenly lights went up in the buildings in the area and from a short distance came the whining sound of a police siren. I ran around the corner to my car, got in and drove away. I drove and drove without knowing where I was going. There was a strange numbness in my arms and legs and I was finding it difficult to breathe. I broke into a feverish sweat and then I began to shake all over. I pulled the car over to the curb, turned off the motor and the lights and sat there. I wanted to move, to get out of the car into the rain-washed night and to breathe in the cool air because my lungs were hot and dry and the pain in my chest was getting unbearable but I didn't have the strength to get out of the car, to open the door, to lower a window. Something in my terrified brain shrieked, "You're dying!" And then I passed out.

I DIDN'T die. I had been hit just over the heart, in a bad spot, and I was lucky. Murphy didn't get a scratch. As we analyzed it later, Tim Murphy's first shot hit me, and after that my reflexes and timing were so far off that I was aiming wide. The boys weren't happy about my messing up the job but it was one of those things. Murphy's report to the police was that he fought off an attempted holdup. But no one was fooled. They knew it was an attempt to get him. And that it wouldn't be the last.

The murder of the two cops had forced Murphy out of the unions he had controlled and he was now without a source of steady income. He was being harassed on both sides—from the gangs that wanted him out of the way, and from the cops to whom he had become useless in every respect.

In order to get the money he needed to keep going until the heat was off him Murphy and several of his boys heisted a mail train in the Dearborn station and got away with more than $300,000 in cash and bonds. This was a government matter. It couldn't be fixed. The Secret Service put their best agents to work on the case and when they had gathered all their evidence it pointed the finger straight at Murphy. The Secret Service agents recovered most of the loot where Murphy had stashed it, and with this evidence in their possession they took Murphy to trial. Judge Kennesaw Mountain Landis, who later became Commissioner of baseball, sentenced Big Tim to six years in prison.

Murphy served his time and was released. He returned to Chicago. Instead of letting well enough alone, restraining his ambitions to pick up where he had let off prior to the mail robbery, Murphy talked big and tough. Al Capone was completely in power now. With the exception of Bugs Moran on the North Side, and the O'Bannions on the near-North Side, Al had Chicago wrapped up. Big Tim Murphy was not wanted. Not by anyone. But Murphy was rash, or maybe too tough for his own good. He also had another fault. He talked too much, and too loud.

On June 26, 1928, a black sedan cruised slowly past Murphy's North Side home. Big Tim was standing on the lawn soaking in some sunshine. In the sedan were Machine-gun Jack McGurn, Frank Nitti, Johnny Hand, and one other boy. Two sawed-off shotguns poked their deadly noses through the open car windows. There was a terrific blast as both guns went off together. The blood spurted out of Big Tim Murphy's body and splattered the lawn and the house. He was dead before he dropped.

He had a nice funeral, with a dozen carloads of flowers and a great number of beribboned wreaths. The one I sent was huge and fancy and worth every dime it cost. I was sorry to see Big Tim go and I expressed my sentiments on the ribbon which was stretched diagonally across the wreath. In golden letters were inscribed these words:

"SO LONG, PAL."

Yes, sir, it was a real nice funeral.

• • •

"You're right, it's not a snowman."

MAQ

MEN'S ADVENTURE QUARTERLY

#9 THIS SUMMER!

WE'RE ON TARGET!

COMICS
MOVIE BOOKS
PULP FICTION
& MORE!!

NEMESIS
THE BOOK OF THE MOVIE

DEATH KISS
THE BOOK OF THE MOVIE

MIKE SHAYNE
PRIVATE EYE

MEN'S ADVENTURE READER

killer

TERROR!

WWW.PULP2OHPRESS.COM

AVAILABLE EXCLUSIVELY ON AMAZON.COM

PULP 2.0

MAN'S

TRUE REPORT: LIQUOR CAN RUIN YOUR LOVE LIFE

TRUE DANGER

NUDE DEATH ORGY OF THE WOMEN CRAZY COSSACKS

35¢ FEB.

THE STRANGE SAGA OF THE WEIRD JEKYLL AND HYDE

KILLER WITH A 100 FACES

THESE "WET-BEHIND-THE-EARS" PUNKS IN SKIRTS MORE THAN EARNED THE NAME OF . . . .

TEENAGE TORTURERS OF TERRE HAUTE

One of the things I love about vintage men's adventure magazines is their straight-faced publication of stories they portray as "true" that are in fact partly or entirely fictional.

Different MAMs went to different lengths to make stories seem to be true. The simplest device was to have subhead saying "TRUE STORY." Another simple ploy was an Editor's Note like the one used for "Killer With 100 Faces." It identifies the author as a real police detective whose story describes real criminals and events. The most creative approaches used photos of the supposed authors, characters and events.

I often can't tell myself whether a "true" MAM story is true or not until I do some online research. For example, when I looked into Dave Mazroff's story in this issue, "I Was Al Capone's Hatchet Man," I was surprised to discover that he was indeed a gangster in his younger days and actually did know Al Capone and the other mobsters he mentions.

By Donald I. Brock
From *MAN'S TRUE DANGER*, February 1963
Cover art and interior illustration by
John Duillo with a spot illustration featuring faces
by Basil Gogos and one or two other artists.

When I looked into "Killer With 100 Faces" I found that virtually everyone and everything in it is the creation of whoever the real writer was. The police detective who was the supposed writer, the central character Johnny Driscoll, all the other characters in the story, and the events described are pure pulp fiction. Even the town mentioned in the opening—Williston City, Colorado—is fictional.

However, like many faux true stories in MAMs, I think it's a fun read. And, I really like the artwork that goes with it.

The cover painting for *MAN'S TRUE DANGER*, February 1963 and the main 2-page illustration were done by the great John Duillo (1928–2003). In the '50s and '60s, Duillo

INTRODUCTION
BY BOB **DEIS**

***A TIME TO FIGHT**, a Western lithograph by John Duillo c.1980*

did scores of MAM cover paintings and interior illustrations and hundreds of paperback covers.

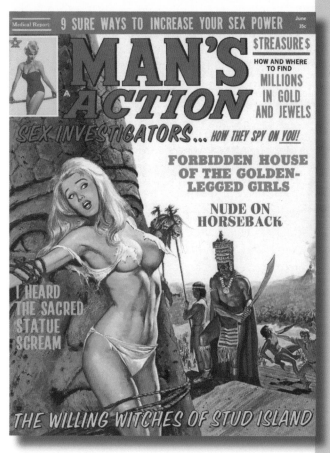

Most of his MAM artwork appeared in the mid-to-low budget "sweat mag" subgenre of MAMs. Those that regularly featured Duillo covers and interiors include titles published by Candar—*MAN'S TRUE DANGER, MAN'S ACTION,* and *WILDCAT ADVENTURES*—and the mags published by Reese Publishing and its sister company Emtee, which have some of the most lurid bondage-and-torture illustrations—*MAN'S BOOK, MAN'S EPIC, MAN'S STORY, MEN TODAY, NEW MAN, REAL COMBAT* and *WORLD OF MEN*. You can also find Duillo covers and interiors in the Natlus, Inc. MAMs *PERIL, RAGE FOR MEN,* and *WILD FOR MEN.*

Duillo also did cover art for the Western history magazine *TRUE FRONTIER.* And, many of his paperback covers were Westerns.

In fact, like a number of his contemporaries who started out doing paperback and magazine artwork, Duillo went on to focus on doing Western and Civil War paintings and limited edition lithograph prints for galleries in the 1970s. In the 1980s and 1990s, his Western and Civil War paintings were being displayed in art shows alongside those by artists like Mort Künstler and Frank McCarthy, who had also preciously worked as illustration artists for paperbacks and magazines. Like them, Duillo actually became best known for his historical artwork and it still sold by a number of galleries and online auction sites.

Duillo was so well respected in the '90s that he was elected to serve as President of the Society of American Artists. Around that time, his wife Elaine Duillo (1928-2021) was at the peak of her own career as an artist.

Elaine started doing paperback cover art in the 1960s and became especially well known for her romance cover paintings. The market for romance and "gothic" paperbacks boomed for several decades after the mid-1970s. Publishers of romance novels like Harlequin were selling millions of copies and paying their cover artists top dollar. Elaine rode that wave and became one of the best and busiest. She did do artwork for other genres of novels, but she's most widely known as "The Queen of Romance Cover Art."

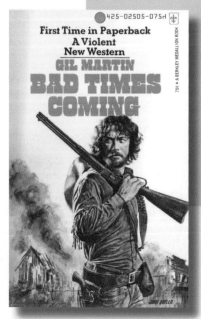

It was her use of the long-haired, muscular male model Fabio Lanzoni on her romance cover paintings that made images of his shirtless bod iconic. And, that led to Fabio's wider fame as a celebrity.

There have been rumors that Elaine sometimes did MAM artwork attributed to John. This has never been verified. However, their painting style is similar and Elaine did once say she repainted the image of a sexy blonde John had done for an obscure 1967 soft porn novel published by Chevron titled *LUST CANDIDATE.* "They asked me to paint the blonde again," Elaine recalled. "Then they stripped it in and paid me well to do this for them."

I don't whether John was too busy to redo the blonde or if the publisher didn't like his version. But it does lend credence to the theory that she *may* have done some of the MAM artwork credited to him before she herself got too busy doing high-paying romance paperback covers.

John's cover painting for **MAN'S TRUE DANGER**, February 1963 is far removed from the realm of romance. The blonde in it is bound and clearly being mistreated, though she's not exactly being tortured quite yet. The women in many John Duillo "sweat mag" cover and interior illustrations usually are.

Naturally, some of the torturers he painted for MAM covers and story illustrations are Nazis. But many of the scores of bondage-and-torture style illustrations he did feature non-Nazi sadists, serial killers, cult members, and other evildoers.

One of my faves is the gonzo interior he did for "Soft Bride for the Slithering Monster From Hell" in **MAN'S BOOK**, August 1963. It features a deformed, legless Nazi who is telling his underlings to feed some hapless, scantily dressed babes to a giant squid in a tank.

By the way, the three heads used for the spot illustration in "Killer With 100 Faces" were not done by John Duillo. They were done by Basil Gogos. Basil is best known for his monster artwork for **FAMOUS MONSTERS OF FILMLAND**. But he also did many MAM illustrations. I'm pretty sure the heads were cut

and pasted from some other story, a common practice of budget-limited MAMs. If you know what they were originally used for, please shoot me an email at MAQeditor@gmail.com and let me know.

•••

OPPOSITE: **MAN'S ACTION**, June 1969 and **BAD TIMES COMING** by Gil Martin featured John Duilo cover art. ABOVE: John Duillo's legless Nazi illustration in **MAN'S BOOK**, August 1963 and an original painting used in **MAN'S STORY**, August 1963. LEFT: Elaine Duillo's artwork for **THE CONQUEROR** by Brenda Joyce (1990), featuring male model Fabio.

KILLER WITH A 100 FACES

By DONALD I. BROCK

Editor's Note: Mr. Brock was an acting lieutenant when he first became acquainted with Johnny Driscoll, who figured in one of the most bizarre cases ever confronted by his 1st Detective Division. His dramatic narration, as recorded by Mr. Slattery, demonstrates that criminals of the old days showed more ingenuity and imagination than the so-called wise-guy punks of today.

WILLISTON CITY WAS A plateau carved out of the shale, sand and rock of Colorado, with a population of 73,000 whose principal source of income was silver mining. Because of the intimacy of its residents, crime or crisis never faced them—but when it did, it had all the impact of a bomb explosion.

Theodore Newell was known only to the hotel clerk when he registered on the night of Oct. 14, 1928, yet, apparently, others were aware that he was a gem merchant, en route to San Francisco. For at 1:32 a.m., a series of gunshots emanated from his room, causing curious guests to spill into the corridor. By the time the

"This is one way to make sure about you," the gunman said.

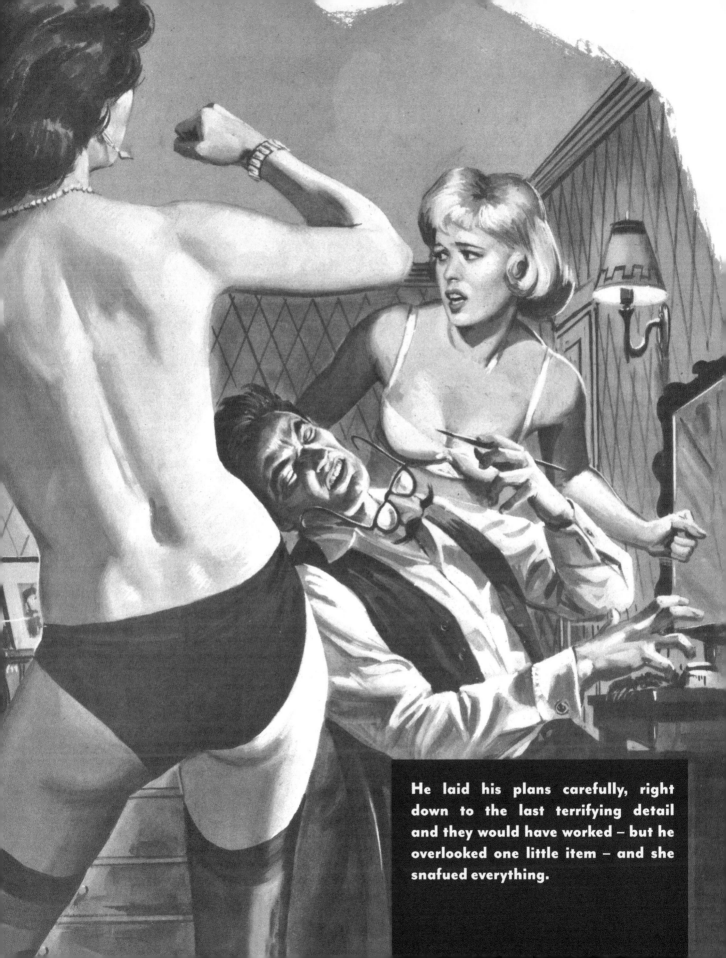

He laid his plans carefully, right down to the last terrifying detail and they would have worked — but he overlooked one little item — and she snafued everything.

The police had eyewitness descriptions of the killers—but did not suspect that all of them were one and the same man.

THAT WAS THE DEBUT of Johnny Driscoll as a criminal, and he was an instantaneous smash hit. As a professional actor, he had been a middling success, more often bordering on failure. He had played insignificant roles on Broadway for such producers as Al Woods, William A. Brady and Dwight Wiman, and his movie career had been limited to a mob scene in a film directed by King Vidor. Burning with indignation, wracked by frustration and confident of his brimming talent, Johnny Driscoll's rejection by the entertainment world plunged him into a new sphere—the underworld.

He was hitchhiking to New York from Hollywood when he made that crime coup in Williston City. It did more than net him 32 grand in gems. It gave him the inspiration to put his twisted talents to a new and dangerous use.

But like most amateurs who pull off a successful job, Johnny was in a dilemma when it came to disposing of the loot. Aware that he risked arrest if he tried peddling it in the west because merchants and police apparently had been alerted to the brazen theft, Johnny hoped to palm off his plunder via the mobs, finks and fences in New York.

It didn't take him long to make contact with Vitoni Montenegro, whose versatility in the rackets ranged from A to Z—arson to zipguns, sold to minors. Vitoni arranged for a fence to handle the negotiations, cutting himself in for a straight 5 per cent of the sale. Johnny was disappointed; he had expected more than the $11,500 paid by the fence, $575 of which had to be given to Vitoni, but he accepted his explanation that the bundle was so hot, the fence had to cut it up and hope he could dispose of it in Europe.

house detective, joined by the patrolman on the beat, entered the room, they found its contents strewn about, and Mr. Newell seriously bleeding from the abdomen. Great gobs of blood gushed from his mouth when he tried to speak.

The open window, leading out to the fire escape, indicated his assailant's means of escape. Obviously he had panicked into leaving the loot behind: $32,000 in uncut stones. The house detective was about to summon the hotel physician when a stranger elbowed through the gaping crowd to announce that he was a doctor. Leaving the two lawmen to pursue their duties, the doctor attended the victim, then left after he had ordered an ambulance. It wasn't until half an hour later, while they were impatiently awaiting the ambulance, that Mr. Newell urged them to bring him his satchel of stones. It was empty!

The house detective and policeman exchanged knowledgeable glances. They'd been tricked, for while their backs were turned, the stranger who posed as a doctor had calmly transferred the gems to his own black medical bag.

JOHNNY's BITTERNESS at his shortlived victory might have caused him to terminate his new career if it hadn't been for Honeychild. She was Vitoni's girl, tall, blonde, and as cool as a Tom Collins on a hot July night. Johnny's dubious claim to fame as an actor thrilled Honeychild, whose latent ambition to express herself was stilled when she was caught in the coils of crime. This kindred spirit fostered their relationship and caused Honeychild one day to reveal an angering bit of news. Vitoni had not fenced the gems but had bought them himself at the bargain-basement price, nabbing the commission as well.

Johnny thirsted for revenge. The incident that touched off the finale occurred on November 21st when Big Ed Borowski sent a couple of stooges around to Vitoni's Murray Hill hotel to announce that he was cutting in on the beer distribution in Harlem.

Vitoni didn't take the order lying down. "You go back to that gunsel and tell him, he muscles in, I'll cut him up in such small pieces. they could bury him in a matchbox!" he roared.

Cunning actor that he was, the situation provided the only cue Johnny Driscoll needed. Some time during the hours of one and three in the morning, he disguised himself as Vitoni Montenegro, taxied up to Big Ed's place in Claremont Park, and managed to slip unnoticed into Big Ed's bedroom. Big Ed's phobia of sleeping in a dark room worked out to Johnny's advantage. Under the glare of the chandelier light, the moment Big Ed felt the cold steel touch his throat, his eyes snapped open, almost popped from their sockets as he saw Vitoni Montenegro scornfully smiling down at him.

The first cut near his jugular was painful; it felt as if his throat were on fire, and it was just as red, red with the blood pumping down his pajama shirt. He felt the sharp point needle into his fat belly, slash it like a stuffed pillow. Big Ed's beefy hands groped, tried to stem the tidal wave of blood and push back his exposed guts. Johnny made sure he'd be heard as he bolted to the window sill. He overturned a chair, sent a lamp smashing to fragments to the floor. He caught his last glimpse of Big Ed, paralyzed with crimson horror, as he fled down the fire escape.

JOHNNY REMOVED HIS DISGUISE in an alley, spent the better part of the night in an all-night diner on 125th Street, reading *The Daily News*

and quaffing several cups of coffee, before returning to Vitoni's. Even as he opened the door and entered the vestibule, he knew his impersonation had paid off. Lights streamed from open doorways, Honeychild was running down the stairs to meet him.

"They shot him, Johnny—Big Ed's boys!" she said, her eyes wide with wonder. "They barged in a couple of hours ago, and pumped him with enough lead to sink a battleship. And you know why? Because they said he killed Big Ed, who was able to identify him before he kicked off." Her cupidbow mouth fell open in astonishment. "But how could Vitoni have done that…when all the time he was here with me?"

Johnny measured her from tousled blonde hair to painted toenail. Her nightgown looked as if she'd been poured into it, her plump breasts were restrained by a small blue ribbon, and her long, firm thighs led to the soft mound of her stomach. He encircled her satiny waist.

"Looks like Vitoni started something he couldn't finish tonight, baby. Let's not have it go to waste."

"But don't you think we should call the cops?"

"What's the hurry? Vitoni's going to be dead a long, long time. Which room did you say was yours…? "

BUT JOHNNY DRISCOLL WAS shrewd enough to realize that such sporadic feats as pilfering the stones back in Williston City and wreaking sadistic revenge on Vitoni Montenegro didn't furnish the firm foundation for building a career. A lone wolf was vulnerable to the fangs and claws of gangster packs; he could be easily isolated, cornered and caught by the law; but if he could utilize his talents for masking and mimicry with an organization, success would be virtually assured.

He tried to tie in with the big ones–Kid Dropper, Dutch Schultz, Johnny Spanish, Pretty Boy Amberg and Bum Rogers–but he struck out every time he tried to step into the big-league batter's box. None of them wanted to have anything to do with such a novel stunt; they regarded him as a kookie. He was making some progress with Arnold Rothstein, the gambler, and had an appointment to meet him and discuss some details at the Coconut Grove, but Rothstein never lived to see that day.

TO THE OUTSIDE WORLD, Jake Jaretzki ran an import-export business from a loft on West 23rd

Street, but the hard, inner core of crime recognized him as one of the biggest traders in narcotics. Jaretzki's office had all the paraphernalia indigenous to a respectable business: a bustling staff that included a switchboard operator, a secretary, bookkeeper, and a dozen shipping clerks. When Johnny brazenly told the operator to tell Jaretzki he had a million-dollar blockbuster proposition, he was invited inside. Jaretzki's first impulse was to kick Johnny out, but then the idea began to appeal to him. Yeah, this handsome jerk could take his place on dangerous missions, when the goods was too hot to handle with any degree of safety.

But Johnny's single reference to narcotics smashed the hopes of any further consideration. Jaretzki slammed a ham fist down on his desk, almost splintering the glass top.

"Narcotics? Who gave you that crazy idea?" he rasped. "I run a respectable business, and no dimpled darling with wavy blonde locks walks in here and tells me he'll take my place when the Feds are breathing down my neck! You don't need my clothes to impersonate me, buddy! What you need is a straitjacket! Now scram, or it's you who 'll be needing a new face!"

Johnny waited patiently in a hallway entrance across the street until Jaretzki went to lunch. Then, he used his nimble, skilled fingers to apply putty and greasepaint to his face, adhesive-taped the hairpiece, added padding to the waist to give him the correct girth, put a pair of rimless glasses on his nose—and walked across the street and up to the loft to make his grand but unobtrusive entrance. In his brief visit, he had studied and mastered Jaretzki's nervous, jack-rabbit gait, his habit of pursing his lips and cracking his knuckles in moments of stress. He could even force his face to turn purple with rage. There was not a hitch to Johnny Driscoll's impersonation; he could have gone home and slept with Jaretzki's wife, it was that perfect.

The telephone operator was surprised to see him back so soon; shipping clerks brought invoices in for his approval; his secretary reminded him they had a date Saturday night, and she had told her roommate to book a hotel for herself that night. Johnny even was bold enough to answer the telephone, leaving his callers stunned or surprised by his double-talk — but they'd swear it was Jaretzki's voice they'd heard.

JARETZKI RAN THE GAUNTLET of bewildered glances when he returned. As he stamped into his office, he came to an abrupt stop. He was looking at his own image! For a moment, his confusion turned to rage, then to smiling acceptance. Johnny Driscoll's exploit that day earned him a job that paid a lucrative fee, and his first assignment. He was to meet Gennaro Romano at the head of the stairs of Track 14 at Pennsylvania Station, accompany him to the newsstand, and switch black bags with him while Romano fished for change in his pocket. Romano's bag would contain a parcel of heroin from the coast, and Johnny's would hold the payola. Romano and Jaretzki had agreed on this subterfuge to outwit the Feds or local lawmen, who might have either one under surveillance.

Johnny was elated by the opportunity to demonstrate his talent on such an important assignment. He switched to Jaretzki's identity in the privacy of the men's room, then slipped out the back door to avoid suspicion. Romano recognized him at once, as Jaretzki, but didn't give the slightest hint. After the bags had been exchanged, Johnny began to stroll off nonchalantly when a terrific explosion rocked the area. Rocky Romano was instantly killed, the newsstand clerk sustained internal injuries that were responsible for his death at Knickerbocker Hospital one week later, a score pf passersby were seriously hurt and removed by ambulance to Polyclinic Hospital. The only pain Johnny experienced was Jaretzki's failure to warn him of the pending blast. If he'd known about the danger involved, he'd have demanded a bigger fee.

Jake Jaretzki tossed a party that night to celebrate his easy acquisition of $150,000 in heroin. Booze and beauties littered the loft. He grudgingly consented to Johnny's demand for a bonus in recognition of the danger he'd endured, but Johnny had a unique method of making not only Jaretzki but his muggs, too, pay in another way. Making sure he was unseen, he slipped out to telephone a warning from a drugstore booth that some of Romano's hoods were en route to get revenge. Jaretzki and his jackal-pack fled in panic, leaving Johnny to help himself to all the goodies.

FIRST, HE DISGUISED himself as Jaretzki, making it seem that he had returned, and locked himself in his private office with his guest, a willowy ingenue who was appearing in a Charles Dillingham musical on Broadway. Then he impersonated each mugg, one by one, enticing their girl friends into the shadows of the shipping room, where he proceeded to make love.

Johnny's legs were wobbly when he'd completed his feat of conquering eleven girls, but his spirits had never been so high. Not only had he scored a new record, but his masterful skill at impersonating anyone had never been put to such a rigid test. And he had succeeded without once being suspected in this most intimate situation.

Somehow, Jake Jaretzki learned of Johnny's duplicity and arranged to dispose of him permanently. On the morning of Feb. 14, 1929, Jaretzki was scheduled to meet a dozen of his dope pushers in a brownstone around the corner from the Hotel Harlem on Lenox Avenue, to collect their weekly take which never was entrusted to a bag man. Feigning some excuse, he sent Johnny in his place. The pushers never for a moment suspected the impersonation, and the innocent-looking brown grocery bag Johnny bore as he exited bulged with $8,000.

JOHNNY QUICKLY DESCENDED THE brownstone's stoop, walked briskly to the corner to hail a taxi when uniformed officers converged on him from all sides.

"Hold it, you! Drop that sack, and put up your hands!"

The cry cut through the Sunday morning serenity, rooted churchgoers to the sidewalk. Johnny's reflexes reacted with pistonlike precision. He pivoted, ducked down a flight of basement steps, streaked through an alley. He sprinted into an apartment house, ascended to the top in an elevator, crossed to an adjoining roof, descended seven flights of stairs to step out to freedom on 126th Street. He was boiling mad.

Besides the pushers, only one person knew about his appointment—Jake Jaretzki, and Jaretzki would have blown the whistle on him to settle the score. But there had been a flaw in Jaretzki's plot. The cops had been late; instead of attempting to nab him before he entered the brownstone, they had set up their stake-out when he'd left with the eight grand in cash. That tidy little error was going to cost Jaretzki exactly that, Johnny reasoned with a grim smile of ultimate victory over his "finger."

The sum of money made life fairly comfortable for Johnny Driscoll for a while, but when his funds ebbed, he began to cast around for another swindle that would demand his extraordinary talent. I had heard about his unique racket through stoolies who collaborated with the police department, but any positive identification via mug shots was impossible because Johnny had never to my knowledge served a jail sentence. How long he might have flourished is a matter of speculation; ultimately, this fanatic with the 100 faces was doomed to be unmasked some time. But the finale began to unfold early in June when a trio of goons heisted the payroll from a safe in a textile house on East 27th Street, off Madison Avenue. In a blazing gun duel between them and a night watchman, one of the thugs—Bobby Youngdahl—was wounded in the head and left to his own devices while his accomplices escaped.

When I reported to the scene of the crime with my Safe & Loft Squad, I found, to my immense satisfaction, that the payroll had been dropped in the confusion. This posed a great opportunity to apprehend the other two fugitives.

I would set a thief to catch a thief. With my captain's permission, I released a story to the newspapers to the effect that the payroll had not been recovered and that the wounded Youngdahl would reveal his pals' hideout to bargain for an easier sentence. I was sure this bait would lure his confederates to the hospital, where they would attempt to silence him.

IT NEVER OCCURRED TO me that this sort of situation also would appeal to Johnny Driscoll's sense of theatrics. Some time during the following day, Johnny entered Youngdahl's room, spirited him to a linen closet, then succeeded in bandaging his head and face, exposing only his eyes, ears, nostrils and mouth. The trap was sprung early that evening when the two hoods, wary of luring officers, entered his room dressed as hospital orderlies—an ironic twist, I later thought, that they disguised themselves, unaware that they were to confront the master of disguises!

I wasn't aware of Johnny's act when I staked out my squad outside his room and in the hospital corridors. And it wasn't until the final curtain closed on Johnny Driscoll that I learned what had happened behind his closed door.

"But we ain't got the dough," one of the hoods protested when they were alone. "I must've dropped it when the old coot opened fire."

"Yeah? So how come the cops never found it?" whispered Johnny as if in pain, to fake his voice. "You guys got it, all right, and you want to cut me out."

"If it wasn't found, maybe you got it," snarled the other thief. "And you wanna make a deal with the law to get off easy so's you can keep it yourself, you doublecrossin' crumb. I ought to plug you—!"

The other was peering closely at Johnny. "Something stinks here. Youngdahl got a cauliflower left ear fighting at St. Nick's. Take a look. This ain't him!" He seized Johnny's arms, held him rigid and helpless. "You're a cop, ain't you?"

"Hey, he saw our faces. He could identify us!" The thug snapped up a roll of heavy gauze bandage and unrolled it. Helpless under their combined strength, Johnny saw his legs and arms bound to the brass bedstead, felt the adhesive tape blot the air from his mouth and nostrils, blind his wildly rolling eyes.

IT WAS SHORTLY AFTER, that the shrill cry of a nurse entering his room and finding his mummified figure sent us barreling inside. A quick phone call to the Reception Desk alerted my men posted at all the entrances. The fleeing felons were picked up as they tried to get away through the Emergency Clinic. One of the interns, Dr. Harold Niemoller, attributed Johnny's death to suffocation. It was strange, very strange indeed, I reflected, as he filled out the death certificate, that Johnny Driscoll, who possessed the uncanny ability to masquerade as a man of many faces, had ultimately perished as a man with no face, no face at all.

•••

HOW to PRAY

and get RESULTS

The true way to mastery will open for you when you know how to ask for and how to accept the gifts that GOD has stored up for those that love and obey Him. Learn

THE MAGIC FORMULA for SUCCESSFUL PRAYER

Here are some of the amazing things it tells you about: When to pray; where to pray; How to pray; The Magic Formulas for Health and Success through prayer; for conquering fear through prayer; for obtaining work through prayer; for money through prayer; for influencing others through prayer; and many other valuable instructions that help you get things you want.

5-DAY TRIAL—SEND NO MONEY

Just send your name and address today and on delivery simply deposit the small sum of only $1.49 plus postage with your postman. I positively GUARANTEE that you will be more than delighted with RESULTS within 5 days or your money will be returned promptly on request and no questions asked. Order At Once.

LARCH, 118 E. 28, Dept. 661-A, New York 16

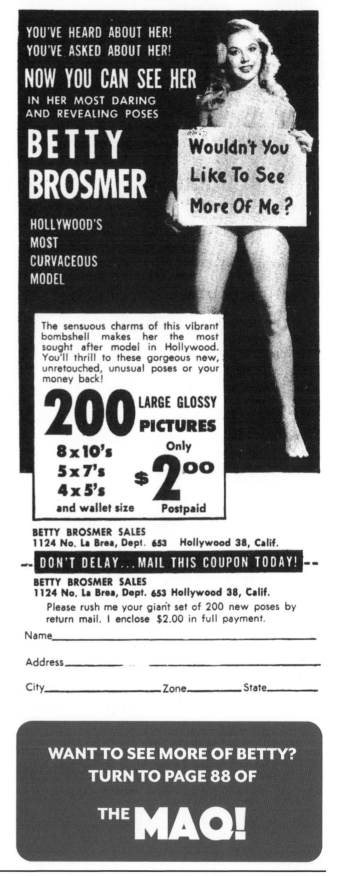

YOU'VE HEARD ABOUT HER! YOU'VE ASKED ABOUT HER!

NOW YOU CAN SEE HER IN HER MOST DARING AND REVEALING POSES

BETTY BROSMER

Wouldn't You Like To See More Of Me?

HOLLYWOOD'S MOST CURVACEOUS MODEL

The sensuous charms of this vibrant bombshell makes her the most sought after model in Hollywood. You'll thrill to these gorgeous new, unretouched, unusual poses or your money back!

200 LARGE GLOSSY PICTURES

8 x 10's
5 x 7's
4 x 5's
and wallet size

Only **$2.00** Postpaid

BETTY BROSMER SALES
1124 No. La Brea, Dept. 653   Hollywood 38, Calif.

DON'T DELAY... MAIL THIS COUPON TODAY!

BETTY BROSMER SALES
1124 No. La Brea, Dept. 653 Hollywood 38, Calif.

Please rush me your giant set of 200 new poses by return mail. I enclose $2.00 in full payment.

Name_____

Address_____

City_____ Zone_____ State_____

WANT TO SEE MORE OF BETTY? TURN TO PAGE 88 OF

THE **MAQ!**

PULPFEST

Celebrating...

MYSTERY, ADVENTURE, SCIENCE FICTION, AND MORE

Chilling SPORTS
And Hero Pulps

AT THE **DOUBLETREE** BY **HILTON**
PITTSBURGH — CRANBERRY
IN **MARS, PA.,**

AUG. 3-6, 2023

▶ **PulpFest**   f **PulpFest**   🐦 **@PulpFest**   📷 **PulpFest**

TRUE WEIRD (November 1955) illustrated by CLARENCE DOORE

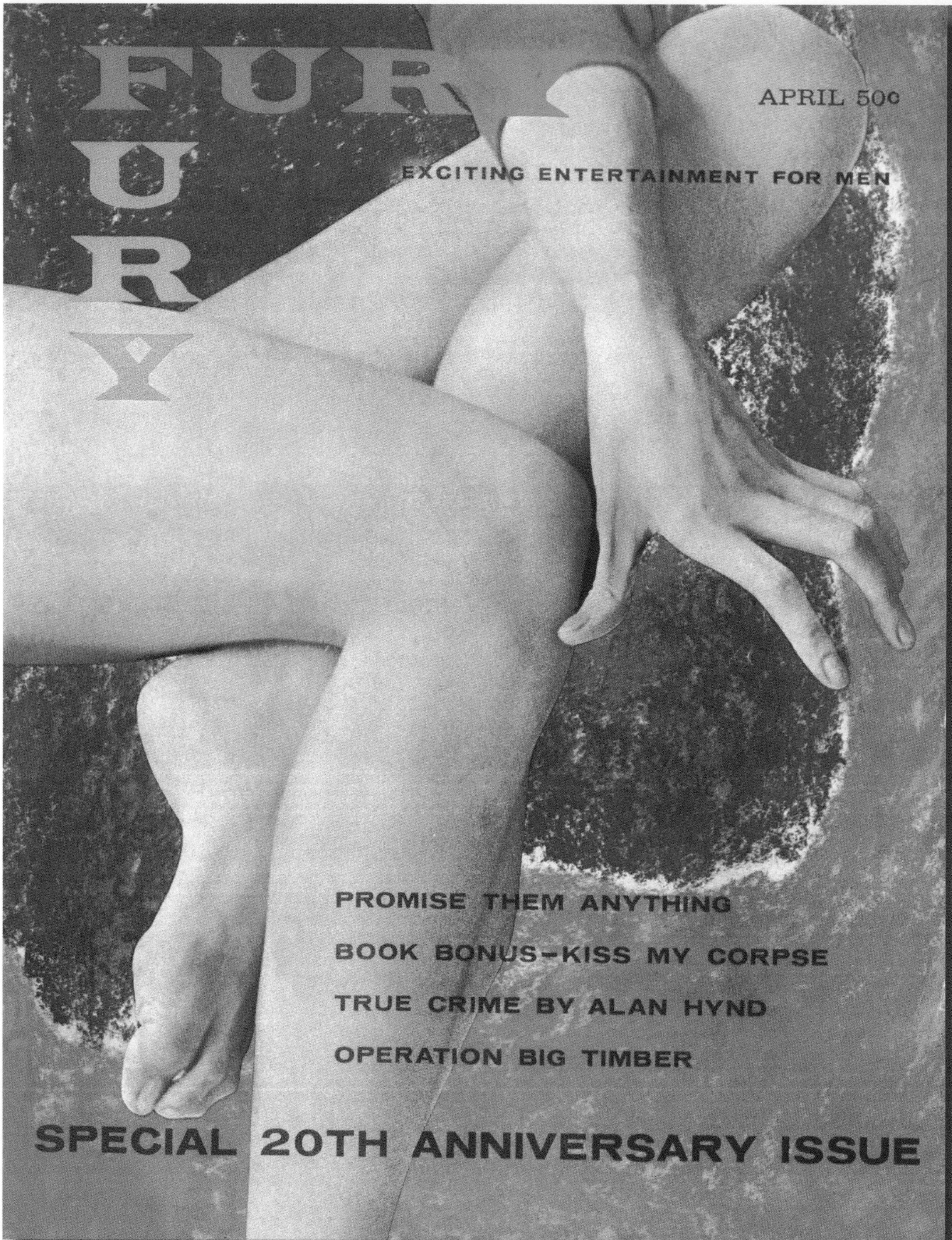

FURY
FURY

APRIL 50¢

EXCITING ENTERTAINMENT FOR MEN

PROMISE THEM ANYTHING

BOOK BONUS—KISS MY CORPSE

TRUE CRIME BY ALAN HYND

OPERATION BIG TIMBER

SPECIAL 20TH ANNIVERSARY ISSUE

"The Specialist" is a neatly crafted yarn with a surprise ending—and it's not the final twist I was expecting.

The writer, George Joseph, worked as a lawyer in New Zealand for 40 years. As a "barrister" he primarily worked as a defense lawyer and was involved in a number of NZ murder trials. On the side, he wrote hundreds of short stories and a number of fiction and non-fiction books, including *HOW TO WRITE AND SELL SHORT STORIES* (1958).

George Joseph

By George Joseph
From *FURY*, April 1963
Artwork Uncredited

INTRODUCTION BY BOB **DEIS**

Most of Joseph's magazine stories were in periodicals published in New Zealand and the UK. The men's adventure magazine his story "The Specialist" is from—*FURY*—was one of the many magazines published by Joseph Weider (1919-2003).

If you're old enough, you know who Joe was. Ads for his Weider bodybuilding system and equipment were in almost every MAM and many other mags aimed at boys or men in the 1950s, 1960s and 1970s.

Weider grew up in Montreal, Canada, where started his bodybuilding career as a young man. In the 1940s, he competed in bodybuilding events and developed his own strength and fitness techniques and equipment. He wrote and published the pioneering fitness magazines *YOUR PHYSIQUE* and *MUSCLE POWER*. He also created an organization to sponsor bodybuilding events that eventually included the "Mr. America," "Mr. Universe," and "Mr. Olympia" contests.

Joe managed his bodybuilding and publishing businesses with the help of his brother Ben Weider.

Together, they were called "The Brothers of Iron."

In 1947, Joe set up an office in New Jersey to be closer to the New York City, the central hub of book and magazine publishing. From there, he launched more magazines. They included MAM-style men's mags that reflected Joe's own unique vision.

In the early 1950s, Joe noticed the rapid growth of the men's adventure mag genre. He decided to create mags that would have *"my own original mix of a muscle magazine and men's adventure."*

The initial results were two hybrid mags that included both bodybuilding and fitness articles and some MAM style fiction and non-fiction—*MR. AMERICA* and *AMERICAN MANHOOD.* He soon created other hybrid periodicals that are unique in the realm of MAMs: *TRUE STRANGE* and *TRUE WEIRD*, which mixed MAM-style stories with tales of the supernatural; and, *ANIMAL LIFE*, *OUTDOOR ADVENTURES* and *SAFARI*, which were part hunting mags and part MAM.

The Weider mag that was most like other MAMs was *FURY*. It was also

the longest lasting. His hybrid mags were all gone by 1959. *FURY* ran from August 1953 to January 1964.

The issues published from 1953 to December 1961 feature great MAM style painted covers. The 10 issues

published after that, including *FURY,* April 1963, have bachelor mag style photo covers with cheesecake pics.

Most of my favorite cover paintings for *FURY* and other Weider MAM-style mags were done by artist Thomas Beecham (1926-2000), a top magazine and paperback cover artist who eventually came to be best known for his wildlife paintings.

In addition to providing artwork for MAMs, Beecham did cover and interior illustrations for mainstream magazine like *READER'S DIGEST* and *NATIONAL GEOGRAPHIC*, and outdoor sports mags like *FIELD AND STREAM* and *OUTDOOR LIFE*.

In the final decade of his career, Beecham was the artist whose work was featured on the popular calendars distributed by the Remington Arms Company. That calendar, which features wildlife paintings, is still being published.

In addition to *FURY*, Beecham also did fantastic cover paintings for Weider's other MAM-style mags. Some are unusual montage paintings with multiple images, an approach not seen on typical MAM covers.

Words don't really do them justice, so look at the examples shown here and be awed.

Another unique aspect of some issues of *FURY* are the full-page, full-color glamour girl photos that were used on the back pages of some issues (13 of the total of 53). The actresses and models that appeared on those back covers included Barbara Nichols, Kathy Marlow, Alice Denham, Jayne Mansfield, Eve Meyer, Anita Ekberg, Lynn Carter, Jo Jordan, Gloria Pall, Lili St. Cyr, Marcia Edgington, Genie Stone and—on the back cover of *FURY*, October 1956—the woman that Joe Weider married in 1961, Betty Brosmer.

At that point, Betty was one of America's most photographed glamour girl models. She gave up modeling after she and Joe wed to help him hype and manage his bodybuilding and magazine empire. She also became a popular female fitness guru herself and wrote articles for Weider fitness mags for the next 30 years.

In 1970, Betty appeared in Weider ads with a protégé of Joe's who became one of the most famous bodybuilders in the world and eventually one of the most famous people in the world, Arnold Schwarzenegger.

That year, Arnold started training under Joe's supervision. He went on to win a long list of bodybuilding competitions sponsored by Weider, including five Mr. Universe wins and seven Mr. Olympia wins.

In turn, Arnold helped pump up the Weider empire by appearing in many Weider magazine ads. He also wrote a monthly column for the Weider bodybuilding magazines *MUSCLE & FITNESS* and *FLEX*.

If you find any of that intriguing, I highly recommend that you read the joint autobiography written by Joe and Ben, *BROTHERS OF IRON: BUILDING THE WEIDER EMPIRE* (2006) and watch the 2018 movie about the Weiders, *BIGGER.*

They're both excellent.

● ● ●

OPPOSITE: The October 1956 issue of *FURY*. Cover art by Thomas Beecham. BACKGROUND: The art for 1958's HOW TO BUILD A STRONG, MUSCULAR BODY – one of the many Weider fitness publications from Joe & Ben Weider.

FICTION

THE SPECIALIST

HE WAS ON TOP OF THE WORLD BECAUSE NOBODY COULD DO HIS SPECIAL JOB AS WELL AS HE DID

VINCE WEBER GRINNED, leaving the neat suburban house that morning. He knew he looked just like any other young guy in the neighborhood, complete with lightweight gray topcoat and medium-brown pebblegrained briefcase.

He was grinning for two reasons; because he did have all the advantages and none of the headaches of a husband, and because of Marion Wiley's childish delusion that luck had anything to do with winning or losing in life.

"Honey, I've entered you in that soap company contest, too!" she'd murmured, happily snuggling into his arms for a goodbye fondle. "The top prize is a vacation for two in the Bahamas. Wouldn't that be wonderful, Vince?"

He'd slipped his hands beneath the folds of the quilted light blue duster, enjoying the warmth of her soft yet firm and erect breasts. "That would be just peachy," he said. His fingers separated from those luscious curves with reluctance. He downed the last of his coffee and reached for his briefcase. She was still smiling dreamily, thinking about winning the contest when he walked out the front door into the overcast morning.

Vince was at the corner, waiting for the transit company car, and there was a damp, chilling breeze off the lake flapping at his topcoat when he heard a familiar hail and turned his head to grin at Ray Albrecht.

"How's the big insurance tycoon today?" the other guy queried, joining Vince. The electric cables above them vibrated as the transit bus rumbled toward the bleak, wind-swept corner where they stood.

"Great. And, what about our promising young banker?" Vince parried good-naturedly. He felt good despite the lousy late summer weather. "Check the anatomy on what's running this way," he suggested, his own gaze flicking expertly over the furiously jiggling bulges beneath the violet jersey sweater and open tan polo coat as the blonde loped along the sidewalk toward the corner opposite where they were standing.

Ray Albrecht sighed ruefully, saying, "Reminds you of a couple oversized grapefruit, don't they? Look but don't touch, buddy. That's one drawback about being married; women are funny that way," he added philosophically, but Vince noticed the lustful gleam in the shorter guy's eyes while Ray kept ogling the girl who was now scurrying across the intersection, her high heels tattooing sharply on the concrete.

Again, Vince grinned. Everyone thought he and the

golden-haired honey sharing the same suburban roof were married. They even had the same last initial. He'd been smart to rent a house instead of planting her in an apartment. It added the perfect touch of respectability.

The flushed, breathless blonde flashed Vince a hurried, grateful smile when he motioned for her to proceed him entering the bus. He stood below the steps with Ray Albrecht. Both men studied the pair of nicely-shaped legs sheathed in nylons, then also climbed inside and paid their fares.

"Busy day ahead for you?" Ray asked when they'd sat down just behind the blonde in the tan coat.

Vince shrugged. "One appointment. Then, a meeting late this afternoon." The heavy, inexpensive scent of the girl's perfume filled his nostrils. She was probably a clerk in some downtown store. Where she bought the perfume, clothes and other gadgets that women need. Vince closed his eyes, resting his head against the top of the seat. At least Marion wasn't in the dime store undies class. Until she'd eagerly accepted his offer for an exclusive arrangement she'd been one of the most successful call girls working for the syndicate.

Ray Albrecht was complaining about his job, as usual. He told Vince how he'd been called on the carpet for a minor bookkeeping error the previous day. "I'm in charge of more than two hundred accounts — what the devil do they expect of an assistant cashier —perfection?" he said glumly. He shifted in his seat, looking at Vince. "You never gripe," he said curiously. "You must like your work, huh?"

Vince was comfortably relaxed. He opened his eyes, his hands folded across the bulky briefcase on his lap. "It's all in a guy's attitude, the way I look at it." he said easily. The blonde ahead of them had been giving him the once-over in the compact mirror while she made out as if inspecting her lipstick. "Me, I consider my job as a real challenge. It's a service business, just like banking."

Ray Albrecht digested the remark, staring through the bus window at the store buildings they were passing. Then, his good-natured grin returned. "You must be a terrific insurance salesman," he said approvingly.

Vince closed his eyes again, passing up the blonde's unspoken invitation to get better acquainted. He heard the angry snap of her compact, and when he next straightened in the seat he saw her wide hips undulate rapidly beneath the coat as she hurried from where she'd been sitting toward the door. Ray Albrecht

got off a few blocks later. Vince watched his fellow-suburbanite march briskly into a bank building. He left the bus himself when it neared the factory district huddled in a smoketinged valley bisected by numerous railroad sidings and bordered by the East River.

THE PROSPECT with whom he had an appointment lived in the better section of the city, but had his office in a shoddy, dismal brownstone building at the fringe of the industrial area. Vince unsnapped the gold-plated lock on his briefcase as he climbed a steep, narrow flight of stairs to the third floor. It was still early morning, so there weren't many people around. A colored janitor was emptying wastebaskets into a cart on wheels in the shadowy corridor. Vince saw the door marked as being the men's washroom. He went in and used the time he waited to slip on his gloves.

The hall was deserted when he came out a few minutes later. He saw a feeble glow of yellowish light seeping through the frosted glass panel of the office door be sought. A burly, semibald guy in a dark brown suit was gnawing on a cigar while he used a stapler on a paper-littered desk.

The guy had been leaning across the desk to use the stapler and he pushed himself away, staring neutrally at Vince in the doorway. "You wanna see me about something?" The cigar scarcely moved between those thick lips.

"I do, if you're Clarence Miller," Vince replied pleasantly, moving far enough into the office so that he could ease the door closed with his foot.

"You a lawyer?"

"No. Are you Mr. Miller?"

"What are you selling, then?"

Vince grinned disarmingly. "My business is insurance. If you're Clarence Miller, I have a little get-acquainted present for you," he advised, his right band slipping inside the pebble-grained briefcase.

"This union writes its own insurance. Don't waste any more of either of our time," the heavy-set man said brusquely, shoving around some of the papers on top of the desk. As far as he was concerned Vince could leave anytime.

"A good salesman has to be persistent, and I do have to file a prospect report with the people I work for," Vince said quietly, unmoving. "I was told to call on Mr. Clarence Miller, president of local 218, and—"

"So, you called on me. Leave that door open on

your way out—it gets too damn smoky with it closed." Clarence Miller had evidently located the typewritten papers he'd been looking for. He flipped back the top sheet and scowled, concentrating on the contents of the second page.

Moments later, a surprised, incredulous expression of pain glazed the fleshy man's eyes and the cigar fell on the desk, scattering sparks and ashes amid the papers. There was a neat, round hole in the sheaf of typewritten sheets he'd been holding, and another much less tidy hole just above the collar of his white dress shirt, directly above the knot of his necktie.

Vince picked up the smoldering cigar and deposited it in the circular brass-ringed ashtray. Assuring himself that all the sparks were extinguished, he glanced briefly again at his prospect while he restored the silencer-equipped .38 cal. automatic to the briefcase.

Outside the building, he turned up the collar of his gabardine topcoat to deflect some of the misty drizzle unloaded from the murky sky. A cruising taxi slackened speed drawing abreast of him as he walked unhurriedly in the direction of the bridge spanning the East River, but Vince motioned for the hopeful cabbie to keep on rolling.

Midway across the trestle type bridge, Vince checked for possible observers, then paused at the railing where he inconspicuously allowed the murder weapon to fall from his hands to disappear in the rain-dotted water far below.

With nothing to kill except time, the tall, bareheaded man who resembled just another junior executive or ambitious young salesman walked leisurely away from the fume-belching smokestacks of the factory district. Of course, he was a salesman. Very successful at his chosen profession, too. Vince Weber. Death insurance salesman.

THERE WERE two other contracts for him as a result of the meeting he attended late that dismal afternoon.

Vince took care of both with his usual competency. Then, at the suggestion of the syndicate employing him, he stayed home and collected unemployment compensation. That money, in addition to the pay for those last three contracts, went into the out-of-town bank savings accounts he'd established years ago when he'd first gone into the business.

Things were dull to the point of boredom after a few weeks of puttering around the house and playing with the golden-haired doll. Marion Wiley's talents didn't include intelligent conversation or much of anything except her sexual skills. For a while, Vince enjoyed being surprised by her knowledge of the many phases of the fine art of passion.

"Whoever heard of doing it this way?" he often muttered, experimenting with some new and varied sensual delight.

"We're—being—pioneers, honey!" Marion would gasp, moaning and shivering with pleasure. She had an extremely low boiling point. If she wasn't a nympho, then exhausted Vince Weber didn't know the meaning of the word!

He was outside watching a flock of geese honk their way south above the city one afternoon when Ray Albrecht alighted from the bus and approached along the dusky sidewalks.

"Did you get laid off or something, buddy? I haven't seen you around in weeks," Ray remarked. His eyes became concerned as he studied Vince. "Hey, you look thinner! Have you been sick?"

Vince's haggard features had tightened. His trouble wasn't entirely from being laid off; part of it was because of too much laying on. He'd just been thinking about ditching the brunette. Walking away from the house some morning and not coming back. She couldn't do anything about it. She was so dumb that she actually believed he was working at some grubby, unexciting job just like Ray Albrecht and the other stupid jerks in the neighborhood!

"Beat it, creep! Who asked you for a physical? Stick to tapping an adding machine and tickling female tellers at that crummy bank—who made you my doctor?" Vince snarled, spinning to stalk back toward the house, leaving the open-mouthed guy to gape after him.

His irritation increased to trembling fury when he phoned the syndicate asking about an assignment, even if it was something in another section of the country. They told him his services would no longer be required. Another equally reliable man had agreed to work for much less money...

"WILL YOU get the door, honey? I'm in here," Marion called from the bathroom after the mellow echo of the front door chimes faded. Vince had been savagely paring at an orange in the kitchen and the small, sharp knife was still in his hand as he yanked open the door.

"Yeah? What is it?" Vince demanded curtly, resenting the boyish, clean-cut guy's friendly grin.

"Hello! Are you Mr. Vincent T. Weber?" The young guy was carrying a briefcase and Vince noticed that his right hand was already inside.

"What do you want?" Vince repeated, his muscles tensing, his hands transferring the paring knife behind his back. He should have known that the syndicate didn't leave loose ends. He was on the opposite end of a contract; just another hunk of perishable merchandise to be disposed of. "Yeah, I'm Vince Weber. What about it, kid?"

"We have to be sure about these things, Mr. Weber. Now, I have something for you," the other guy said cheerily.

Vince was watching the hand inside the briefcase. When it moved, so did he. The slim, sharp point of the paring knife slid smoothly through flesh in a quick, whipping motion that thrust upwards through the chest.

The brunette named Marion screamed and kept on shrieking like a hysterical factory whistle. Vince was still holding the bloody knife and staring numbly down at the dying man when two patrolmen brushed through the frightened, babbling crowd of onlookers and grabbed him.

He blinked, seeing the blurred circle of horrified faces as if through a swirling reddish haze. "I—I won first prize in that damn soap company contest, the guy told me," Vince whimpered pathetically. He started to laugh when he looked down again at the certificate awarding a vacation for two in the Bahamas that had fluttered from the pebble-grained brown briefcase beside the last guy he'd killed.

He couldn't seem to stop laughing.

•••

ZULU MONSTER DOLL
So Ugly, We Dare Not Print Its Picture!
Your blood will run cold when you see this pocket-size nightmare. Your flesh will creep when you touch its incredibly death-like "skin". Caution: Do not show your Zulu Monster Doll to your children. Do not order if you suffer from heart disease or a weak stomach. Rush $1.00 cash, check or M.O. today. Zulu Monster Doll is guaranteed to make women scream . . . strong men feel faint . . . or money back!
VALO CO., Dept. 506, 587 Seventh Ave New York 36, N. Y.

BASS FISHERMEN WILL SAY I'M CRAZY — *until they try my method!*

JUST ONE TRIAL WILL PROVE THAT I MAKE EVERY FISHERMAN'S DREAM COME TRUE!

I have no fishing tackle to sell, I make a good living out of my profession. But fishing is my hobby. And because of this hobby, I discovered a way to get those giant bass —even in waters most fishermen say are "fished out."

I don't spin, troll, cast or use any other method you ever heard of. Yet, without live or prepared bait, I can come home with a string of 5 and 6 pound beauties while a man twenty feet away won't even get a strike. You can learn my method in a few minutes. It is legal in every state. All the equipment you need costs less than a dollar and you can get it in any local store. The chances are no man who fishes your waters has ever used my method—or even heard of it. When you have tried it—just once—you'll realize what terrific bass fishing you've been missing.

Let me tell you about this method—and explain why I'm willing to let you try it for the whole fishing season without risking a single penny of your money. There is no charge for this information— now or any other time. But I guarantee that the facts I send you can get you started toward the greatest bass fishing you have ever known. Send me your name today—letter or postcard. You've got a real fishing thrill ahead of you. Eric O Fare, Highland Park 65 Illinois.

SELL Advertising Book Matches

FULL OR PART TIME!

No experience needed to earn Big Daily Cash Commission plus premiums for both you and your customers. Be a direct representative of the world's largest exclusive manufacturer of advertising Book Matches. Every business a prospect for new Tenorama, Glamour Girls, Hillbillies, safety series and dozens of other styles. All wanted sizes 20, 30, 40 stick matches. Quick daily sales, steady repeat business. New FREE Master Sales Kit makes selling easy. WRITE TODAY for full details.

SUPERIOR MATCH CO.
Dept. E-1161, 7530 S. Greenwood, Chicago 19

MAN & WIFE TEAM

If you have a camera, you can earn the kind of money you have always dreamed of. Complete Literature $1.00.

ARTEK, Dept. 776
836 N. FAIRFAX, HOLLYWOOD 28, CALIF.

FREE BOOK TELLS HOW

CLOGGED SEWERS
CLEANED INSTANTLY
SAVES PLUMBING BILLS

Anyone can trigger new Flush Gun shooting air & water impact on difficult stoppages in pipe ½" to 6"; Rags, Grease, and Roots melt away when struck by hammer-blow in Toilets, Sinks, Urinals, Bathtubs, & Sewers 200 ft. Amazingly effective when air hits running water. Save Costly Plumbing Bills or start your own Business. Tear out Ad now & write address beside it for FREE BOOKLET or phone Kildare 5-1702, Miller Sewer Rod, Dept. ST 3, 4642 N. Central Ave., Chicago 30, Ill.

THE LOOK YOU WANT, WHEN YOU WANT IT!

You will be Amazed at the Exciting Change in your Personal Appearance!

The Natural Look of these sideburns, mustache, van dyke and/or beard actually allows you to select the way you want to look, Older, Younger, Distinguished, Cool, Suave — you name it! Wear each one independently or combine them for the effect you desire — sideburns and beard, sideburns alone, van dyke alone, van dyke and mustache. The combinations are limitless!

All items are made of simulated natural hair to exacting professional standards. Firmly self-adhering. Can be worn with self confidence anywhere, anytime. They are so life-like you will have to remind yourself that they can be removed.

FREE with each order, a complete guide that tells how to naturally wear your sideburns, mustache, van dyke and beard.

SIDEBURNS
wear alone or with mustache and/or van dyke **$1**

MUSTACHE
wear alone or with any item **$2**

Wear Any Combination

VAN DYKE
wear alone or with mustache and/or sideburns **$2**

FULL BEARD
wear alone or with mustache **$2**

MAN INTERNATIONAL Dept. 5369
1800 No. Highland Avenue, Hollywood, California 90028

Yes, I want to choose my own appearance. Rush me the items I have checked below. I understand that I must be completely satisfied or I may return the merchandise within 10 days for a full refund. Check items and color shade you want. **If not sure of your hairshade, enclose hair sample with order.**

SEND ME THESE ITEMS:
☐ Mustache $2
☐ Sideburns $1
☐ Van Dyke $2
☐ Full Beard $2
☐ All items $5 (Save $2.00)

MAKE ITEMS THIS COLOR:
☐ Light Brown
☐ Medium Brown
☐ Dark Brown
☐ Black   ☐ Auburn (Red)
☐ Blonde   ☐ Silver (Grey)

All orders under $2 enclose 25c extra postage and handling.

Name . . . .

Address . . . .

City . . . . State & Zip . . . .

A PACIFIC WAR SAGA OF WILD ADVENTURE

"SGT. KELLY IS LEADING A WOMEN'S BRIGADE"

TRUE Book Bonus:

stag IND.

AUG.

COMMANDO RAID INTO CHINA: FIRST EYEWITNESS REPORT

FROM HOUSE DETECTIVES' CONFIDENTIAL FILES:

VICE GIRLS WHO HUSTLE HOTELS

35¢ 40¢ IN CANADA

ADMIRAL RIVERO: **U.S. NAVY HERO THE REDS HATE MOST**

Some hitmen are stone cold professionals. Then there was Benjamin "Bugsy" Siegel.

The author of this next story, Anthony Scaduto, described him like this:

"Bugsy was as vicious as a Gestapo agent. Even after he had parlayed arrogance, suaveness and contempt of danger into a spot on the board of directors of the National Crime Syndicate, Bugsy would still take time out from his million dollar enterprises to handle a 'contract' for execution. He derived as much pleasure from killing as he did from the desirable women who clung to his arm and shared his bed."

By Anthony Scaduto
From **STAG**, August 1963
Cover art by Mort Künstler
Interior illustration by Samson Pollen

Some hitmen wisely keep a low profile. Then there was Benjamin "Bugsy" Siegel.

As described in Scaduto's account of the bloody rise and fall of that legendary mobster, when Bugsy wasn't in the news for being charged with crimes, he enjoyed generating gossip and news stories by hanging out with actors, actresses and other wealthy socialites in Hollywood or at the pioneering Las Vegas Flamingo Hotel and casino he conceived, built and managed for his Mafia bosses.

INTRODUCTION BY BOB **DEIS**

Bugsy was indeed an amazing character, and his fairly brief life seems too wild to be true. But most of the things in Scaduto's article about him are indeed true—with the probable exception of his hookup in the hospital with the hot and horny nurse mentioned in the opening.

Bugsy did check into a hospital after Tony Fabrizio, a hitter for a rival mobster tried, but failed to blow

Hollywood's Face Is Red—Folks Call It the Home of No. 1 Gangster

In the garb of the "wealthy Hollywood sportsman" he was reputed to be, but looking a bit worried, is Benny (Bugsy) Siegel, above. He's pictured after being removed from his luxurious Holmby Hills home for questioning in the gangland murder of Harry Schachter.

'Bugsy' Siegel Dies in Blast Of Gunfire

Nation's 'No. 1 Gangster' Killed

BEVERLY HILLS, Cal., June 21 (UP) — Benjamin (Bugsy) Siegel, 42, dapper man-about-Hollywood rated as the nation's No. 1 gangster, was slain last night by a hail of machine-gun bullets fired through a window.

Police had no clue to the killer's identity or motive for the slaying. Footprints found beneath the window indicated more than one man was involved. A neighbor heard an auto "really traveling" after the shooting.

The assassin, standing next to the glass, let loose a burst of fire that shattered the window, ripped through Siegel's body and lodged in the wall. One pierced a huge oil painting of a nude woman holding a drinking glass.

IN HAPPIER DAYS—Movie Star George Raft, right, and Gangster Benjamin "Bugsy", Siegel, are shown with the actor placing an arm around the shoulders of the racketeer. Siegel was shot to death last night in a luxurious Beverly Hills mansion.

him up with a bomb. It's also true that Bugsy wasn't seriously hurt by the explosion. Checking into the

ABOVE: Bugsy Siegel and actor George Raft. Siegel was well-liked in Hollywood circles.

hospital after surviving that attempt was his clever idea for an alibi. It's also true that Bugsy snuck out of the hospital briefly to shoot and kill Fabrizio. However, I suspect the nurse was an embellishment Scaduto added to fit the usual sex factor men's adventure magazine readers expected.

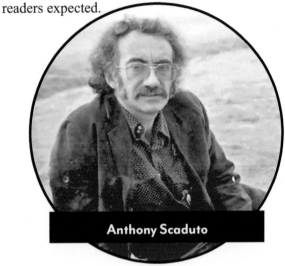

Anthony Scaduto

Anthony Scaduto, who died in 2017 at age 85, was an interesting writer. He was a longtime police reporter and investigative journalist for the *New York Post* who focused largely on stories about crime, criminals and celebrities. On the side he wrote mostly fact-based articles for magazines, under his own name and the pseudonym Archer Scanlon.

He had many stories in men's adventure mags, including *ACTION FOR MEN, CLIMAX, MALE, MAN'S MAGAZINE, MEN, STAG,* and *TRUE ACTION*. He also wrote stories for men's bachelor mags, like *PLAYBOY* and *PENTHOUSE.*

However, Scaduto became best known for the books he wrote. In 1971, he made a splash with *BOB DYLAN: AN INTIMATE BIOGRAPHY*, the first serious biography of Bob Dylan. In 1976, he got a lot of attention for his book *SCAPEGOAT, HOW THE WRONG MAN*

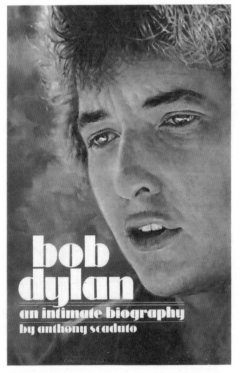

WAS FRAMED FOR THE LINDBERGH BABY KIDNAPPING, which persuasively contended that Bruno Richard Hauptmann was wrongly executed for the kidnapping of Charles Lindbergh's baby.

He also wrote books about The Beatles, Mick Jagger, Frank Sinatra, Marilyn Monroe and mobster Lucky Luciano. (The latter three were originally published under his other pseudonym Tony Sciacca.)

The artwork associated with Scaduto's story in the August 1963 issue of *STAG* is by two artists I've the good fortune of knowing personally: Samson Pollen and Mort Künstler.

Sam was a top MAM illustrators from the mid-1950s to the mid-1970s. He specialized, by choice, in doing interior illustrations for them, like the cool red duotone used for the Bugsy Siegel story. Over the decades he did several hundred of them, mostly for Martin Goodman's Magazine Management MAMs (*FOR MEN ONLY, MEN, MALE, STAG,* etc.).

Sam did do a few MAM covers, but most of his cover art was done for paperbacks. He painted roughly 200 of those from the '50s into the '90s. They included many genres, but I am naturally partial to those he did for men's action/adventure paperbacks, such as the *RENEGADE* (aka *CAPTAIN GRINGO*) series, the *C.A.T.* and *HAWK* series, and the *EASY COMPANY, SPUR* and *BUCKSKIN* Western series.

I sought out Samson Pollen in 2016 and asked if I could do some art books featuring his MAM work as part of the Men's Adventure Library book series I co-edit with Wyatt Doyle, head of the New Texture indie publishing company.

Sam said yes and we collaborated with him on two books before he passed away in 2018, *POLLEN'S WOMEN* and *POLLEN'S ACTION*. Sam's original painting for the Bugsy Siegel story and many others are included in those books. Recently, Sam's wife Jacqueline gave us permission to publish a third book featuring his MAM artwork, *POLLEN IN PRINT: 1955-1959.*

The cover for the *STAG* issue the Bugsy story is in was done by another one of the top MAM and paperback artists, Mort Künstler. Unlike Sam, Mort did many MAM covers, as well as many interiors. He later became widely known for his historical artwork, especially his Civil War paintings. Mort is one of the greatest artists in all of those realms.

I've had the pleasure of talking with Mort by phone a number of times and the honor of visiting him at his home in New York a few years ago. One result of our association is the art book Wyatt Doyle and I co-edited with him, ***MORT KÜNSTLER: THE GODFATHER OF PULP FICTION ILLUSTRATORS***.

As I write this, Mort is still alive and doing well for someone who is 95 years old. Not long ago, he gave Wyatt and I a long reminiscence about his late friend and mentor, artist George Gross. It's in our book ***GEORGE GROSS: COVERED***, which features 100 classic MAM covers by Gross.

Like the ***MAQ***, the Pollen, Künstler and Gross art books are available on Amazon worldwide or via my *MensPulpMags.com* online bookstore.

•••

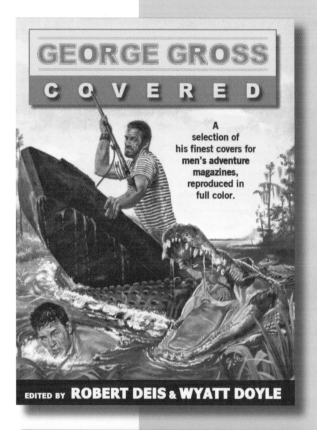

OPPOSITE: Author Anthony Scaduto and the hardcover edition his 1971 book *BOB DYLAN: AN INTIMATE BIOGRAPHY*, which features cover art by Peter Caras. LEFT: The Samson Pollen art books *POLLEN'S WOMEN* and *POLLEN'S ACTION*. ABOVE: The book *GEORGE GROSS COVERED*, which showcases men's adventure magazine covers with artwork by Gross. The Pollen and Gross books are available via Amazon worldwide and Co-Editor Bob Deis' MensPulpMags.com website.

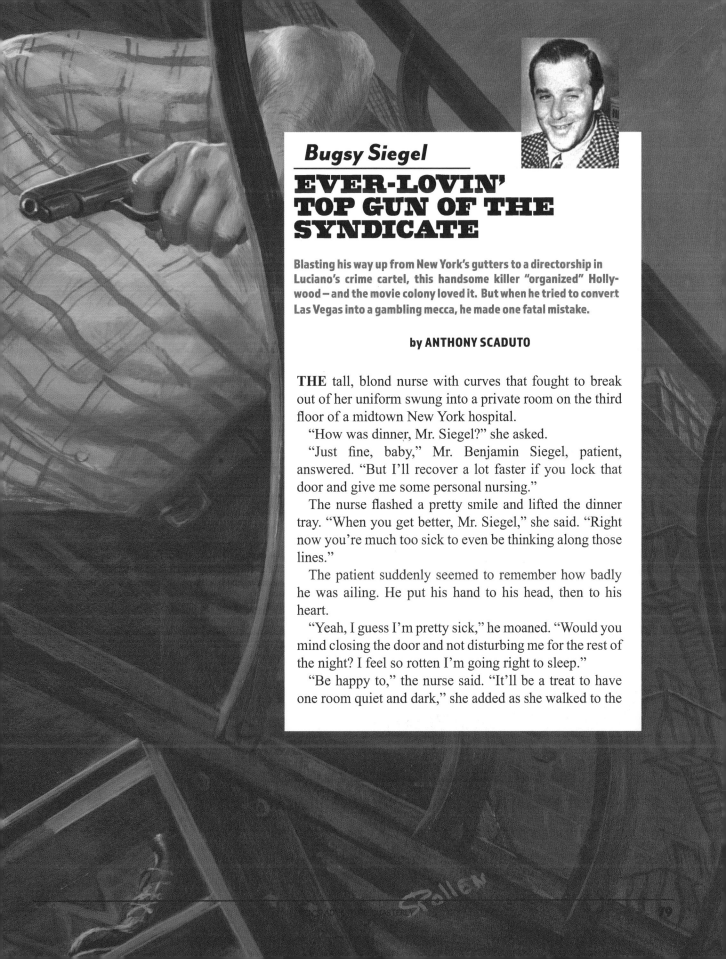

Bugsy Siegel

EVER-LOVIN' TOP GUN OF THE SYNDICATE

Blasting his way up from New York's gutters to a directorship in Luciano's crime cartel, this handsome killer "organized" Hollywood – and the movie colony loved it. But when he tried to convert Las Vegas into a gambling mecca, he made one fatal mistake.

by ANTHONY SCADUTO

THE tall, blond nurse with curves that fought to break out of her uniform swung into a private room on the third floor of a midtown New York hospital.

"How was dinner, Mr. Siegel?" she asked.

"Just fine, baby," Mr. Benjamin Siegel, patient, answered. "But I'll recover a lot faster if you lock that door and give me some personal nursing."

The nurse flashed a pretty smile and lifted the dinner tray. "When you get better, Mr. Siegel," she said. "Right now you're much too sick to even be thinking along those lines."

The patient suddenly seemed to remember how badly he was ailing. He put his hand to his head, then to his heart.

"Yeah, I guess I'm pretty sick," he moaned. "Would you mind closing the door and not disturbing me for the rest of the night? I feel so rotten I'm going right to sleep."

"Be happy to," the nurse said. "It'll be a treat to have one room quiet and dark," she added as she walked to the door, hips wriggling.

The patient watched in fascination until she was gone. He lay back and closed his eyes for a few minutes. Then he slipped out of bed, went to the closet and pulled on a shirt and pair of slacks over his silk pajamas.

He carefully stuffed pillows under the blankets. When he was satisfied that his bed would look occupied if someone peeked in the door, he put on a coat, shut the light and climbed out the window onto the fire escape. Seconds later he hopped into a car that was waiting out front, motor running.

"Ready, Ben?" a man in the back seat asked. The patient nodded as his hand closed around a .45 caliber pistol the man offered him. The driver threw the car into gear and sped towards the Brooklyn Bridge.

A little more than a half hour later, they pulled up in front of a small apartment house off Fort Hamilton Parkway in Brooklyn where Tony Fabrizio lived. Tony was a minor bootlegger and major killer for the rackets bosses. He was, in fact, one of the two men who cut down Vincent "Mad Dog" Coll with machineguns.

Tony had spent more than half his 40 years in the rackets. Recently, though, Tony had begun to have doubts about his future. He wanted out. But he knew a gunman couldn't just walk out on the mob and go straight. So he decided to write his own insurance policy against getting bumped off —a diary that implicated top mobsters in about 50 killings in which he had a hand. Once his biography was safely tucked in a vault, he figured he would be immune from underworld retribution.

Unfortunately, Tony made the mistake of mentioning his brainstorm to a couple of friends before he put pencil to paper. His friends immediately tipped off mobland's leaders. Mr. Benjamin Siegel —who will forever be remembered as Bugsy —was commissioned to blue pencil Tony's literary career

The budding author opened the door when Bugsy knocked. Recognizing his visitor, his jaw sagged, his knees gave way and he started to slip to the floor. Bugsy gave him a helping hand. He raised his cannon and blasted four holes in Fabrizio's head.

Bugsy was rushed back to the hospital. He climbed the fire escape to his room—and almost fell out the window when he saw the blond nurse in her panties

HE RAISED HIS CANNON AND BLASTED FOUR HOLES IN FABRIZIO'S HEAD.

washing herself at the sink. Her uniform hung nearby on the open closet door. She turned as he climbed into the room—not bothering to cover up.

"Mr. Siegel's been a naughty boy," she said, smiling warmly. "And Mr. Siegel doesn't look the least bit sick to me."

"Hell," the dapper Bugsy Siegel said, hiding his gun as he unbuttoned his expensive shirt. "A guy can go crazy in a joint like this. He's gotta get out and have some fun."

The nurse turned her mouth into a stage pout. "And what about the little girl you left behind?" she asked. "It's not very gentlemanly to proposition a woman and then abandon her," she teased.

Bugsy pulled the blonde towards him. "I'm gonna show you I'm no gentleman," he laughed as he pushed her on the bed.

"I hate gentlemen," she said, pulling Bugsy to her.

Later, when the curvaceous nurse slipped back into her uniform, Bugsy asked, "You're not gonna say anything down at the office about my little pleasure cruise on the town, are you?"

"Not if you promise you won't mention my pleasure cruise to my husband," she said.

BUGSY laughed. "Baby," he said, "you're my kind of woman."

Though he had made a remarkable recovery, Bugsy Siegel remained a patient at the hospital a couple of days longer. When he checked out, he had a date with his nurse, and a perfect alibi.

For the rest of his life, Bugsy would laugh wildly when he bragged to other hoodlums in gray flannel suits about the alibi the cops couldn't crack.

"I'm the only guy alive who would think of a beauty like that," Bugsy always wound up his story. "A beautiful nurse to play with and a beautiful alibi. I'm a genius."

That was Bugsy Siegel—a vain, egotistical playboy, and one of the most feared killers in organized mobland. In his own way, Bugsy was a man of distinction. He was the last of his breed, the missing link between the old fashioned plug uglies who damned the consequences and handled their own artillery, and the soft-spoken gentlemen mobsters who pulled strings from behind the scenes.

Bugsy was as vicious as a Gestapo agent. Even after he had parlayed arrogance, suaveness and contempt of danger into a spot on the board of directors of the National Crime Syndicate, Bugsy would still take time out from his million dollar enterprises to handle a "contract" for execution. He derived as much pleasure from killing as he did from the desirable women who clung to his arm and shared his bed.

Bugsy's ego was his most memorable feature. Darkly handsome, his hair wavy and thick, he even had his toenails manicured twice a week. Whenever he was praised for his brilliant handling of a murder job, his chest would swell and his eyes gleam. And although his nickname was pinned on him in underworld praise for his complete disregard of the risks of his trade and his fearless use of a gun, Siegel would grow livid if anyone called him Bugsy. He considered the name degrading for a man of his stature, and it has always been rumored that more than one young hood was obliterated because he said "Bugsy" to Siegel's face.

Bugsy Siegel was deadly, but he could also be most charming.

When Bugsy was transferred to Hollywood in the late 1930's to bring the wild, virgin west into the Syndicate's corporate setup, his matinee idol looks and his sinister charm helped make him the intimate of the top actors and actresses of the day. Especially the actresses.

He was idolized by them, invited everywhere by them, and he slept with many of the most beautiful of them—while at the same time his racketeer organization was muscling them out of about $500,000 a year. They coughed up, and they loved it.

The glamour boy of the Syndicate was filled with paradoxes. Though he was so cold-blooded it was said he'd kill his grandmother if the price was right, Bugsy was protective toward his hired gunsels. He was the kind of mob boss who spent $250,000 to put in a political fix so that two of his gunslingers would get a life term instead of the chair, and then spent another $35,000 to hire someone to case the possibilities of breaking them out of prison.

"My men are worth it," he explained when Frank Costello told him he was carrying sentimentality and loyalty too far. "They always gave me their best."

Yet, there were other sides of Bugsy's largesse. Once, the story is still told by Hollywood oldtimers, Bugsy was on the way to a love nest he shared with a young pretty redheaded actress who has since become a top box office star. They stopped at a grocery store and his playmate asked for a can of salmon. Bugsy exploded.

"What happened to the salmon I bought you last week?" he demanded.

A FEW months later, the actress decided there was no percentage in a life with Bugsy in spite of the furs, jewelry and cash he eventually gave her. She suddenly ran off and married another man. Instead of oiling his .45, Bugsy went out and bought a $50,000 mansion as a wedding present for the bride and groom.

The contractor who built Bugsy's personal monument, the Flamingo Hotel in Las Vegas, once

Bugsy Siegel's first mug shot for the authorities. There would be many more.

said of Bugsy:

"He was a remarkable character—tough, cold and terrifying when he wanted to be, but at other times a very easy fellow to be around. He told me one night that he had personally killed 12 men. But then he must have noticed my face, or something, because he laughed and said that I had nothing to worry about.

"There's no chance that you'll get killed,' he said, 'We only kill each other.'"

Siegel was born in 1905 in New York's lower east side, a neighborhood so tough that infants teethed on brass knuckles and pistol barrels. His early career has faded into the obscurity of the young-punk phase of all top mobsters.

His first recorded brush with the law was right after New Year's Day, 1926, when he was charged with rape. Bugsy beat the rap, as he was to do with monotonous regularity all his life. In 1928, Philadelphia cops arrested him for carrying concealed weapons, but the courts discharged him. A year later he was picked up in New York on a narcotics charge, but was again set free.

In 1930 a Miami judge made something stick

on Bugsy, for he paid a $100 fine for gambling. The next year Miami had another try at him, this time for hanging around with known criminals, but the charge washed out.

Obviously, the handsome, personable and very deadly young man had made some influential friendships by this time. Most important among them were other young mobsters on the way up, like Lucky Luciano, Frank Costello, Louis Lepke, Joe Adonis and Albert Anastasia in Brooklyn, and Abner (Longy) Zwillman in New Jersey.

Plus Meyer Lansky, another product of the teaming lower east side. Some time in the late 1920's Siegel and Lansky teamed up and formed a powerful gang with interests in bootlegging, gambling, narcotics, general racketeering and organized murder.

The Bugs and Meyer mob, as it became known with a great deal of fear in gangland, was the forerunner of Murder, Inc. In fact, the execution division of the Syndicate was patterned after the coldly efficient Bugs and Meyer mob, which gave up contractual murders only after its two leaders graduated to bigger and better things.

Siegel was just shy of 26 in April, 1931, when he completed a business deal for which Lucky Luciano was extremely grateful, and which assured Bugsy a top spot in the syndicate Lucky put together.

At that time Lucky was an underling, although a rather important one. He was the right hand man to Joe (the Boss) Masseria, an aging Mafiosa with a thick Sicilian accent who was undisputed king of the rackets in Brooklyn and lower Manhattan.

Joe the Boss had a number of weaknesses in his character and in his approach to his hazardous trade. For one thing, Masseria was so old-fashioned that he was content to get rich on booze and gambling, leaving narcotics, organized prostitution, and labor rackets to younger mobs whose leaders were not too conservative to stick their necks out.

ANOTHER defect in the Boss was his old country bias against forming allegiances with non-Sicilians—Jews like Lepke and Bugs and Meyer, or Irishmen like Owney Madden and Vannie Higgins. It was Lucky's considered opinion that Joe the Boss was a "Mustache Pete," an immigrant with no class and no vision.

Masseria's major failing, however, was that he trusted his chief assistant too much.

"I'm promoting myself," Lucky announced one night at a secret meeting of the younger mobsters; "And when I'm in, we're all gonna form one big combine to grab all the action going."

"Count me in," Bugsy said. "And I wanna personally hand the Boss his walking papers."

The vote was carried unanimously: Joe the Boss had to go, and Bugsy would hasten his departure.

It happened on a pleasant Saturday evening. Luciano, Costello, Adonis and another young hood on the rise named Vito Genovese, invited Joe the Boss to a Coney Island sea food house. They fed him well and filled him with wine. After dessert, Luciano rose.

"To the Boss," he toasted.

His companions cheered. Pleased, drowsy with wine, Masseria accepted his due. He reached for his glass. Before he could raise it, Bugsy Siegel slipped into the private dining room, held his gun a couple of inches from Masseria's head and fired six slugs into his brain.

After the formalities of police questioning, the younger generation picked up the empire Joe the Boss had left behind and immediately expanded into other fields. A share in the kingdom and a seat on a newly formed Syndicate's board of directors went to the Bugs and Meyer mob.

Siegel was now a criminal executive. But he didn't give up killing, because it would have been like giving up breathing, or women. For example, some 17 months after the younger mobsters promoted themselves over Joe the Boss' body, Siegel gunned down Tony Fabrizio, the killer with literary ambitions. And according to the hoods who squealed on Murder, Inc., years later, Bugsy was responsible for some of the dozens of bodies that were being dropped on the sidewalks of New York at that time.

Because of his undeniable ability with a gun and his fearsome reputation, Bugsy became chief troubleshooter for the Syndicate, keeping his experienced eye on the mob's widening business properties and fastgrowing enterprises.

Within a year after the Syndicate was founded, it held full control of the east coast from Maine to Florida. Under the prodding of Lucky and Costello, Chicago's Capone mob, Detroit's Purple Gang and mobsters in every other major city joined the crime cartel, creating an interlocking national organization that coined millions each year.

All good things must eventually come to an end, however. By 1937, rackets buster Thomas E. Dewey was coming up with a headline a day in his investigation into organized crime. Luciano was in jail for running a compulsory prostitution ring. Lepke's narcotics business was Dewey's next major target. And, from informers planted right in the prosecutor's office, the Syndicate learned that Bugsy Siegel's specialized role in the mob's operations was coming under scrutiny.

It so happened that the Syndicate had just discovered the golden west at this time. Reports of rich profits and sky-high salaries in Hollywood constantly hit the newspapers, and, to the Syndicate, it seemed a crying shame to let the boobs hold on to their bank accounts.

"Ben's the guy to handle it," Lepke said at a meeting of the board. "He's sharp and he knows the angles. He's got guts, and he's smooth enough to put up a good front. And with the Brooklyn crowd (Murder, Inc.) handling the hits, we could spare Benny."

"And another thing," Costello added. "We could grab all the gambling. I hear that movie crowd spends a mint."

After getting the okay of Lucky, who was in Dannemora, the Syndicate selected Bugsy Siegel to open a branch office in Hollywood.

Bugsy proceeded to outdazzle the tinseled world of the movie colony. His fantastically inflated ego was a natural in the land of egotists. Bugsy dressed better than the stars, and he out-talked them. He made quite a splash.

Like most gangsters of the era, he was a big spender and lived in high style. He had barely arrived on the west coast before he built himself a luxurious 35-room mansion in the elite Holmby Hills area. It cost him $250,000—a pre-war 250 grand.

Bugsy spared nothing. His special pride was a huge Roman bath, done in imported maroon marble set off with solid gold plumbing fixtures. Bugsy also installed indirect lighting behind the dressers in his ballroom-sized dressing room so that his $25 shirts would be properly displayed.

While he was captivating the hearts of movieland, he stole from its inhabitants. Through a phony labor union run by local hoods and imported torpedoes, Bugsy organized the movie extras and shook down stars and studios for about $500,000 a year.

BUGSY got away with his dual role of thief and pal of the stars simply by dazzling a Countess, who was Hollywood's leading hostess and whose command performance parties were attended by everyone important—or else. The suave, mannerly mobster became her "protege," and she almost single-handedly put down all rumors that Bugsy was still an active mobster. Her efforts were so successful, in fact, that Hollywood columnists referred to Bugsy as a "sportsman," and Hollywood's elite accepted him in the inner circle.

His name was soon linked romantically with some of the most famous screen heroines of the day. He was always a very charming person around women, and he wouldn't permit anyone to use obscene language in their presence.

During one fabulous party, a well-known cowboy star got loaded and began telling off-color jokes, punctuating every line with four-letter words. Bugsy grabbed him by the throat and dragged him into the wine cellar. He pulled out a .38 and stuck it under the cowboy's nose.

"Clean up your language, or I'll blow your head open," Bugsy ordered. The cowboy cleaned up his language, pronto.

The debonair playboy didn't neglect the Syndicate's business, however. His shock troops visited every bookmaker and gambling den operator they could find from San Diego north to San Francisco, whispered "Bugs sent me," and the Syndicate soon controlled most of the gambling in the state. Bugsy used the same tactics to muscle out competition and gain a near-monopoly over the tons of narcotics that crossed the border from Mexico.

Staying completely behind the scenes, Bugsy was able to play the role of Hollywood sportsman while keeping his unsportsmanlike activities hidden from view. Early in 1940, however, his facade of respectability began to crumble.

The chain of events started back in New York a year earlier. Lepke was a fugitive from a narcotics indictment and got tired of hiding out. Before surrendering, though, he wanted to cover all bets. So he and his Syndicate partners decreed the murder of all minor mobsters believed weak enough to crack under the prosecutor's pressure.

One of those on the purge list was George Greenberg, known as Big Greenie, who had been associated with Lepke in garment industry shakedowns. Big Greenie fled before he could be knocked off, but the mob traced him to Hollywood.

"Let Ben handle it," Lepke suggested.

The murder contract was promptly delivered to Bugsy by Murder, Inc. killer Allie Tannenbaum, who flew to California to assist on the job. On Thanksgiving eve, Big Greenie left his hideout apartment for the first editions of the morning papers. When he returned in his car a man in a slouch hat stuck a revolver through the open window and blasted him.

Six months later, Abe "Kid Twist" Reles, a young executive killer in Murder, Inc. became a canary, Anxious to keep himself out of the electric chair, Allie Tannenbaum also began to sing. Tannenbaum named Bugsy Siegel as the man who had planned Big Greenie's murder.

"While the triggerman's blasting away," Tannenbaum said, "I'm sitting behind the wheel of Siegel's new Caddy. Siegel himself decides he wants the Caddy to be the crash car, to block off anybody chasing the getaway car we stole. Siegel's sitting right with me, squeezing his finger like he's got a gun and saying, 'Give it to him, give it to him,' all the time Greenie is getting blasted."

Siegel and his partners were indicted for murder. For the first time in his life, Bugsy was tossed into a lockup for more than an overnight stay. He made the best of it, however.

One afternoon, about two months after checking into the county jail, Siegel was spotted lunching with a famous British actress in a high-class eatery on Wilshire Boulevard. A deputy sheriff was acting as chaperone.

When reporters began asking questions, it was learned that Bugsy had never spent an hour in his cell. He lived in the infirmary, from which prisoners who were actually sick were barred so that Bugsy wouldn't catch their germs, and he slept in his silk pajamas on a soft hospital bed.

THE JAIL'S VIP guest also had his personal barber come in to trim his hair, and paid another prisoner to act as his valet. Special meals also were brought in for Bugsy, including his favorite dishes, caviar and roast pheasant.

The official explanation for the fact that Bugsy had made 19 trips outside the jail in the 50 days he spent there, was that he was getting his teeth fixed. Bugsy's choppers, however, were perfect. It turned out that the prison physician was an old chum of Bugsy's, and they had sometimes shared rooms at the Waldorf on trips to New York. The doctor had personally okayed his mobster friend's outside trips.

Everyone got fired, and Bugsy was slapped into the dirtiest cell in the place. He didn't stay long, though. The murder indictment was dismissed two weeks later when squealer Abe Reles developed "ulcers" and refused to make the trip west.

Some months later, the murder charges were revived. But by the time the case came up for trial, it turned out Reles was a canary who couldn't fly. Despite a full time guard in a Coney Island hotel, Reles "fell" from an 11-story window while playing a "trick" on his protectors, according to the official version. The case against Bugsy went out the window with songbird Reles.

The Syndicate charm boy returned to his racket empire, and he suddenly discovered Virginia Hill.

One of 10 children of an Alabama tombstone polisher, the full-bosomed honey had a strange partiality for alliances with some of the top mobsters in the country. Virgy first caught the public's eye as a slightly-clad, 16-year-old showgirl in the Chicago Fair of 1933 and 1934.

After the Fair closed, she ran through a couple of quick marriages and soon blossomed as an all-American girl of the Syndicate, becoming quite palsy with both Fischetti brothers, in turn, and then with Luciano, Costello, Joe Adonis and other mobland bosses. By the time she got to Hollywood, she was well enough in the chips to rent Rudolph Valentino's old hilltop mansion.

Virginia caused as much of a splash around Hollywood and Vine as Bugsy had done years earlier. She threw $10,000 parties, got her name in the gossip column as the "female Diamond Jim Brady," and became Bugsy's favorite bunny.

The Syndicate's beachhead in California had grown into a fairly complete operation sometime after Pearl Harbor. Then Bugsy discovered Las Vegas.

At the time, Las Vegas was little more than a desert town with a couple of poker and crap tables. Bugsy, however, was a man of vision. What he could foresee was a billion-dollar-a-year Paradise, where there would be so many suckers bleating to be fleeced that some of them would have to be turned away. The Paradise was to be run by Bugsy, of course. He rushed to New York and convened a meeting of the board.

"Monte Carlo won't be in the same league with this town," Bugsy said. "We're gonna build the biggest, most fabulous hotel ever seen, and it's gonna be stocked to the rafters with slots and crap tables and the wheels. There's a fortune waiting there, and we gotta get in on the ground floor."

His enthusiasm was catching, and the mob leaders agreed to invest $3,000,000 in Bugsy's dream palace. The result was the plush Flamingo Hotel.

Bugsy, a man with an obsession, refused to believe such things as war-time priorities could stand in his way, and he paid black market prices to satisfy his demands for the finest materials in the world. By the time the Flamingo opened, it had cost Bugsy and his backers $6,000,000.

The Syndicate was unhappy, and Bugsy was in trouble. He began to lose his head and really live up to his nickname. Bugsy, in fact, went haywire.

For many years, Bugsy had held the West Coast franchise of the Continental Press Service, which relayed to bookmakers the split-second race results without which they couldn't operate. As the Flamingo was nearing completion, the Chicago branch of the Syndicate set up a rival race service, killed off the front men of Continental, and merged both wires. The Syndicate now had a nationwide monopoly.

Astoundingly, Bugsy refused to go along. He defied the cartel, ran his own wires independently in California, and siphoned off all profits into the Flamingo.

"I put the wire together and I'm gonna run it," Bugsy told the boys back east. "It's all mine."

THE Syndicate was patient. Bugsy, after all, was a member of the board. To kill him would not be the same as exterminating one of the lower echelon hoodlums. Another deterrent to hasty action against Bugsy was the fact that his chief lieutenants—old-line mobster Jack Dragna, who had learned at the feet of the mighty Capone himself, and a brash punk named Mickey Cohen—backed Siegel up all the way.

Bugsy was given a little time to come to his senses. But he was still reeling like a schoolboy in love, except that he was now 42 and his only big love was the Flamingo.

The gambling palace opened a couple of months after Bugsy had thumbed his nose at the Syndicate bosses. On opening night, after a Hollywood-type premiere with stars and spotlights and Roman candles, the casino handled more than $250,000 in play—and it lost an unheard of $5,500.

Back in New York, Costello, Zwillman, Lansky, Adonis and other Syndicate kings went pale with disbelief. Bugsy Siegel, member of the board of directors, had not only disobeyed the majority's wishes on the race wire, but was now obviously holding back some of the take from the Flamingo.

Bugsy was summoned to New York for a meeting. Frank Erickson, the human adding machine who was manager of the Syndicate's gambling empire, cited columns of figures to show the Flamingo couldn't possibly have come up with the loss Bugsy reported.

Bugsy said nothing. Costello finally spoke.

"You got 30 days to get up a million and a half," he said. "That's final."

Bugsy scrounged around everywhere he could, putting the bite on every friend he could contact.

"I gotta go into hiding if I don't get it," he told several people he approached for loans.

But he had no luck. He even tried banks, and was turned down because he was already mortgaged to the hilt.

When Bugsy's 30 days were up a meeting of the board was held in Havana, where Lucky Luciano had been secretly living for several months. Lucky had been deported to Italy after serving several years of a life sentence for compulsory prostitution. Before the board—now a kangaroo court—voted on the Siegel question, Lucky called Bugsy in Las Vegas. Underworld informers later told Federal agents the brief conversation went something like this:

Lucky: "Wise up, Ben. You know what has to happen if you don't."

Bugsy: "I don't give a damn. I got enough on all you guys to send you to the chair."

Lucky reported back to the other Syndicate directors: "Ben's blown his stack. He's gotta be hit." The decision was carried by unanimous vote.

Late in May, 1947, two high members of the Chicago mob visited Hollywood and summoned Bugsy's staunch supporters, Jack Dragna and Mickey Cohen, to a secret meeting. When the conference was over, Dragna and Cohen suddenly became neutrals. They flew off to Florida for a vacation.

AND Virginia Hill, apparently possessed of a woman's intuition, ran off to Paris on June 14.

Four days later, on a Friday night, Bugsy returned from a Hollywood night club to the 16-room Beverly Hills home Virginia had rented a few months earlier.

Bugsy had a gold key to the door, and he kept some of his clothing in an upstairs bedroom. He apparently had come to town to clean out his expensive duds and take them back to the Flamingo.

Accompanying Bugsy was Virginia Hill's younger brother, Charles, her secretary, and Bugsy's pal Alan Smiley, a character with a long police record who had a small piece of the Flamingo.

Hill and the secretary went upstairs to pack Bugsy's things. Siegel and Smiley went into the sumptuously furnished drawing room. As Smiley sat down on one end of a long, flowered sofa, Bugsy drew the drapes on a side window. They missed coming together completely by about six inches. Bugsy dropped onto the other end of the sofa, loosened his tie, and picked up a newspaper.

It was exactly 11:15 p.m. when a darksuited man braced a high-powered Army carbine against the rose trellis along the driveway of the house next door. Rapidly, he squeezed off nine rounds.

Smiley dived to the floor at the first sound of shots.

"Shut the lights," he screamed to Bugsy.

When the fusillade ended moments later, Smiley picked himself up. The lights were still on. Bugsy Siegel was lying back on the sofa, his hands in his lap and the newspaper between his legs, catching the blood that poured from two bullet holes in his head and two in his body. Bugsy's left eye was across the room.

With Siegel out of the way, the men of the Syndicate breathed a little more comfortably. Whether they regretted the need to execute a member of the board of directors for the first time is not known. They probably did, for Bugsy was as popular as he was vicious.

It was left to the two women in his life to write his epitaph. The words were spoken long before Bugsy came to his sudden end, but they sum up his life so well:

"Ben Siegel may be brutal to some, but to me he is a charming, delightful man," the Countess once remarked.

"I don't see where people get off calling him tough," Virginia Hill said. "I sleep in the raw and he sometimes sleeps in my silk nighties."

●●●

THAT OTHER BETTY

A CELEBRATION OF BETTY BROSMER BY GARY LOVISI

Many fans of the sexy glamor gals of the 1950s – the young women whose gorgeous images graced the covers of so many books and magazines of the era – fondly remenber Betty Page – however there is another lovely young lady who had just as much impact on the glamour field. That was Betty Brosmer.

I first noticed Betty in photos on early Novel and Merit paperback covers. These were from 1961 and 1962 and had titles like *BRUTAL ECSTASY* and *BED CRAZY*. Betty's photos showed a lively and charming young woman with the classic hour-glass figure. Later on I was to learn her measurements at that time were an amazing 38-18-36. But it was the bright and sunny disposition of this young woman that came through in her book and magazine cover photos. Betty had a fresh and playful, girl-next-door type of look, and she looked like she was having fun hamming it up for the photos.

I often wondered just who she might be. As I was not really into pin-up or "glamour" photography, and since her photos were on books from 50 years ago, I thought it might be impossible to discover who she was – much less find her, and interview her. It was destined to take me quite a few years before I found Betty Brosmer.

Eventually I discovered her photos on the covers of some Chariot Books, and on other Novel Books and Merit Books, all soft-core sleaze paperbacks. I also found many covers with her image on magazines of the late 1950s and early 1960s – then she seemed to have disappeared. I began to wonder, where did Betty go?

It seemed strange that after about 1963 I could not find any paperbacks or magazines with Betty on the cover. Since I knew by then, that her name was Betty Brosmer, I used the Internet and did a Google search under that name.

That search lead me to BettyWeider.com. I wondered who *she* could be. This Betty Weider had the same first name as Betty Brosmer, but not the same last name. It turned out that Betty Brosmer was now Betty Weider, after marrying bodybuilding maven, Joe Weider.

Around 1960 she met bodybuilder, publisher and fitness guru Joe Weider when she modeled for his *BEAUTY AND FIGURE* magazine. The two were married soon after in April,1961. They have been

THE MAQ GAL-LERY

Figure
QUARTERLY

ONE DOLLAR

PHOTOGRAPHY
SCULPTURE
PAINTING

SPECIAL
LIGHTING
ISSUE

PETER GOWLAND'S
UNDERWATER
NUDE
STUDIES

THE MODEL
IN CARTOONS
BY
JEFFERSON
MACHAMER

BEN STAHL
DRAWS THE
FIGURE

VOLUME ELEVEN

happily married for over 40 years. Betty quit glamour modeling soon after her marriage and only did modeling for ads in Joe's magazines. There's even one famous ad with her and Arnold Schwarzenegger, the future star and "governator" of California who Joe was instrumental in first bringing to the United States from Austria in 1968. The rest, as they say, is history.

Betty Brosmer was now Betty Weider. The glamour girl of the 1950s had done photos that were on over 300 magazine covers, she had been on television and won numerous beauty contests. She was an incredibly popular model. At one point in the 1950s Betty was the highest paid pin-up model in America – she had turned down *PLAYBOY* because of her rule of never doing anything more than just cheesecake glamour shots and no nudes. Betty always brought grace and class to everything she did. Her pleasant smile and sweet girlish charm gave a classic sexy image that always evoked innocence and good clean fun. She was into physical fitness and nutrition, even before she met her husband, Joe, and later also co-authored several books on fitness and exercise as well as being a magazine columnist.

In 2007 I was able to interview Betty for my magazine *PAPERBACK PARADE* (issue #70) and the following material comes from that article and subsequent information I have gathered over the interveening years.

I found Betty to be an amazing woman, warm, friendly and quite charming. She was a joy to speak with and I hope you enjoy this interview with glamour pin-up legend, Betty Brosmer.

Gary Lovisi: Can you talk a bit about your early life and how your modeling career got started?

Betty Weider: It started when I was very young, 14 or 15 years old. I went to New York City with my Aunt Annie. We lived in Los Angeles then, and went to Maine in the summers. In New York when I was 14 my aunt met with a gentleman and showed him photos of me and he said I photographed beautifully. That was for Ewing Galloway, they had hundreds of thousands of stock photos, whatever the subject, and he said to put me in the photos. I thought that was nice and I went to the studio, did some head shots. They printed them and recommended I go to an agency. A head shot from that shoot was in ads in *TIME, LIFE, FORTUNE,*

One of the many glamourous shots Betty posed for in her career.

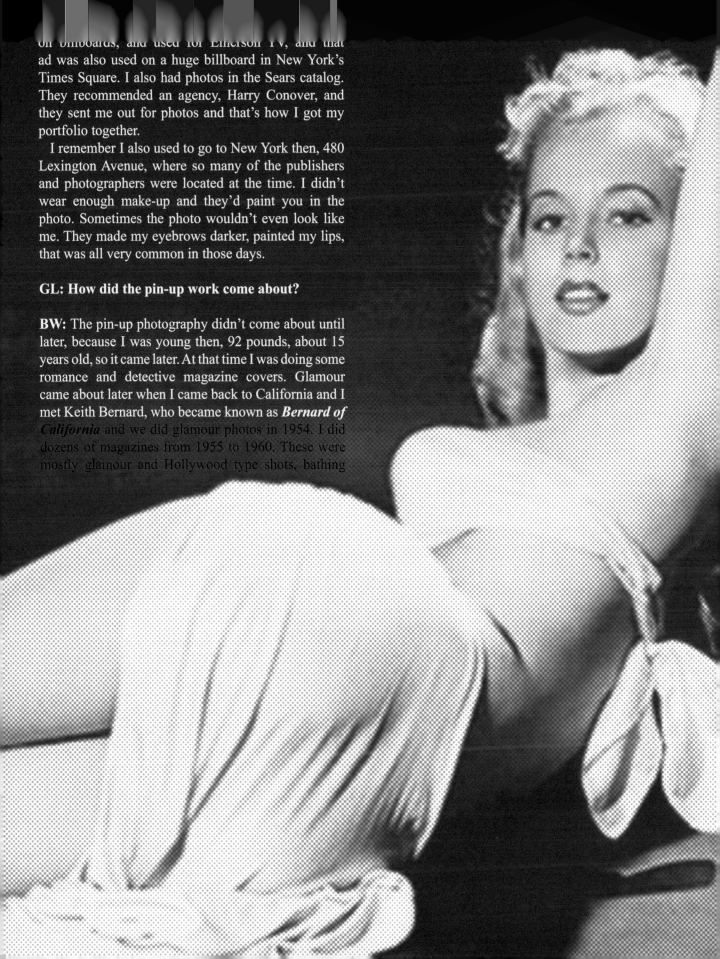

on billboards, and used for Emerson TV, and that
ad was also used on a huge billboard in New York's
Times Square. I also had photos in the Sears catalog.
They recommended an agency, Harry Conover, and
they sent me out for photos and that's how I got my
portfolio together.

I remember I also used to go to New York then, 480
Lexington Avenue, where so many of the publishers
and photographers were located at the time. I didn't
wear enough make-up and they'd paint you in the
photo. Sometimes the photo wouldn't even look like
me. They made my eyebrows darker, painted my lips,
that was all very common in those days.

GL: How did the pin-up work come about?

BW: The pin-up photography didn't come about until
later, because I was young then, 92 pounds, about 15
years old, so it came later. At that time I was doing some
romance and detective magazine covers. Glamour
came about later when I came back to California and I
met Keith Bernard, who became known as *Bernard of
California* and we did glamour photos in 1954. I did
dozens of magazines from 1955 to 1960. These were
mostly glamour and Hollywood type shots, bathing

suit shots, and Bernard was the one who popularized me and my name.

When I came into Bernard's studio and showed him my portfolio he was impressed and wanted to use me for glamour shots. He asked me my fee, my rates then were New York rates which were high for California. Bernard said, "Oh, no, I could never pay that kind of money, it would bankrupt me!" But his agent, George Posner, spoke up and proposed we should do a partnership. Eventually we worked it out so that I would get 33% of anything we sold, Bernard would get 33% and George would get 33%. We all thought that was a great idea and it worked out very well.

GL: Did you have an agent?

BW: My agent was the Harry Conover Agency until I left New York. In California, I was with the Mary Webb Davis Agency but the main person I worked for here in California was Bernard of Hollywood.

GL: How did you get along with the photographers?

BW: Most photographers treated me well and they were very professional. I was lucky because I had my Aunt Annie and she went with me to every shoot in New York and California. I was always treated well, probably better than some of the other girls who just went to shoots by themselves. I think I met Bernard when I was 19.

GL: Since PAPERBACK PARADE is a book collector's magazine and I read in a bio that at 17 you said you, "fell in love with art auctions and rare book stores in New York" and that you love book stores, can you talk about your interest in books? Do you collect books?

BW: I always liked books and I always liked history. I like to learn when I read. I used to go to Bartfield First Editions for rare books in New York City. I've always been interested in antiques and collectibles, swap meets, flea markets, yard sales, I love them all, it's like a treasure hunt. You never know what you will find. I tried to collect first editions of Mark Twain and Brett Harte, I also am interested in books on California history, the Gold Rush, and the pioneer era.

GL: Did you ever know Bettie Page or any of the

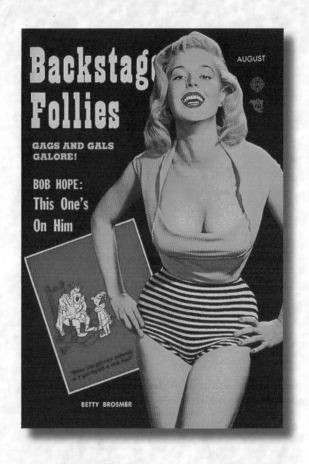

OPPOSITE: Betty Brosmer became the new "Cover Girl" 3-4 years after Bettie Page. She also negotiated residual rates for her posing, something Bettie couldn't do. Here she poses for **BACKSTAGE FOLLIES** and **GALA** magazines. THIS PAGE: Often these photo shoots were of the "Sexy Housewife" variety - cooking, cleaning, or as this picture shows, waiting for her man to come home from work.

TAB

THE POCKET PICTURE MAGAZINE

APR. 25c

MEET LIBERACE'S "SWEETIE"

Stalking the TUSKED TERROR

The Siren Who WOULDN'T STAY DEAD

BETTY BRASMER

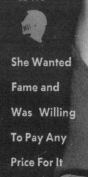

LENS GIRL

CB-199

She Wanted

Fame and

Was Willing

To Pay Any

Price For It

by

E. S. SEELEY JR.

50c

THE SHOCKING STORY OF A FLAMING BEAUTY
WHO BECAME A HELLION BEFORE THE CAMERAS

TV GIRLS and GAGS

NOVEMBER 1955

15¢
ANC

Betty Brasmer

Lust for women and money inspires
an incredible scheme of deception

LUST LODGE

An Original By
Arnold Marmor

ADULT READING

Tony Martin Goes West

PICTURE

SCOPE

They Run
The Raging
Congo

FIRST FOTOS!

OPERATION ON
A HUMAN BRAIN

Destruction
Derby

Calling All
TViewers

other models of that era?

BW: Bettie Page was a little earlier than I was, about 3-4 years before my time. I came into the glamour modeling in the later 1950s. I don't remember hearing about her then when I was in New York. In California I met some models, they were really more actresses than models: Iris Bristol, Diane Webber.

GL: Were you aware your photos were used on the covers of some paperback books?

BW: Not really, the paperbacks never used my name, the magazines did. I do remember *LENS GIRL*, and there may be five or six others. Several were also with my photos but they made artwork out of it. I was also on a movie poster the same way. It was for Kim Novak but they used my photo and used her head on my body – but it was artwork not a photo. That kind of artwork also had me on some calendars. Earl Moran took photos of me and he put the transparencies in a machine that blew up the image larger and then he painted them. That way I didn't have to stand there and pose.

GL: What do you think of your glamour photo covers today?

BW: It think it is interesting, it seems trendy, girls buy

compacts with the pin-ups, it's a retro revival. They find it charming. It's amazing how many fans I have who are really young, they think it's cool. I think even Bettie Page did some wild things but she always did it in a light and fun way. I never went that far but that's what I wanted to do, make it happy and fun and that still works today.

GL: How did you feel about being a model when so young?

BW: In the beginning I really disliked it, I was extremely shy and it was hard for me to get in front of the camera. The photographers told me not to be afraid of the camera and when I realized that, I started to enjoy it. One of my first photo shoots in New York City was in a long studio with art directors or ad agency people present. When I came out – I was very young and shy – I heard them comment about me. They asked why did the photographer hire me. They said I had no sex appeal and that I was too young. They thought I couldn't hear them but I could and I was so devastated I wanted to quit right there. They wanted a dark-haired girl, more mature, sultry and seductive and I was too young and blonde. But I made up my mind that I was going to show them, so I posed and it was like a transformation, whatever I did worked. When the camera came on I came alive. It could have ended

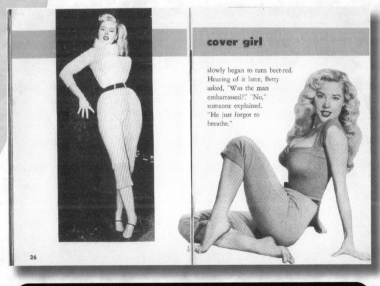

Photos of Betty Brosmer appeared on covers and in interior photo spreads of hundreds of magazines, on paperback covers, and in ads.

From one of the many photo shoots Betty posed for Weider fitness magazines. She eventually married Joe Weider, the head of the company, and became the shape of female fitness.

Betty Chloe Brosmer was born August 6, 1929 and is now about 93 years of age. Sadly, Joe Weider died in 2013 at the age of 93.

my career had I responded differently. The photos came out fine, they were for a golf magazine or golf shoes. The agency wanted a more mature girl but when they saw my photos they were very happy with me. The photos came out cute.

I went to another shoot, my second shoot, my aunt was always with me. I remember this photographer saying how my jaw was too wide and that it should be broken and then reset. He said I should have surgery to break my jaw and have it reset. I would never do that. But it was interesting, because Bernard who made me famous, loved models with broad jaws like Farrah Fawcett, who had a broad jaw also. So what one photographer said was a detriment, Bernard told me was an attribute.

I want to thank Betty as well as Harold Forsko, her most ardent fan, for their input in this article. To find out more about Betty visit her website: BettyBrosmer.com

●●●

Betty Brosmer wasn't only the shape of female fitness, she was its glamourous face.

MUSCLE, FITNESS AND ADVENTURE!

THE JOE WEIDER MUSCLE ADVENTURE MAGAZINES

ARTICLE
BY BOB **DEIS**

Betty and Joe Weider

Magazines were one part of the amazing business empire created by brothers Joe and Ben Weider, with assistance from Betty Brosmer after she married Joe in 1961. The "Brothers of Iron" helped create the modern bodybuilding and fitness industry and made millions from their bodybuilding contests, courses, equipment and nutritional supplements.

Ads for "Weider System" products and publications, which often featured a photo of Joe in his bodybuilding heyday, are as common in vintage men's magazines and comic books as ads for rival bodybuilder Charles Atlas.

The Weider brothers played a major role in shaping the bodybuilding and fitness magazine genre by pub-

lishing a long list of popular muscle mags, starting in 1936 with the groundbreaking magazine *YOUR PHYSIQUE.*

In the 1950s and 1960s, Joe and Ben also published men's pulp adventure mags, like *FURY, OUTDOOR ADVENTURES* and *SAFARI*, and men's bachelor mags, such as *JEM* and *MONSIEUR.*

Two of the Weider men's mags, *MR. AMERICA* and *AMERICAN MANHOOD,* were unusual hybrids: *part bodybuilding magazine and part men's pulp magazine.*

For both of these magazines (and most Weider periodicals) Joe focused more on the creative aspects, while Ben focused more on the business management aspects.

In the fascinating joint autobiography written by Joe and Ben, *BROTHERS OF IRON: BUILDING THE WEIDER EMPIRE* (2006), Joe Weider explained how these hybrid periodicals originated.

He said that by the early Fifties their first popular magazine, *YOUR PHYSIQUE*, seemed "too French-sounding and soft for U.S. readers." One of the

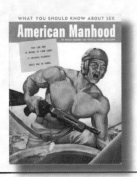

recent publishing trends that got Joe's attention was the growing number of men's adventure pulp mags. He decided to remake **YOUR PHYSIQUE** into a men's pulp magazine, with "my own original mix of a muscle magazine and men's adventure." Joe first tried this mix in the magazine **MR. AMERICA** in mid-1952.

> *"The combination seemed to make sense, because young men bought both kinds of magazines, and guys who read tough stuff would want to build their bodies to get tough,"* he wrote in **BROTHERS OF IRON**. *"It didn't work, though, because the two genres had different readership. And even guys who bought both kinds of magazines didn't want them together."*

The men's adventure version of **MR. AMERICA** ceased publication in the fall of 1953, although the Weiders later revived the title as a pure bodybuilding magazine heavily associated with the Mr. America contests they sponsored. (This was a forerunner of their Mr. Olympia contest, which helped make Arnold Schwarzenegger famous).

• • •

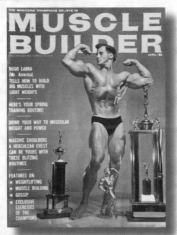

Examples of Weider magazines, and an ad with Betty Brosmer on Arnold Schwarzenegger's shoulders.

À **MÃO** BONUS

BETTY BROSMER

CC
02400

GIRLS IN FULL COLOR
Plus More Stories Than Any
Other Men's Magazine

20 LOVEMAKING TURN-ONS (ILLUSTRATED)
No Woman Can Resist Them All

MALE

Nov.   75¢

$6.95 TRUE BOOK BONUS
I HIT THE HIT MEN
Brutal Life of the Mob's Most
Feared Super-Killer. "What it
feels like to kill...By a '50-timer'
who rubbed out the world's most-
wary victims..." –POLICE REVIEW

4 Lustful Men and a Girl
Buried Alive in a Lost Gold Mine
SEALED HIDEOUT
1974's Strangest Survival

Have Flying Saucers Shifted
to Underwater Invasion?
THE NEW MYSTERY OF U.S.O.'s-- UNIDENTIFIED SEA OBJECTS

YOUR NEIGHBORHOOD NYMPHO
There's At Least One
On Every Block

Extra!
SPECIAL FICTION
NAKED IN THE WOODS

Hitler Called Them Filthy Butchers
G.I. "RIVER RATS" WHO BLASTED THE NAZIS' SEX CIRCUS VILLA

JANIE JONES:
THE WORLD'S MOST SEX-OBSESSED FEMALE
Exclusive Story and Photos of Her

PLUS: You And Women,
Inside For Men, It's A Strange
World, You And The Law,
Headline Happenings

By Jerry "Red" Kelley as told to
Win P. Morgan
From *MALE*, November 1974

Here's another hit man story that's portrayed as true. In this case, it's said to be the reminiscences of a freelance hitter who killed dozens of people, Jerry "Red" Kelley, "as told to" writer Win P. Morgan.

According to an "Author's Note" at the end of the story, it's transcribed from audio tapes Red made before he died. Morgan indicates that Red's younger brother gave them to him and that a book based on them was planned.

The story is so full of believable details and anecdotes, that it certainly seems like it could be true. But there's no way to know for sure. Morgan says in his note:

> *"Needless to say, various names and locales were changed, though a thorough check of newspapers and police files prove that the details of the tapes were accurate. For every hit described by Jerry 'Red' Kelley, there is a corresponding unsolved murder case in law enforcement records."*

I might have accepted that if I could have found some info confirming that Win P. Morgan was a real person or if I could have found some book published in the '70s that is based on the memories of a hit man.

INTRODUCTION BY BOB DEIS

However, the only other trace of Win P. Morgan I found is one other MAM story credited to that name. A biker story in *MALE*, May 1972. And, I could not find any book that has an "I Hit the Hit Men" theme. So, I'm guessing it's Morgan is a pseudonym for one of the many writers who penned stories for *MALE* under pseudonyms.

That doesn't take away from the fact that the story is a well written, interesting and entertaining yarn. The issue it's in, *MALE*, November 1974, is a good example of what the MAMs published by Magazine Management were like in the '70s.

During that decade, *MALE, STAG, FOR MEN ONLY, MEN,* and the other remaining Mag Mgt, MAMs struggled to hold onto readers who were increasingly drawn to men's mags with more explicit photos of female models and more explicit articles about sex.

Thus, instead of a big cover painting, the main image on the cover of *MALE*, November 1974, like others from the '70s, features a photo of an almost nude woman. The artwork is reduced to two small lifts from interior illustrations shown in inset panels, plus a couple of photos from the issue's "non-fiction" articles..

On the positive side, Mag Mgt. issues from the '70s printed the interior artwork used for stories in full color, rather than as the duotones or black-and-white illustrations that were typical in the '50s and '60s.

Earl Norem's vertical art for "G.I. 'River Rats' Who Blasted the Nazis' Sex Circus Villa" from *MALE* November, 1974. Read it in *MAQ* #5.

And, the two color illustrations in *MALE*, November 1974 are quite awesome.

The first is an eye-popping scene painted by Earl Norem for the gloriously gonzo story "G.I. 'River Rats' Who Blasted the Nazis' Sex Circus Villa." A small photo of the original Norem painting is shown on the cover. Inside, its printed sideways in a vertical 2-page spread. If you've read *MAQ* #5, the "Dirty

Missions" issue, you've seen that Norem art before, since we reprinted it and the story in that issue.

This issue's second full color illo was done by another top MAM artist, Bruce Minney. It goes with the story "Sealed Hideout" which tells the tale of *"four men and a girl buried alive in a lost gold mine."*

Like many Mag Mgt. from the '70s, this issue also has full-color, multi-page "beaver"-filled photo spreads featuring completely nekkid women—a far cry from the comparatively mild cheesecake photos MAMs featured from the early 1950s to the late 1960s. They're a bit too porny to show in the *MAQ*. Sorry.

The rest of the stories and articles in *MALE*, November 1974 are illustrated with photographs. A couple of those, in addition to "I Hit the Hit Men," are pretty interesting. One, titled "We Were Trapped in Killer Bear Country," is in

the classic MAM animal attack mode. Another, "The New Mystery of U.S.O.'s— Unidentified Sea Objects," is a cool variation on UFO stories, which are fairly common in MAMs.

MAMs often had sexology, sex exposé, and sex advice articles. In the '70s, such stories were a bit racier than they were in the '50s and '60s. The examples in *MALE*, November 1974 include "Our Neighborhood Nympho," "Lovemaking Turn-ons: No Woman Can Resist Them All" and "Janie Jones: the World's Most Sex-obsessed Woman." There's also a soft porn fiction story, "Naked in the Woods."

Two other stories are similar to the types of "reader beware" exposés MAMs published in previous decades: "A Rip-off Lawyer Can Ruin You—Legally" and "I Can Frame You as a Homicidal Driver."

Like most MAMs from every decade, this issue includes a number of the news roundup articles and features that were common in *MALE*, like the long-running regular feature "Inside for Men."

"Inside for Men" was basically a series of headlines and mini-articles about recent events and people in the news. The example in *MALE*, November 1974 includes one particularly noteworthy entry. It's about the porn actress Marilyn Chambers. It notes that Marilyn had been the model for mother holding the baby in the image shown on boxes of Ivory Snow laundry detergent in the early '70s. You know, the soap that's "*99 44/100% pure.*"

After Marilyn became famous for her appearance in the 1972 porn classic *BEHIND THE GREEN DOOR* Ivory stopped using that illustration. The editors of "Inside for Men" advised readers to save some boxes of Ivory with Marilyn on them, saying *"in ten years,*

they'll be collectors' items."

They were right. On eBay, Ivory Snow boxes with Marilyn's image now sell for $150 or more. I saw one she autographed before her death in 2009 offered for $399!

• • •

OPPOSITE FROM TOP: The Cover to the 5th issue of MAQ, the "Dirty Missions" issue. Art by Earl Norem. "The Sealed Hideout" story by Jeff Grant. Art by Bruce Minney. *MALE, Nov. 1974* also featured a "U.S.O." story, an underwater version of UFOs. **THIS PAGE:** That issue (un)covered the fact that adult film star Marilyn Chambers had posed for the mother on boxes of Ivory Snow before she became (in)famous and correctly predicted they'd be collectors items some day.

BRUTAL LIFE OF THE MOB'S

I HIT THE HIT MEN

By JERRY "RED" KELLEY
as told to
WIN P. MORGAN

MOST FEARED MURDERER

PETE Benton was a creature of habit. That's the reason he's dead today. Looking back, what's odd about his death was how easily it might have been avoided—if, as I've said, Pete Benton wasn't a creature of habit.

He couldn't bear to alter his schedule. Every Thursday afternoon at 2:30, he drove to the Four Winds Motel outside Los Angeles, parked in front of a stucco bungalow, made sure that the bosomy Julie's convertible was parked outside, took a good look around and went in.

Usually, blonde Julie was just stepping out of the bathroom after a shower wearing no more than some quick squirts of perfume between her full breasts. Sometimes, if she'd arrived just a few minutes earlier than Pete Benton and hadn't had time to shower, she'd

be wearing those transparent bikini briefs with no crotch and a half-bra which didn't get anywhere near covering half of her breasts.

No matter how Julie appeared, though, she would have already ordered frozen daiquiris for Pete Benton and herself. This routine was never varied. Unfortunately for Pete Benton. Because all I had to do was wait five minutes after he went in, knock on the door dressed like a bar waiter and carrying a tray of drinks.

To give Pete Benton his due, he didn't exactly throw open the door. He'd been too good a hit man in his time to get altogether careless. Instead, he kept the chain on and opened the door as far as it would go.

Now a chain is pretty good protection against a junkie burglar, but it won't help if someone wants to

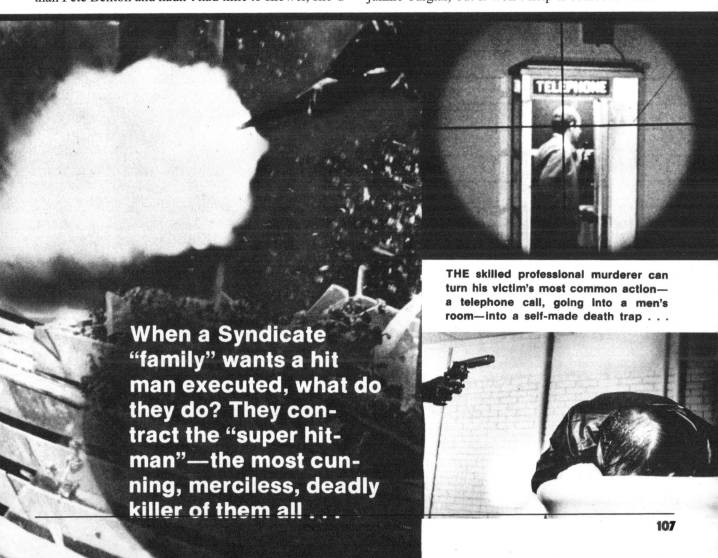

When a Syndicate "family" wants a hit man executed, what do they do? They contract the "super hit-man"—the most cunning, merciless, deadly killer of them all . . .

THE skilled professional murderer can turn his victim's most common action— a telephone call, going into a men's room—into a self-made death trap . . .

kill you. Even though the door is still locked, you have to stick your face in the opening to see who's there. And that's what Pete Benton did. He looked. I pressed a silencerequipped .38 against his forehead and pulled the trigger. Just like that. His eyes were wide open as the bullet plowed into his brain.

Julie, who'd been watching TV, I guess, hadn't seen the action. As a matter of fact, she didn't even know Pete Benton was dead because he'd caught his arm on the chain and was slumped against the door. By the time the broad figured out that her Thursday lover was a corpse and started screaming her lungs out, I was in my car and headed out onto the highway with all those thousands of other cars doing 85 m.p.h. No sweat. I was approaching San Diego when the 5 o'clock news came on saying Pete Benton had been shot to death in a motel outside Los Angeles.

I remember Pete Benton better than most of my hits because he was first of 38 hit men themselves on whom I'd had a contract in the last eight years. I'd collected a fee of $30,000 apiece. That might seem like a lot of dough, but you've got to remember that I'm talking about hit men, and they're not as easy to take out as some ordinary punk whose big crime was he stepped out of line or welshed on a deal or got caught with his hand in the till.

Anyway, it was the summer of 1966, right after the World Series in which Baltimore took the Dodgers in four straight and I lost $20,000 to the bookies. I got a call from Chicago's Terry Carpenter. He ran an operation with another guy, Monty Monaster, strictly narcotics, on the fringes of the South Side.

"What are you doing these days?" Terry asked me casually.

"Retired," I told him. Which was true. At the age of 39, I figured why push your luck. I owned a $45,000 fishing boat I sailed up and down the coast of California. It was safer than any house on land, there was money in the bank, and I wanted to enjoy life.

"Would a thirty-grand job coax you out of retirement?" Terry wanted to know.

It might," I replied, taken by surprise. My fee in the old days had been $10,000 plus expenses, tops. I wondered if the victim was a politician or a judge.

"Pete Benton," Terry said.

"Pete Benton!" I exclaimed. "What the hell is going on? He's out here in Los Angeles, not in Chicago. What's he got to do with you?"

"I'm phoning for a friend," Terry explained.

THEN I got it. Someone in California was looking to do Pete Benton, a hit man for the Lusk-Sordo organization, but rather than use one of their own organization's hit men, they were contracting the job through Chicago to avoid the impression of gang warfare.

"No deal," I told Terry. "I don't do jobs by remote control. Face to face with the client. If the Lusk-Sordo guys find out it's me, which is always a possibility, I got no client to go to for protection. So long, Terry," I added, hanging up on him.

I'd expected that to be the end of that piece of business, but it wasn't. A week later when I berthed my boat at a Los Angeles marina, I was told there was a guy in the parking lot waiting to see me. At first I thought it was a ship-to-shore radio salesman who wanted to show me the latest model I'd asked about, but when I got to the parking lot and saw the big Chrysler Imperial, I knew for sure he wasn't a salesman. They didn't go in for expensive cars with big, rough chauffeurs. I approached the Imperial and looked in the back door window.

"How are you these days, Jerry?" asked the deeply-tanned, portly man seated in the back.

I recognized my visitor immediately.

His name was Dick Lusk, Tommy Sordo's partner in the Lusk-Sordo organization.

Lusk had a big grin on his face. He said, "Terry Carpenter told me you wanted to meet the client. Get in the car and let's take a little drive."

I did what I was told. A few minutes later, we were cruising along the shore highway. I said, "Pete Benton is your boy, isn't he?"

Lusk shrugged. "He says he is," he replied, "but I'm not so sure. He's getting big ideas, Pete is, like setting up his own operation in our territory. Sordo and I aren't particularly interested in competition. Do I make myself clear?"

Lusk made himself all too clear, as far as I was concerned. He had a hit man he couldn't control, a sort of Frankenstein monster, and that was a real problem because he couldn't use another organization's hit man to solve it. I told Lusk I'd let him know within two weeks.

I wasn't being cute or indecisive about letting Lusk know. I needed time to size up the situation. Pete

Benton was a pro and it wouldn't be a case of walking up to him and taking his head off with a shotgun.

You read and see a lot of crap in movies about ingenious hits, like poison in fingernail polish, juke boxes exploding when you play a certain record, but it's all made up by writers. What actually happens in a well-executed hit is not only different, but a hell of a lot more simple.

Basically, the key to whether or not you can hit a guy is whether or not there comes a moment where he's vulnerable. If you take the average fellow on the street, there's more moments in a day than you can count. He's got to get in the mail every morning, go to work, eat lunch, come home, go to the movies, sleep. With a racket guy, those moments decrease rapidly. For one thing, he's usually armed or has armed guys around him. For another, he has someone else doing things for him like driving him to work, going out for sandwiches (or checking out the restaurant before he goes in), and there's few ways of taking him in the safety of his house at night.

What I was looking for in Pete Benton's case, then, was a moment of vulnerability, preferably a moment that was part of an established routine.

His meetings with Julie was it.

What made it a perfect moment was the combination of unique factors. Julie was married to an accountant who handled the Lusk-Sordo books, so if Pete Benton wanted a roll in the hay, he'd have to show up at the motel alone. Second, he'd been balling Julie regularly every Thursday and felt safe. Third, you don't ball wearing any other gun but the one you were born with. Fourth, they both liked a little pre-sex cocktail to calm them down and cool them off. Fifth, and most important, a gentleman like Pete Benton didn't send a naked or erotically clothed chick to the door to turn on a bar waiter: he went himself.

Driving to San Diego that afternoon, it occurred to me that if Pete Benton had liked a drink afterwards rather than before, he would have died a happier man.

WITH Pete Benton's hit, I was officially out of retirement, but to put the whole scene in perspective, it's worthwhile talking about what I did before I decided to call it quits for an easy life on a fishing boat. I didn't come out of the Army a full-blown killer, for example, like you're always hearing or reading about. With my reform school background and arrest record, there was no chance of my serving my country in uniform. Nor was I ever a psycho fascinated with death and destruction. I got into being a hit man the way 99% of all hit men do: by coming up the ranks from a bodyguard to an enforcer to an interfamily hit man. You were "promoted" because you were efficient. At any point along the way, I could have said no without any hard feelings, but as each step up the ladder carried a corresponding pay raise, I had no reason to refuse.

I was going on 28 years of age when I got my first contract, though contract might be too fancy a word to describe it. I was at the time an enforcer for a family (who'll remain nameless) in the East Bronx, though they did a business in all five boroughs of New York City as well as areas of New Jersey and Connecticut. By and large, the family confined itself to bookmaking, shylocking and a bit of prostitution, leaving narcotics for another organization. It was lucrative, not because there was so much going, but because there was no competition around.

Competition did, however, raise its ugly head in the form of the now defunct Sapinski family, made up primarily of some young Turks who had split off from an older Newark family. Its guiding light was Alfie Sapinski, a sort of forerunner of the later Crazy Joe Gallo. Alfie was a borderline psycho, unpredictable, possessing a hair-trigger temper. He was not the kind of guy you cut your eye-teeth on, but the price was right and I figured I knew a way to take him. A pal of mine, Jackie Golden, told me I was nuts to take the contract. "Alfie doesn't go anywhere without Big Marty," Golden said. "You hit Alfie and Big Marty gets you as sure as night follows day."

I could see why Jackie Golden was scared I wouldn't be able to pull it off. Big Marty was fiercely loyal to Alfie and one hell of a marksman with his .38 Magnum. If I got close enough to Alfie to nail him, I was close enough to Big Marty for him to return the favor.

Still, I had my reasons for thinking I could do it. And I wasn't saying how.

My driver Benny Albertsen wondered aloud why I had two shotguns in the car the night we drove to a restaurant in the East Bronx that Alfie and his top lieutenants favored for the spare ribs and chicken. "Don't worry about it," I said. "You handle the driving, leave the rest to me."

We parked about a block from the restaurant at 9

o'clock. Although he didn't do anything else routinely, Alfie liked to eat on time. In 15 minutes, his chauffeur-driven Buick would pull up in front of the restaurant and Big Marty would get out to size up the situation. If it looked O.K., Alfie would come out of the car and the two of them would go in and eat. There were always a couple of his guys in the restaurant waiting, so the only critical time was when he was between the Buick and the door.

"Pull up alongside the car when Big Marty gets out," I whispered to Benny.

"What for?" he asked, growing alarmed. "Alfie's going to be in his bullet-proof car. We'll get our ass shot off."

"Do what I told you," I snarled.

Alfie's Buick came down the block from the opposite direction at 9:15, right on time, and I ordered Benny to get going. He was sweating like a pig, but he obeyed. By the time we reached the restaurant, Big Marty was looking up and down the pavement.

I let him have both barrels at once and blew him through the restaurant window.

"You got Big Marty," Benny Albertsen screamed, and was just about to pull out of there quick when I shouted for him to stay put. I was counting on something, and that something was Alfie's temper.

Sure enough, the crazy bastard, seeing Big Marty get it, jumps out of the Buick with his pistol drawn. By then, I had the second shotgun ready, and it was like shooting ducks in a barrel. Alfie was dead before he hit the ground.

"Now we go," I said. As we turned the corner, I saw Alfie's boys pouring out of the restaurant to see what had happened to their boss and his bodyguard.

WITH Alfie and Big Marty gone, the mopping-up operation on the Sapinski organization took only a few months. Alfie's cousin Fat Fred bought it in his car when a Detroit bomb specialist wired his Chevrolet while it was being repaired at a garage. The rest of their boys split for safer shores.

"But how did you know Alfie would come out of his car?" my pal Jackie Golden asked me a little later when we were drinking in a saloon near our headquarters.

"Alfie had a bad temper," I answered. "Nine out of ten guys would have hit the deck when their bodyguard got it, but not Alfie. He had to come to the rescue like a hero because he was sore as hell that anyone would take out Big Marty. If he had stayed put, he'd be alive today. It was his weakness, you see. It left him vulnerable. Everything depended on getting Big Marty first and then Alfie. Not the other way around."

Taking out Alfie on my first assignment made my reputation in the family. It was a reputation, as I had hoped it would be, for brains. Despite what people think, the "mad dogs" don't last long. I've seen a dozen of them come and go in my time, and the reason for their short careers isn't hard to understand.

They like to live up to their reputations. Or, to put it another way, they die up to their reputations. Because they've been tagged "mad dogs," they behave like "mad dogs." They take foolhardy assignments, assignments guys like myself turn down cold, and they do everything the hard way to prove they've got nothing but guts. If they can hit a guy with a high-powered rifle and scope at 200 yards, they won't. Instead, they'll get within 20 feet to throw a knife. No brains, no patience, no cunning. They've got to be spectacular, leave their signature all over a job. I remember one guy, Phil Breen, who got so worked up over being regarded a "mad dog" that it cost him his life. His bag was to take out a victim piece by piece, blow off the kneecaps and the testicles and the elbows before finishing the guy off. Well, he was just about to let the victim have it between the legs when the victim's bodyguard severed Phil's spine with a .45. I'd. have been a mile away before the bodyguard came on the scene.

But to get back to the early days before I went into my first retirement, I continued to hit for this family, picking my spots, taking my time. No one, not even the head of the family, could rush me. I had it in my mind that the only thing that counted was to be successful, to get results. Sometimes it took months to figure out how to get a guy. Planning was everything. For every minute it took me to hit, I spent days looking for the right way, the sure way. Hitting was a job, not a suicide mission. In short, I wanted to survive.

There's a myth today that a hit man is at the beck and call of the organization or family he works for; that is, if he's told to hit, he does. Let me tell you it just isn't so, at least not for a hitter. An enforcer, yes, he has to obey orders. That's why he's pulling down $20,000 a year. But, hell, there's no risk involved in leaning on a shopkeeper or double-teaming some longshoreman who's behind on his loan payments. Because the sucker knows that if he puts up too much resistance, there's a hit man coming and that means a bullet instead of a couple of teeth loosened.

A hit man, though, has a different role within the organization. His life is on the line, especially if he has a contract for a guy in the rackets who's protected. Have I ever turned down a job? Yes, I have.

His name was Paddy the Priest, and I can mention it because not so long ago Paddy was taken for a ride by his own organization. There's speculation he was beaten to death with a tire chain, then dumped into the foundation for the Verrazano Bridge that spans the New York harbor between Brooklyn and Staten Island.

Paddy the Priest was, as far as I was concerned, simply unhittable. A family man, he never chased the broads or got drunk in gin mills or went out to eat. He stayed at home every minute he could, and home was a big Long Island estate with wire fences, guard dogs, and enough ammo among his bodyguards to supply a regiment. I spent two months studying his movements, but there was just no way to get at him.

So I cancelled the contract on him, telling them to find someone else if they still wanted him. My argument was simple. I was a top-ranked hit man, not an up-and-coming enforcer. That made me a champion, or at least a contender rather than a preliminary fighter, and I called the shots, not my manager.

This is not to say my refusal to hit Paddy the Priest didn't make waves. I remember a cousin of the head man in the organization called me chicken in front of everyone. All I did was pull out a gun, stick the barrel in his ear, and ask him to repeat the charge.

He went as white as a ghost and didn't say another word. The whole thing was over before it started. He, too, wanted to survive.

WHICH brings me to the second myth about hit men. The general but false impression held by a lot of people is that all hit men have a suicidal streak, and their lives were without pleasure or interest.

Well, that's crap too. In most ways, they're just like everyone else. They marry, have girl friends, go to ballgames, eat in restaurants and drink in bars, and some even raise families. With me, though, a wife and kids wasn't on, but that had more to do with my character than my occupation.

There was also the fact that I needed a succession of women to keep myself loose and easy. They're very easy to relax with, or so I find them. I know that among the general public, there's a tendency to think that a hit man's sex life is warped, based, I suspect, on the notion that if a man's work is unconventional, so too must be his erotic practices. Like all he wants from a woman is oral sex, or he likes to beat up on her, or subject her to degrading scenes.

Maybe guys like that do exist, but I never met any of them. The ones I knew regarded sex as something pleasant, something diverting, something necessary, like anyone else.

The really interesting question, though, was not what turns on a hit man, the style or anatomy he favors, or when and where he prefers to give expression to his sex drives. It's what the chick sees in a hit man.

By and large, they're fascinated!

You don't go too far afield to find broads because it's unsafe. Most of them you lay know or have an inkling what line of work you're in. Let's face it, how many hit men are there in this world? The broad that beds one down is taking on a guy who's unique, different, done something few people other than hangmen or G.I.'s do, which is cutting short the lives of his fellow men. They want to see your action in bed, gauge your reactions, and, if they have big egos, like a lot of chicks, they want to please you. Maybe somewhere deep down inside themselves, they're secretly frightened of displeasing you. I don't know the answer to that question, but they do try harder to please, and they withhold nothing at all. You might even say they get up for sex with hit men in a way they'd never do for anyone else. And I never paid for it in my life.

I hit 43 guys before I retired the first time. Some made the newspapers, but most didn't because they were clean, and the cops were just as happy to let the case drop if the victims were hoods. I mention this for a reason. As a hit man for a family, my main targets were other family or organization guys. I was no free-lancer willing to knock off a cheating husband or partner in a business that the other one wanted to get rid of. Which is the way I wanted it. I never did see the purpose of hitting anyone outside the rackets. All it did was get the public's back up. There's enough money in organized crime without going in for marginally profitable pursuits like hitting for the squares. It's bad business.

Of those 43 guys, most of them went with a revolver,

shotgun or, occasionally, dynamite. There was one I nailed with a high-powered rifle and scope when he made the mistake of taking an earlymorning swim on a deserted beach, but on the whole I relied on the tried-andtrue methods. It always amuses me to hear about how hit men use ice picks and garrotes but on the whole the only time those hand-to-hand weapons come into play is when you've got the victim all tied up in a basement and you don't want to make any noise.

Like other hit men, I spent a considerable amount of time practicing with a pistol, shotgun and rifle. They were the tools of my trade and it was only natural that I wanted to use them well. But I was never what you could consider a crack shot or a fast-draw expert. I didn't have to be. My hits depended on timing and planning, not aim. Anyone who's ever hunted deer knows that the shorter the shot, the more effective. When you have to depend on aim or a long shot, lots of things can go wrong. Hitting a twig, a sudden gust of wind can throw off a shot with a .30-06 more than a foot at 150 yards. On the other hand, you can take out a herd of deer at 15 yards with a sawed-off shotgun. So the trick, as I saw it, was to get close. There might be a lack of finesse, but who the hell cares?

NOT too long ago, I saw a scream of a movie about this hit man who tried to make each hit look like an accident. More crap, I assure you. A hit is a hit—period. It's the results, not the methods that make you a success in this business. It doesn't matter that the cops or a rival organization know that they've been hit. The cops couldn't care less how a mobster buys it, and it's much more effective in scaring hell out of another organization if it does look like a hit. Every hit is supposed to convey a message, usually clear out and don't come back. It's a lesson, and it doesn't have to be subtle.

Does a hit ultimately have to kill the victim? It's an interesting question. I was paid twice when the victim survived by the way, although I should add that in the first case, the guy who managed to live spent his life as a vegetable with an inoperable bullet in his brain and the second was paralyzed from the waist down with a severed spine. The head of the organization figured that despite the fact that the targets lived, they were as good as dead. Again, it's a question of aims and results. He wanted them out of action, and out of action they were—permanently.

So we come to the point of my first retirement and the reason why I decided to pull out. It was, oddly enough, the same one that brought me back into action—the odds on survival. When I left the job, they were getting short. When I came back, they were long again.

Take the initial retirement first. When you're a hit man for an organization, your primary targets are other organization members. Well and good. But you have to make sure the organization doesn't retaliate, which means hitting enough key men to weaken the structure and brains.

For the first six years I worked, we didn't have much trouble. Taking out a few key men usually meant the rest lost nerve or had no stomach. Once in a while, they'd "go to the mattresses," that is, they holed up somewhere expecting us to make a frontal assault. We hardly ever bothered. Shoot-outs are costly. We always figured that while they were holed up, you could reestablish your supremacy over the territory, lean on a few wavering shopkeepers, catch a few defectors that couldn't stand the tension of defending the fort, so to speak. In any besieged organization, there are almost certainly two wars: one with the guys outside trying to get in, another among the guys inside deciding whether or not to surrender, make peace or fight it out to the last man. Usually, the peace-makers have the final say, and the war is over.

But then, a new factor was on the scene. Blacks, Puerto Ricans and other ethnic groups were coming to the fore, and they weren't willing to concede a thing to the criminal establishment. In the old days, too, when you had driven out an organization from your territory, you usually had a year or two of peace. But no longer. As soon as you removed one upstart, another took his place. Instead of making two or three hits a year like I used to, I was tripling that figure. That's three times the risk.

Not only was my organization threatened, it was threatening. The drug rackets were just too inviting for the leadership to resist. So we started to compete, and that meant we were being hit as well as hitting, fighting defensively as well as offensively. How risky our new tactics were became all too obvious.

Three of us—the head of our organization, his bodyguard and I—were coming out of a health club on East 83rd Street where we'd gone for a workout, massage and steam bath. Without warning, the street became a battlefield. The bodyguard got hit by at least 20 shots, while the boss and I somehow managed to get behind a parked car.

"They're firing from the windows across the street!" I yelled to the boss over a second fusillade. We were trapped like rats, and our only chance was to stay put. I was thankful that the dumb s.o.b.'s were so inexperienced that they hadn't nailed us all in the first exchange when everyone opened fire on the bodyguard instead of spreading it around evenly.

I didn't think they'd try a charge—which meant dashing across an open street—but to be sure l reached with my right hand for a revolver I carried. It was then I realized that I'd been hit after all. My arm dangled uselessly, and a big stain of blood was spreading out over my chest. The funny thing was that there was absolutely no pain. Just my arm hanging limp. We heard police sirens in the distance, and got out of there. The gunmen had the same idea, so there was no more gunplay.

I SPENT about a week in a private hospital. Doctors assured me that no muscles or nerves had been permanently damaged, and that if I did some post-operative physical therapy, I'd have full use of my shoulder within six months.

Actually, I wasn't too worried about 100% or 50% use anymore. Lying there in bed, I got to thinking about how the odds were no longer in my favor, that the law of averages had almost caught up, especially since I was not only a hunter but the hunted. The guys who had missed killing the boss and me outside the health club had been novices, but they would learn from their mistake. The next ambush they set up wouldn't allow two of the three targets to survive.

I started to figure out my own personal economics. Between the hits and basic pay, I'd made roughly $75,000 a year tax-free for the last l 2 years, plus some big profits on 'stocks when I had inside information about rigging the price. I had never been a big spender, not because l'm cheap, but because in my line it pays to live simply, without flash. Get known as the guy who drives the Ferrari, and you could be advertising for a death certificate. Besides, I had no family, no big house with the mortgage to keep up, no long vacations on the beaches of Miami or San Juan. So I had about a million dollars in a Swiss bank. There was no reason

in the world for me to starve in my retirement—even though there was no pension or Social Security benefits to look forward to.

I could retire on a million as easily as two million. So that was that. I told the boss I was quitting and he wished me luck.

Already I can hear someone yelling, "Hey, no one ever quits." Yes, they do. All the time. You don't go over to another organization, but you can leave your own. The guys in the rackets are too good as businessmen to want anyone to stay on whose heart isn't in it.

If I didn't need the money when I got out the first time, what brought me back? Simple. I got bored.

Sure, the life of leisure was great. Relaxing; too relaxing. Something was missing, something important. Excitement? Kicks? Some sense of purpose? I don't know, but I was bored. And the Pete Benton job was intriguing—hit man vs. hit man, with no chance of revenge against me because the contract came from Benton's own chief.

The whole thing appealed to me for other reasons. During a gang war, no one is going to get rid of their hit man and weaken their organization at a critical time. If they were going to dump him, they'd do so during a lull-the time when the hit man wasn't really on his guard.

The element of surprise was my edge, and I needed it. Good hit men are basically cautious and thinking. The fact that they're drawing breath is a testament to the care they exercise in both killing and staying alive.

Still another edge I had was that the fat fee of $30,000, plus expenses, meant I could do fewer jobs, say four a year, and have more time to plan for each.

Take Bob Henshaw, for example, the second hit man I went for after Pete Benton. I spent more than three months, night and day, keeping him under observation. I knew him like a book, maybe better than he knew himself. I could name his favorite foods, type of women, clothes, cars, movies, books and magazines, even his underarm deodorant. I knew the names of his accountant, doctor, lawyer and dentist.

It was the dentist I was really interested in. Bob Henshaw had lousy gums. When I broke into the dentist's office one night and studied the hit man's X-rays, I was surprised how bad they were. He was only 29 years old. But bad they were, and he needed treatment for them every two months. I found that out when I went through the dentist's appointment book and saw he was due for a visit in a while, and that his appointment was the last one of the day.

I suppose the dentist's nurse who acted as a receptionist thought when she saw me with the stocking over my face and the gun in my hand that I was a junkie breaking into the office in search of drugs. Anyway, she did what she was told, which was to ask the dentist to step out for a moment and leave his patient—Bob Henshaw.

AFTER locking them in a closet and saying I'd kill them if they make a sound, I went back into the room and saw Bob Henshaw lying in the chair, his eyes closed and his neck bared. I'd honed my knife to a razor-edge, and the gash it made on the hit man's throat went through the jugular and windpipe as if they were butter.

Later on, his boss asked me to describe the death he had bought for his employee Henshaw. When I did, he started laughing so hard I thought he'd choke. "It's that big mouth," he finally managed to get out, "that did him in."

At first, I thought the delighted client was referring to Bob Henshaw's teeth alone. Then I got the joke. The contract had been taken out on the victim because while drunk he'd told a whore about a hit, and the news of his being talkative had got back to his boss. Hit men who drink too much, then talk about their work to casual acquaintances are very poor risks to an employer.

Looking through my records (I kept a file on the habits and movements of each of my hit man contracts), I find that the third, fourth, fifth, sixth, seventh, and eighth contracts were dispatched by gunfire. Maybe it was the long lay-off, maybe advanced age, but numbers three and four did not die immediately; they lingered in hospitals for a few days before giving up the ghost. This kind of carelessness sent me to a pistol range where I burned off the skin between my thumb and forefinger of my trigger hand firing some 500 rounds of magnum ammunition in an effort to improve my failing markmanship. I'm pleased to say it did get better.,

There was nothing particularly remarkable about that group of six killings except for the poor shooting in two cases. I carried out the assignments, I got paid, and the bosses, looking sorrowful, attended the funerals of the men whose deaths they had ordered.

It's time to discuss why the hit men had to go. Three out of four times, the victims were suspected—rightly or wrongly, I never really knew for sure—of going over to the competition or wanting to take over the organization. In essence, then, they were potential threats to the powers that were. However, there was the minority of hit men, the one out of four, who died for other reasons than personal treachery. This group was made up of hit men who were no longer reliable or had muffed one too many assignments. Among them were guys who started drinking heavy because of the pressure or started shooting off their mouths or simply were getting so sloppy that they had to go—terminated with prejudice, as the government agencies put it so nicely.

Frankly, taking out the one of four who'd lost his nerve or talent was a lot easier than hitting the organizational traitors. For one thing, they generally were getting careless. Like Number 23, for example. His drinking habit was getting so serious that I was able to poison him by slipping in a bottle of scotch laced with strychnine in a case he had ordered, knowing that at the rate he drank—some two bottles a day—it would take less than a week to finish him off.

The traitors, on the other hand, were different. Because they were in some cases contemplating a double-cross, they were especially wary because they never knew if their intentions to betray had been discovered.

Perhaps the most interesting of the traitor class was Bart Cope, a New Orleans hit man who became Number 29 of my successfully executed contracts. It went like this:

His boss, Andy Turner, a French Quarter kingpin with his finger in most of the strip joints, gay bars, and mobile bordellos, got in touch with me when he found out that Bart Cope was making noises about the poor leadership of the organization. It turned out that Turner was an old buddy of Dick Lusk, who had hired me to get rid of Pete Benton. Anyhow, would I take the job?

I told Andy Turner to send me a first class ticket made out in a phony name and $3,000 for traveling expenses, and I'd come to New Orleans, size up the situation, and let him know. As usual, I'd contact him rather than the reverse to give my final answer.

Two weeks later, I had a meeting with Andy Turner in a hotel room I'd reserved in the phony name. "I'll take the job," I said.

Turner, a wiry guy with a toothy grin, was delighted with my decision. "Great," he said. "Have you been tailing him?"

"I have," I replied.

"Then what's he been doing these days?" asked Turner, interested, I thought, to find out what organization Bert Cope was representing.

"He's been tailing you," I said evenly.

The look on Turner's face was one of complete shock. "He's been doing what?" he finally demanded.

"He's been tailing you," I repeated. "He's looking to hit you."

Andy Turner swallowed hard. "You better get him quick," he said.

"No hurry," I told him. And then I let him know what I had in mind for Bart Cope. It was borrowing a page from my first hit, the one on Pete Benton.

"Andy, you have to get yourself a girl," I said.

Andy Turner looked incredulous. "A girl?" he mumbled. "I'm a married man."

"Forget about your marriage vows," I went on. "I want you to start taking one of the girls from your clubs to a motel every Wednesday afternoon. You got to be there from 2 o'clock to 4 o'clock."

"What am I going to do in a motel?" protested Andy Turner.

"That's up to you," I shot back. "You can do what I'd do or watch TV or read or just sleep. Doesn't matter. The important thing is that you order drinks the minute you get there."

Andy Turner did just what he was told to do for three straight weeks. At 2 o'clock each Wednesday, he met this incredibly big-breasted topless dancer at the motel and went through the routine we had rehearsed. Each week, stationed at another motel bungalow, I saw Bart Cope's car drive up and park for the two hours Andy Turner and the chick stayed inside.

On the fourth straight Wednesday, there was one little difference in the scenario. When Bart Cope got out of his car, he was wearing a waiter's outfit.

That was the moment, of course, when he was a dead man. As he walked toward the motel bungalow door, he was thinking of only one thing, which was nailing his boss Andy Turner. Forgotten was everything else. He was, as I've said before, completely vulnerable. He didn't hear me open the window, he didn't see me sight along the barrel of a .247, and he didn't feel a thing as the bullet struck him in the ear.

The cops, I heard. from the grapevine, wondered what the hell the corpse of Bart Cope was doing in a waiter's outfit and why the safety on his Luger was off. Andy Turner paid me off and I was all set to fly back to L.A. Just before I left, though, Andy said with a grin, "I've got another job for you.",

"Who's that?" I asked.

"My wife," he answered. "That little topless dancer Dolores is fantastic."

"You'll have to get someone else for your wife," I told Andy Turner, laughing like hell. Then I added,

"But if I were you, Andy, I wouldn't meet Dolores at the same time and the same place in the future."

AFTER Bart Cope, there were jobs in Miami, Detroit, San Francisco, and even one in Montreal. Of all, the one in Miami was the most complicated. It involved scuba equipment, wet suit, and a bit of my swimming through Miami's Biscayne Bay to set an explosive charge on Tim Jordan's boat's keel. It was a lovely yawl, and it was sort of sad to watch it blow up into splinters with Tim Jordan standing there at the wheel. They never found the body, so I guess the sharks that come in each night to the bay must have eaten him.

Blowing the boat was the first time I used explosives. It's a method more and more coming into practice. You can kill from afar and be gone before the hit takes place. The power of these new charges, too, leaves little room for missing. And what's even more important, today's detonators are as foolproof as anything can be in this electronic age.

The main problem, though, is you can take security measures against them, and the equipment for detection has developed apace. The trick is planting them. I've managed to get one in the tire of a private plane that blew the wing off when it reached an altitude of 5,000 feet, as well as two under the hoods of cars, but it wasn't easy. Worse, it blew apart a hit man's girl friend riding in the front seat with him, which to my way of thinking is messy.

Author's Note: The remarkable story of hit man Jerry "Red" Kelley, transcribed from tapes, ends abruptly at this point for the simple reason that it became too painful for the narrator to continue in his terminal

stage of cancer of the throat. (Continued)

Why precisely Jerry "Red" Kelley decided to set the record straight as his life drew to a close is a question I've asked myself many times. The closest thing to an explanation might be to regard this unvarnished glimpse of a hit man's career as a deathbed confession. The tapes were discovered among the personal effects of Jerry "Red" Kelley by his younger brother Robert whose initial reaction was to destroy them. It took a great deal of argument on my part to allow publication. Needless to say, various names and locales were changed, though a thorough check of newspapers and police files prove that the details of the tapes were accurate. For every hit described by Jerry "Red" Kelley, there is a corresponding unsolved murder case in law enforcement records.

The edited tape transcripts and the accompanying verifying documentation are scheduled for publication in book form on the 1st of December, ironically the anniversary of Jerry "Red" Kelley's death due to throat cancer in the Los Angeles County Hospital.

• • •

MEN ONLY!

We have the most **unusual** items and **novelties** for men ever offered. Sample assortments, only $2.00. Catalog only 25c, refunded on first order.

ARTCO MFG. CO., Dept. 1154
5880 Hollywood Blvd., Hollywood 28, Calif.

NEW! SENSATIONAL!
PARTY RECORDS

WOW! A torrid selection of "special numbers" recorded strictly for adults. Racy ditties and gay parodies about those spicy, intimate moments. Shocking, but delightful. **EIGHT "Exclusive" SELECTIONS** on finest quality 45 or 78-rpm records (state choice), sent prepaid in plain sealed wrapper for $4.95 (no c.o.d.'s). **SPECIAL OFFER:** Two Different Sets of 16 Recordings only $8.95. For a thrilling adventure in adult entertainment, order yours Today!

NATIONAL, Dept. 35-F, Box 4241, TOLEDO 9, OHIO

BE TALLER

You will begin to see an increase in your height within 10 days after using the world-famous HEIGHT INCREASE SYSTEM! This is a new, natural method. No drugs, pills or mechanical apparatus.

Add inches to your height. Send for FREE trial lessons which actually get you started on the road to becoming taller. Positively guaranteed for young or old. Send 25c to cover cost of postage and handling to:

HEIGHT INCREASE INSTITUTE
G.P.O. Box 1902, Dept. SM-3
New York 1, N. Y.

Men! Men! Men!

We don't care about your age. Just tell us kind of woman you wish to meet. Our women are screaming to meet you.

MARRY RICH!

In about five days after we receive your application you'll start receiving letters.

Send me a stamp —

Your Friend, Ruth

NAME ....
Address ....
City .... Zone ....
State ....

Write us a letter telling us about yourself. Also send in above application. This offer will not be repeated if we can get enough men for our women.

Remember our slogan: "No man is any good without a woman."

Girls! Send us a snapshot.

HELP COMPANY CLUB
4554 Broadway   Chicago 40, Ill.

WHY BE LONELY

If its Friends, Romance or Companionship you want, let America's foremost Club arrange an introduction for you. Nationwide membership. Confidential, Reliable. Write for sealed information, sent free.

PEARL J. SMITH
P.O. Box 2732-H   Kansas City 42, Mo.

Publisher of ~
PAPERBACK PARADE

Now in Its 37th Year!
The Longest-Running Magazine
Devoted to Collectible Paperbacks

Read
Paperback Parade!
Advertise in
Paperback Parade!
Subscribe Today!

Visit "Gary Lovisi"
Vintage & Collectable Paperbacks
On YouTube! Give it a look, a 'Like'
and SUBSCRIBE!

www.gryphonbooks.com

FOR MEN ONLY

CC
02401

15 FULL COLOR PAGES, 12 EXPLOSIVE STORIES
MORE THAN ANY OTHER MEN'S MONTHLY ADVENTURE MAGAZINE

ONE DOLLAR

MARCH

"Scoring" Isn't Everything, It's The Only Thing
MEMOIRS OF A SUPER BOWL HOOKER

Known Only To The Godfathers Of The 5 Families
THE HIT MAN WHO TURNED OUT TO BE A WOMAN

Basic Training For Better Orgasms
UNIQUE 7-DAY CRASH COURSE TO IMPROVE YOUR SEX LIFE

BULLET-HARD BOOK BONUS Hired Killers Use Bulldozers As If They're Assault Tanks
THE "OIL SWAMP" MASSACRE

Sue Anne
SEE PAGE 17 AND DISCOVER WHY SHE'S BEEN NAMED FARMER'S-DAUGHTER-OF-THE-YEAR

The Midwest Is Her Territory, Small Towns Her Beat
I DRIVE A MOBILE MASSAGE PARLOR

WW II's Most Unsung G.I. Hero—He Was The Only Male P.O.W. In A Female Prison Compound
TODAY THEY CALL HIM FATHER ITALY

10 STARTLING RESULTS FROM FMO'S NATIONAL WIFE-SWAPPING SURVEY

Exclusive Full-Color Photo Essay
THE BIGGEST PILE-UP IN THE WORLD!
Islip Raceway: Where Smash Is King

I'm a big fan of movies in the "gals killing gangsters" genre. Films like *KILL BILL I* and *KILL BILL II* (2003 & 2004), *COLOMBIANA* (2011), and *PEPPERMINT* (2018).

I also enjoy films involving female government assassins or freelance contract killers, such as *LA FEMME NIKITA* (1990), *GUNPOWDER MILKSHAKE* (2021) and *KATE* (2021).

OK, I admit it. I like just about any movies with heavily armed, good looking women blowing away and/or slicing up bad guys. I even liked the recent Netflix movie *THE MOTHER* starring Jennifer Lopez. (Don't judge me until you've watched it.)

"The Hit Man Who Turned Out To Be A Woman" is definitely a "gals killing gangsters" story, but it's not told from the female killer's perspective. It's told by a cop who's given the unwelcome assignment of trying to track her down and stop her. Although it doesn't fit the modern movie mold, I still enjoyed reading it.

The other thing I like about this story is the half color/half black-and-white illustration by artist Bruce Minney. The use of full color on one page and a single color on the opposite page in a painting done for a two-page spread is something that popped up every once in a while in issues of *FOR MEN ONLY* and other Magazine Management MAMs.

From what I've been told by men's adventure magazine artists I've talked to, it wasn't done for purely artistic purposes. It was more of a small cost-saving device.

By Craig Campbell
From *FOR MEN ONLY*, March 1975
Artwork by Bruce Minney

Every page printed in full color cost the publisher a little more, and the Mag Mgt. MAMs had more limited budgets than those at the top of the MAM food chain, like *ARGOSY* and *SAGA*.

However, even if not an artistic choice per se, examples of such illustrations are very interesting from an artistic perspective.

The artists painted them half full/half one color at the direction of the magazine's art director. Sometimes instead of being black and white, the page opposite the full color page was a single color, such as blue or red, another option that was still just slightly less expensive to print.

One of my favorite examples of a half color/half blue illo is the painting Mort Künstler did for the story "The Great Ranger Raid on Pantagian Prison" in the February 1959 issue of *MEN*, another Mag, Mgt, mag.

I also especially love the one done later that year by Mort's friend James Bama, for a story titled "Shirt-Tail Rangers Who Held the Philippines" in *MEN*, July 1959.

INTRODUCTION BY BOB **DEIS**

CLOCKWISE: Examples of the "Hitwoman" subgenre of movies that we like include the classic 1990 film *LA FEMME NIKITA* (1990) and more recent movies like *GUNPOWDER MILKSHAKE* (2021), *THE MOTHER* (2023), and *KATE* (2021).

When I look at the original paintings Künstler and Bama did for those 2-page spreads, I am awed by the way they delicately transitioned the scenes from full color into all blue.

I have never seen the original half color/half B&W painting Bruce Minney did for "The Hit Man Who Turned Out To Be A Woman," and the transition in that case is abrupt.

It's really two scenes linked together by the arm of the hitwoman and the cape she's wearing as part of her disguise as an old lady. But it comes off pretty well on the printed pages IMHO.

I don't know who the female model was for the right

hand scene. It shows the hitwoman looking into the mirror, applying makeup mimicking the wrinkles on an old lady's face. But one of the funny things about the full color scene at left is that the model for both the victim who's helping the "old lady" by picking up her purse and the "old lady" who's about to stab him was probably Steve Holland. I'm fairly sure that Bruce had Steve do both poses and just painted him with the woman's face.

If you're fan of MAM and vintage paperback cover art, you probably know that Steve Holland was the most frequently used male illustration art model in the 1950s, 1960s, and 1970s. He was the favorite of Minney, Künstler, Bama and scores of other top illustrators who did artwork for MAMs and paperbacks in those decades.

His face and body became especially well known when James Bama used him as the model for Doc Savage, in the paintings he did for the Bantam paperback series. He continued to be used for Doc Savage covers done later, by artists like Bob Larkin and Joe DeVito.

When an artist booked Holland for a reference photo session, they often took photos of him to fit all of the male characters that would be in the scene they were going to paint. That was half as expensive as hiring two male models. When the scene called for a man and a woman, artists usually booked a female model to pose with him. But the pose and face of the "hit woman" in Minney's painting for "The Hit Man Who Turned Out To Be A Woman" definitely looks like Holland to me.

BACKGROUND: James Bama's "transition" illustration for "Shirt-Tail Rangers Who Held The Philippines" in *MEN*, July 1959. ABOVE: From one of the multitude of reference photo sessions featuring model Steve Holland. This is for the *SPIDER* series reboot in the 70s by Pocket Books. In this case, it was for *SPIDER #3: THE CITY DESTROYER*. He was also *DOC SAVAGE*, *CONAN*, and others.

BACKGROUND: "The Great Ranger Raid on Pantagian Prison" in the February 1959 issue of **MEN.** Artwork by Mort Künstler. OPPOSITE: Michael Stradford's library of books on Steve Holland, the male model artists used for thousands of paperback cover and magazine illustrations.

If you want to learn more about Steve Holland and the artists who used him, you need to check out the series of books done about him by our friend Michael Stradford. Michael knows more about Holland and the artwork he modeled for than anyone in the world.

He's shared that knowledge in a series of four well-researched, lushly illustrated books that showcase hundreds of illustrations Holland modeled for, interviews with Holland and artists who used him, artist reference photos he modeled for, and much more.

Those books are:
- **STEVE HOLLAND: THE TORN SHIRT SESSIONS** (2021)
- **STEVE HOLLAND: THE WORLD'S GREATEST ILLUSTRATION ART MODEL** (2021)
- **STEVE HOLLAND: COWBOY** (2022)
- **STEVE HOLLAND: PAPERBACK HERO** (2023)

Michael's books are a huge contribution to both knowledge about Steve Holland and to the history of paperbacks and illustration art. I highly recommend them all. They're available on Amazon worldwide. MAQ co-editor and designer Bill Cunningham did the layout for **THE WORLD'S GREATEST** and designed the cover for **PAPERBACK HERO.** For more about Bruce Minney, get the must have book **BRUCE MINNEY: THE MAN WHO PAINTED EVERYTHING**, edited by his son-in-law Tom Ziegler.

• • •

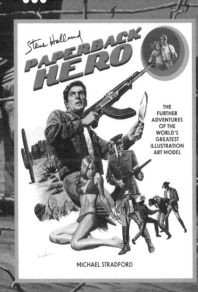

Lush-bodied and calculating, she knew how to use whatever was necessary to lure her mark for the kill. But Ross was one "male-chauvinist" cop who wasn't about to let this cold-blooded executioner get away with even one more murder

THE HIT MAN WHO TURNED OUT TO BE A WOMAN

Known Only to The Godfathers of the 5 Families

An expert at disguises, Delpha applied makeup to look like an arthritic old woman.

By CRAIG CAMPBELL

ART BY BRUCE MINNEY

WHEN SHE got out of her car she showed leg all the way up and Vario, who had been watching football on TV, turned to look. It was probably the only thing in this world that could have gotten his eyes away from the tube. She left the car door open and the motor running, stared up and down the street, seemingly confused, and then in his direction as if seeing him for the first time. She started up the driveway and the closer she came the better she looked, and he got up from the patio lounge chair then. In addition to the very short skirt she seemed to be wearing a see-through blouse, which were as rare as palm trees in this fashionable

HIT MAN

"Do you know where...?" She was still some distance from him and the TV was so loud that it was difficult to make out exactly what she was saying. But it definitely was a see-through blouse and, despite himself, Vario swallowed his Adam's apple as he felt the impact of the large firm breasts, the round spread of nipples and their hardened pips.

"...the Aragons live?" he thought she said. In addition to the TV being so loud her voice was very soft and low. There was a Southern quality to it, and by then she was standing directly in front of him and he was staring down at the boobs, like some goddamn high school kid. staring at them, swallowing again. thinking that he should turn the goddamn TV off.

It was the last thought Vario ever had because when he looked up he realized she was holding a small pistol in both her hands and was pointing it directly at his head. He was so surprised, the great legs and then the boobs and now this, that he just stood there mouth open, not too long but long enough so that she could steady the gun and then coolly and deliberately fire it. The shot came just as someone on the TV caught a long pass and began running for a goal, bringing the crowd to its feet roaring. The bullet entered just at the bridge of his nose and he fell like a loosefilled sack rather than timber, dead before he hit the patio floor. There was surprisingly little blood, more of an ooze, which was, of course, his brains leaking out.

She returned the gun to her purse and walked calmly back down the driveway, got into her car and drove away just as if Vario had told her where the Aragons lived.

Vario's wife screamed and dropped the tray with the two cans of beer and the pretzels that he liked her to bring out at about this time on football Sundays. She knelt beside his body, brought her hands up to her face but didn't scream again. Like the wives of all men who make their livings out of crime she always knew that it would happen this way, if not by the police then by their own kind. Louise, which was her name, had always half-dreaded it and half-hoped for it. Now that it had happened and even though she cried while on her knees beside the body she suddenly felt a release, something heavy had been lifted from her, she had gotten a reprieve from that strange, awful, illegal world that she had never quite gotten used to.

His instructions had always been, "If something should happen to me call Frank first thing." Frank was his brother and she called him now, her finger almost too light for the dial. Frank's voice changed immediately. From a sort of stupid sounding adenoidal voice it suddenly became very clear, very serious, very wise. He told her to lock all the doors and not to let anyone into the house, or answer the telephone.

"What about the police, Frank?" she asked.

"No, not now. You do as I told you and I'll see you in about 20 minutes."

It was only when she had hung up the receiver and sat down on the couch that she realized Frank hadn't once asked how she was. Yes, inside she knew that it was going to be a blessing.

Frank had calls to make. First to Tom Weis who was their contact with the man they called the big "G" or just Mr. "G". Frank had only seen Mr. "G" once, and that time at a distance. Even though he more or less worked for him, or at least gave him a good percentage of every truckload of merchandise he hijacked, he was still not quite sure what the "G" stood for. At first, he had thought it might be the first letter of his last name, Grazzini, Graziani, something like that. But people said that it stood for Godfather and others, with joking, simply thought it stood for God. Tommy Weis didn't say anything when Frank told him what had happened to his brother, just grunted and hung up, which bothered Frank a lot. At least he might have said, "Gee, Frank. I'm sorry." It was only when he called his younger brother Ralph that he began to feel the real pain.

"They hit Carmine, Ralphie," he said, crying by then, slobbering over the telephone, getting it wet. "Someone got him this afternoon. No, fir crissakes, how do I know who? Look, go over to the house and tell momma and poppa, but take it easy, understand?"

What made it even worse was that Ralphie started crying, too, screaming and cursing into the telephone saying that if it was the last thing he ever did he was going to get his revenge.

LOUISE WAS still sitting on the couch when Frank rang the doorbell. She had not cried since that first time, nor had she gone out again to look at the body. She had been sitting there in a not unpleasant sort of daze and once or twice she had smiled without realizing it. She let Frank in and then followed him to the patio. He stared down at the body and started to cry all over again, got down and put his face on his dead brother's chest and sobbed his name and for some reason hit it several times hard with his fists.

When he got up, he wiped his eyes with his fingers and without a word went inside. Then, with Louise following, not sure of what he was going to do, he went from room to room, going to certain drawers for which he had the keys and to hiding places she didn't even know existed in her own house. He took out thick wads of cash, she could clearly see fifty and one-hundred dollar bills, and envelopes and papers and plastic packages that contained white powder which she knew was heroin. After a while he said curtly, "Go get me something to carry this in, " just like that, just like Carmine used to talk to her. She went downstairs to the storeroom and picked out a battered and dust-covered canvas bag with a zipper that she had been meaning to throw away for several years now; there are gentle ways of getting even and Louise was gentle. And she brought it up without dusting it, too. She had never seen so much money in her life and when he was finished the bag was packed so tight that the zipper wouldn't work. "OK, Louise," he said at the front door. "In about five minutes call the cops. Just answer their questions because you don't know anything anyway. The only thing, don't tell them is that I've been here. Got that? AII right. Now don't worry about anything. The big "G" 'II take care of you. You'll be all right."

When he was gone she sat at the telephone until the clock had ticked off the five minutes. Louise, she told herself as she dialed the emergency number, this is going to be the best thing that has ever happened to you, you'll see.

The big "G"' and the four other men who among themselves controlled all organized criminal activity in the three state area met regularly once a week, each one taking turns at being host. The meetings were more for the benefit of the various law enforcement units than anything else. Regular meetings as friends, they thought, were preferable to suddenly called special meetings every time a problem arose. These would only serve to warn these police task force men who made careers tracking them and keeping detailed records of all their activities. This particular meeting was hosted by a man named Larner who controlled prostitution and pornography in the area. His was a luxurious estate in what had once been the very best neighborhood in St. Louis. They played their usual poker game with the 20 cents limit they had recently raised it to to reflect the inflation in the economy. The procedure was to bring up their problems, or conflicts or differences among them while they played. Carmine Vario's murder was so unimportant that it wasn't even mentioned at that meeting, as a matter of fact things had been going so well for them that this was the fifth straight meeting that no business was discussed, a sort of record. The big "G" won $17.80 that night, which he took as a good sign for the coming week.

The first police to respond to Louise Vario's call belonged to the suburban village in which she lived. As ridiculous as it might sound the suburban police force consisted of 12 uniforms. When someone left the department, usually to find a better-paying job elsewhere, his uniform remained behind to be used by the man who took his place. Though neither the chief nor the village councilmen would admit it, probably the most stringent requirements for new recruits was that they have the same size neck and waist as the unform they were to fill.

All except Chief Hotaling, who had been on the job for close to 30 years and who, in addition to getting a pretty good salary, and being able to buy everything from groceries to gasoline at a discount from village merchants, also got a uniform allowance, though he used it to pay for his vacation trip to Miami every year.

There was very little crime in the village, an occasional breaking and entering, a fight every now and then in one of the four local taverns. But that didn't mean there weren't any criminals. Vario had been one and with him gone there were at least three others that the chief knew about who were involved, in one way or the other, with the rackets. And there was someone who was bilking millions of dollars from the federal government through phony FHA mortgages. and a woman who was suspected of having accidentally-on-purpose run her car over her old man, and a married man whose pregnant girl friend's body had recently been found on a garbage dump all the way in in East Cicero, Illinois. The chief had reports on all of these and whenever some law enforcement unit carried out an investigation in his village they notified him, as a courtesy.

After stationing one of his men at the body with orders not to touch anything or walk around too much the chief went into the kitchen where Mrs. Vario was sitting to wait for the State police who investigated serious criminal activity in the village. He sat opposite her and they looked at each other but neither said anything. At least she could offer me a cup of coffee, the chief thought. It wasn't as if they were strangers. He had seen her a great deal in the village, shopping or at church. It used to amuse the chief that he and a big-time crook both belonged to the same church.

The State Police mobile lab arrived 33 minutes after he had notified them of the homicide and he made a note of the time because he would use it in his report. The St. Louis Police Department meat wagon, which took care of his corpses, showed up exactly seven minutes later. The morgue attendants stood on the sidelines while the lab boys went to work. Funny, the chief thought as he watched the activity, how at first all these men looked alike but as soon as they got out their equipment and went to work they suddenly developed identities, Like the fingerprinting man blowing powder on likely surfaces like an artist, no more than three white grains wasted. And the two photographers moving around taking pictures, really involved in what they were doing. And the guy with the metal detector, wearing earphones, listening as if to great music, going over every inch of ground for the slug. In the kitchen, the two CID men, one tall and blond, the other short, ugly and dark, taking turns at questioning Mrs. Vario.

MRS. VARIO told the same story no matter how the expert investigators worked on her, and it was mostly the truth. Her husband always watched football out on the patio on Sunday afternoons when the weather was good, No, she hadn't heard any shot, just the noise from the TV set. No, she didn't care for football, she liked to go to the movies once in a while, but that was all. Oh, she added, maybe if her husband had encouraged her to watch with him she might have but he liked to watch football and basketball and things like that, alone. When she went out with a tray he was dead. Yes, of course she was aware of what her husband did for a living, he sold insurance for the Thomas A. Dell Company in St. Louis. No, she didn't

know that her husband had any enemies. Yes, he was a good husband and provider. When they asked if she knew that her husband was the main importer of heroin into the St. Louis area she seemed shocked and said no, she didn't, and they must have made some mistake because Carmine would never do anything like that, and her eyes filled with tears just for them.

There were no clues. The patio surface was not the kind that would retain any usable fingerprints, there were no footprints of any kind and not even the metal detector could find the spent slug even though it did pick out bottle caps, buried nails, hair pins and coins. The unit began packing their equipment about the same time that it started getting dark and the technicians turned into anonymous men again, mostly overweight and balding. When everyone had left Louise Vario started making her dinner and it was so peaceful that hardly anyone would believe that she had just lost her husband a few hours before.

SHE KILLED Brodkey in a restaurant. Since the first murder everyone who was in anyway involved with the St. Louis underworld was keeping low and cautious. Most of the men wouldn't go out alone and even those who did business at night hesitated going anywhere after dark. But she was experienced and had anticipated that things would tighten up after the first one. So that was why she killed him in the restaurant.

It was called Richard's and it was a very expensive place that specialized in $15 steaks which were brought in from Kansas City especially for them. It was far too expensive for an ordinary tile and floor-covering salesman, which Brodkey was. But Brodkey had a very lucrative little sideline. He loaned money at exorbitant rates, 10 percent a week, which came to 520 percent a year. And that was only one way to look at it. Those people who borrowed from Brodkey were people who could not get loans from banks and finance companies, not only because they were poor credit risks but also because the money they needed was usually not going to be used in legitimate ways. Which is why they were willing to pay $500 a week for a $5,000 loan, But quite often the schemes that these men put the borrowed money into went sour, a horse came in last rather than first, a sure-thing stock fell rather than rose, a partner would disappear with the assets. In that case they could come back to Brodkey and say that they needed another week to pay back their loan. Brodkey would smile and his beautiful white teeth would flash. Sure, he would say and then explain that they now owed him $5500 of which interest for the week came to $550, which all together added up to $6050. And if the same thing happened the following week, the figures changed again, to $6550 for the principle, $655 for the interest, and on and on until it reached a point where Brodkey would take possession of the person's business, or home, or car, or whatever tangible assets there were. And if the poor soul was unfortunate enough not to have any tangible assets his bruised and mutilated body would be found in a ditch someplace. And even that had some value to Brodkey because it would serve as a warning to others who thought they might get away without paying their loans back. So that was how he could afford to eat at Richard's every day.

She chose a Tuesday because Richard's was less crowded on Tuesday, for some reason. She had studied Brodkey's behavior like a scientist studies a bug and she knew that the first thing Brodkey did when he came in was to shake hands with those people he was meeting for lunch and then go back and wash his hands. He was an extremely tidy and clean man and he was the kind who liked to go to the bathroom alone.

He did it on that Tuesday, too. He walked back to the small men's room, locked the door behind him and walked right over to the sink. She had been crouched in the booth on top of the toilet seat and suddenly he looked up in the wash basin mirror and saw her standing behind him. He was so surprised to see a woman in the men's room that it didn't occur to him that he was in danger. He was thinking about it when she struck hard with the piece of pipe, catching him on his right temple, in just the spot that contained both a nerve and a blood vessel. He wasn't dead, just unconscious and would remain that way for at least six minutes. She dragged him by his shoulders over to the booth and stuck his head into the toilet bowl, face down, then took the heavy marble tank cover off and put it on top of his head to keep his nose and mouth under water. She used toilet paper so as not to leave any fingerprints. In three minutes or so he would drown.

She looked up and down the corridor through a small hand mirror she had placed on the transom, and all was clear. She retrieved the mirror as she walked through the door. She had already finished her meal and paid the check, leaving a normal tip, not too large, not too small, nothing to cause anyone to remember her. She got her coat from the check room, and walked casually to the area of the parking lot where she had left her car. There was a chance that someone would remember that she had been there but it would be a rare cop who had imagination enough to picture a woman entering the men's room.

THE FIVE men met in the big "G"'s house that week. It was an old-fashioned house in a slum neighborhood and most of the furniture dated back to the 1920's, but it was immaculately kept and when one of them dropped a cigar ash the big "G" picked it up and dusted the spot with his handkerchief. They played cards on the big round dining room table but the game wasn't successful because it was obvious that each man looked at the other with suspicion. Two deaths in a row. Someone was deliberately killing off their men. Not that they worried very much about their men's welfare, each and every one among them had had their soldiers killed. But each man that was killed meant that much less money. And, what made it worse was that the killings could only have been done by one of those sitting around the table. Who else would be doing it, and for what reason? The big "G" lost $42 that night, in his own house, the most anyone had ever lost in these games. At the end of the last hand he threw his cards down angrily and said, "We got to go back to playing a nickel and a dime instead of ten and twenty." No one answered him. They all stood up to leave then, nodding to one another. And they made their way out to their limousines and cars without talking.

The combined police forces took the Brodkey killing seriously, too. The state representative also had the Vario folder on the large, oval, government issue desk waiting for the others when they came in. As it was the most important business facing them they took it up first.

"That's two," one of them said.

"Like I said last time," someone answered, "couldn't happen to nicer people. You ever get a look at the stiffs when Brodkey's goons had worked them over? Boy, I couldn't eat a decent meal for two weeks. A real bastard that man, believe me, no one's going to miss him."

"But the point is," the federal man put in. "That makes two. As much as I like seeing them dead we are supposed to be protecting everyone, them as well as our own children. No, strike that. I'm not explaining it right. Let me put it this way. This is obviously a gang war. We don't care what happens to crooks but gang wars have a way of harming innocent people. What if some everyday citizen gets in the way of one of these bullets? If that happens we are responsible. Law and order, remember? And so if a congressional committee or someone from the state legislatures ever looks into it they are going to say, to us, what did you do to stop this? And we're going to look like horses' asses sitting there in front of the cameras and the lights when we say, "Well, sir, we thought that these were crooks." It won't wash. Just for the record we got to put someone on this. Just in case, you know what I mean?"

They chose Ross to do the job. They argued back and forth that they were working under a tight budget and they couldn't afford to put one man full time to act as bodyguard for the very people they were trying to destroy. But in the end, and after a great deal of debate, they all agreed. Ross was a state undercover man and the state representative gave a little bit about his background. He was a dedicated cop, a guy who hated the underworld like few other people hated it. And he had a reason. When he was a kid his daddy used to own a gas station, and he was one of those independent people who refused to pay protection to a mob that was "organizing" all the gas stations in the area. So one Saturday morning, early, they came in and killed his daddy, shot him down just like that. And it just happened that the kid had gone to work with his daddy that morning and watched the whole thing from behind a stack of tires. That was Ross.

HE WAS a big, soft-spoken, quiet guy, with large ears, feet and nose, and reddish-sandy hair that was beginning to thin out. He had thick, strong fingers that didn't let go once they grabbed hold of someone. He was there when they buried Brodkey. It was a lavish casket, something like the one they buried Napoleon in. There were enough flowers to give everyone within the radius of a mile hay fever and Ross stopped counting after the fiftieth limousine. One of the more touching sights was Brodkey's widow and two children. The widow had been a dancer in Las Vegas, where Brodkey, had met her. Among the better customers of the club in which she worked she had been known as "big mouth." She wore black silk that day which, in addition to symbolizing grief, showed off her figure to its best advantage. But those mourners who looked at her with the idea of paying a later call of condolence were already too late; a certain distributor of soft drink products had been doing so for more than two years now.

Ross stopped at the first telephone booth he came to after he had left the cemetery. He dialed a number from memory and when the receiver on the other end was picked up he said, "This is the red one, what are the odds on the JetsDolphins game?"

"Dolphins by seven," the voice on the other end said.

"I'd like to put a C note on the Jets," Ross said and hung up. He hadn't really made a bet, it was the way he got in touch with Wente.

Wente was a small, thin bald man with the kind of fussy moustache that would look better on a ladies shoe salesman than on a very small-time bookie. Ross was already seated at the counter of the diner on the outskirts of St. Louis which was their meeting place when Wente arrived. He sat at the far end of the counter away from Ross, ordered a piece of Dutch apple pie and a cup of coffee and didn't look his way once. When Wente was down to his last bite of pie Ross paid his check and walked out. Wente had parked his car next to his but facing in the other direction so that the drivers' windows were opposite one another. Wente came out a minute or so after Ross.

"I want to know about the two hits in the past month," Ross said as soon as Wente was in hearing distance.

It was as if Wente had been expecting the question, or rather had been programmed for it. He began spieling the answer very fast and in a monotone. When he came to a name Ross wrote it down on a three-by-five card. Vario had been into heroin, everyone knew that. But the stuff that he brought into St. Louis was costing him too much money because there were payoffs in New York and Chicago before it got here. By importing his own Vario would be able to add at least 50 percent and maybe more to his profits. So he got together six men he knew, sent one of them to Marseilles, France, and arranged for a $4 million shipment to be brought to St. Louis directly by air freight.

"Brodkey and White in on the deal?" Ross asked.

"Yeah. Brodkey supplied part of the money, White had connections with the freight handler's union."

"Who are the other three?"

"Lawrence Gontar, Alfie Gargulio, William H. Mohr."

"Who's doing the hitting?"

"Don't know."

"Coming from Chicago or New York?"

"Don't know:"

"Why don't the big bosses put a stop to it?"

"They don't know who's doing the hitting either. The plan was kept from them. Someone in New York or Chicago wants to make them very nervous. Maybe come in and take a piece away from them, too."

"Anything else I should have?"

"You got all I know." Wente then started his car and drove off.

Ross put the three remaining names through the St. Louis Police information bank and the statistics began coming back almost immediately.

There were four aliases for Lawrence Gontar: Larry Gobbie, L. Martin Grosby, Lance Grove. His arrest record went back to 1945 when he was 15 years old. He had been indicted for everything from murder to armed robbery to rape and had served a sentence of seven years for assault with a deadly weapon. He had at one time or another been involved in prostitution, white slavery, truck hijacking, pornography, running card and dice games, fixing horse races and extortion. His current occupation was listed as proprietor of The French Quarter, which was described as a massage parlor. The address was given as well as an estimated gross income. The report also stated that Gontar ran a gambling operation on the premises and as he had no known home address it was guessed that he also used the place for his living quarters. A recent photograph showed him to be a rather good-looking man with black hair cut in the modern fashion and eyes that were too close together.

Alfred Gargulio had no aliases. He was president and sole owner of the Gargulio Chemical Company, which specialized in the sale of chemicals to neighborhood dry cleaning stores. The Gargulio Chemical Company had a monopoly in St. Louis and the surrounding area on the fluid cleaners use to get the dirt out of clothes. In addition to buying the fluids from Gargulio the dry cleaners were also forced to buy fire and explosion insurance. Those who didn't couldn't get the fluids. Those who had managed to bring fluids in from elsewhere had their businesses destroyed by either fire or explosion, or both. It was as simple as that. The combined task force had been trying to put a stop to Gargulio for years but they could never get a dry cleaner to swear out a complaint. In 1967 one man did and the following day he and his wife were killed when a truck ran over their car.

GARGULIO HAD once served three years in a state prison for extortion, but that was when he was 19 years old and though there had been other indictments there were no other convictions. There was a recent photo of Gargulio and a notation that he was a ladies' man of some reputation. In addition to the apartment he lived in he also had one that he used for dates and he paid yearly rental on a room in the Hotel Stanhope luxury hotel not far from his office. He used the room at the Stanhope for dates during the lunch hour or midafternoon.

William H. Mohr was a real estate man. He had been indicted by various grand juries 74 times, which was thought to be some kind of a record. But he had never once been convicted of any crime. Mohr's difficulties with the law always involved property. Several people had complained that when they wouldn't sell their property to Mohr at his price they were visited by squads of goons who first threatened them and then acted out their threats, stopping only when they agreed to sell at Mohr's price. Mohr had also been indicted as a co-conspirator in arson, and in bribing or offering bribes to public officials. Once, two apartment houses that he had constructed fell apart a year later. Seventeen people were killed and an investigation showed that all of the materials that had been used in the construction were inferior and didn't meet the city standards. Mohr was indicted for second-degree murder but the trial ended in a hung jury. There was a suspicion that the jury had been tampered with but there was not enough evidence to prove it. Mohr was married and had one son, now 16 years old. He lived in a simple home in a modest section of the city. The report added that he had no known vices, no friends or relatives, he had never gone on a vacation and it was not known how he spent his spare time. The accompanying photograph of Mohr seemed to prove everything his record said.

When he had read the last page Ross put his feet up on the desk and laced his fingers behind his head. Crazy world, he thought. He has always wanted to be a cop to get scum like these and now that he was a cop he was assigned to protect them, act as a bodyguard, see that they didn't get killed. Crazy world? Insane.

It was obvious that these three men were candidates

for the grave. They had committed the unpardonable sin of the underworld, they had cheated on someone who was stronger than they were. The plan he would use almost suggested itself, watch them and just before they were hit, grab the would be killer. Use them as bait, as lures. The problem was that he couldn't watch all three at the same time. Oh, well, he thought, he would just have to do the best he could.

It didn't matter which one he watched. He looked at his watch and as it was close to four in the afternoon he decided he would start with Gontar because the area where The French Quarter was located didn't really come to life until about six. So he went home and took a shower, changed his shirt and made himself an onion omelette. Stakeouts were the most boring and tedious part of police work and more than one detective he knew had asked to go back into uniform rather than sit through another stakeout.

The French Quarter sign on River Street also said, "upstairs one flight." Downstairs was a small luncheonette, a paint store and the office of a trucking company. He drove around the block once to see if there could be a rear entrance but as far as he could tell there was none; a fire escape on a side street seemed to provide the only other exit than the door on River Street. So he parked where he could watch both. He had Gontar's photo with him and he placed it inside the Racing Form he had brought with him and sat in the car and pretended to be picking out the next day's horses. He had no idea where Gontar was but he guessed that he might be arriving at any time now to get The French Quarter ready for that night's business. Once he arrived Ross was certain that there would be enough muscle upstairs to make it difficult for anyone to get him. Once he was upstairs Ross would leave, get some sleep, and begin following either Gargulio or Mohr. When he was more familiar with their routines he would be better able to dovetail his stakeouts.

As he sat there thumbing through the Racing Form, making marks every now and then with his pencil, he watched the activity in the streets around him pick up. Lights were turned on and vehicular traffic thickened. Several hookers stepped out of a sleazy looking hotel, yawned and began looking for customers. A car parked at a curb and six gangling high school athletes got out and started hitting each other in the arm out of embarrassment or because they had nothing better to do. The police patrol car moved slowly down the street, not affecting the activity one bit.

While he watched a cab pulled up across the street from him and, to his surprise, an old woman with gray hair got out. Old women are usually out of place on sin streets and he guessed that she might be the mother of one of whores, or maybe one of the girls who worked in the massage parlors. She was bent at the shoulders and she walked slowly, her left leg seemed to be giving her trouble. Arthritis, Ross guessed. His own mother had suffered from arthritis and she walked the same way. The old woman had her pocketbook clutched under one arm. She looked up and down the street and then at the address number in front of her. Then she started walking in the direction of The French Quarter entrance.

A taxi pulled up before The French Quarter just about the same time the old lady reached it. A man got out, Ross couldn't see him very well because the taxi was between them, but he could see that he was well dressed, in mod-style clothes. The old woman again looked at the number of the building and as the man finished paying the cabbie and turned his back on Ross she approached him. Just as she got to him, she dropped her bag. The man bent down to get it for her. Then something happened that Ross couldn't see. The man seemed to fold, grab at his midsection and then crumble to his knees. The old woman seemed to be doing something to him, again and again, and by the time Ross realized that she was jabbing him with either a knife or an ice pick it was too late because he had dropped to the pavement and she was running down the street, white wig askew. When she arrived at an alleyway she turned into it and disappeared.

Ross was out of the car like a shot. He paused where the man had fallen, recognized him immediately as Lawrence Gontar, saw that he was dead, then ran to the alley. He followed it for 200 feet where it made an L-shaped turn then continued running until it came out at the next street. There was no evidence anywhere of the man—or could it be a woman? —who had murdered Lawrence Gontar.

A CROWD had formed around Gontar's body and the patrol car, its lights flashing, had just pulled up at the curb. Ross did not stop but returned to his car where he sat for a while with his hands on the wheel. Was it a woman who was methodically and systematically murdering these hoodlums? And how could he, Ross, have been so goddamned stupid, so slow to react, to be sitting there and watching while Lawrence Gontar was being stabbed to death?

The only change Ross made in his plan was to tell the two remaining hoods that he would be following them. He figured it would save him time and energy not having to dodge both the marks and the killer, and it would allow him to work closer to them.

Alfred Gargulio's huge chinless face, which reminded Ross of the underside of a toilet bowl, turned even whiter when Ross showed him first his badge and then his identification card. He had had a big smile on his face when Ross had first walked into his huge, expensively decorated office. He was wearing a striped tailor-made suit and shirt and a blue silk tie that looked like it had been woven to match the color of his blue eyes. He had recently been shaved and barbered and manicured and he smelled like a whore bent over. But despite all of this he was an ugly man and no amount of work could make him otherwise. What bothered Ross the most, though, was that his stomach rumbled and he passed wind all the time Ross was in his office.

"I came to help save your miserable life," Ross said before Gargulio could speak.

"Thanks," the mobster said sarcastically.

"But I want to make it clear from the beginning," Ross went on. "It isn't my idea of the way I would like to be spending my time. As a matter of fact I would give half an arm to be helping whoever it is that's after you. But that's the way things sometimes turn out in this life.".

Gargulio didn't bat an eye lash and Ross went on to explain that from now on he would be following him.

"Everywhere?" the mobster asked.

"Everywhere."

"Look. there's this one thing. I got to have my sex. I got to have it every day or I get sick. I don't feel right. You going to be around when I'm balling, too?"

"Not under the sheets," Ross answered.

"No," Gargulio said. "I don't want that. That's too much. I'll take my chances. I got a gun, I know how to use it. I'm not scared."

"Look, Pal," Ross said then. "You don't have a choice. We're not really interested in your miserable hide, we just don't want someone to be hurt by a stray bullet that was meant for you, understand? And if you give me any trouble I'll close this place down so tight you'll have to go back to stealing hub caps. I'll have

G-men here, and T-men, vice squads, people all the way down to the Red Cross checking out your blood to see if it's legal. Do you understand?"

Gargulio didn't move.

"Understand?" Ross shouted, getting up from his chair and leaning across the desk.

Gargulio hesitated then shook his head up and down, his wattle shaking like a turkey's.

He told Gargulio then that he could go about his normal activities, business as well as balling, but that she would ignore the fact that Ross would always be close by. When he was finished and the gangster had reluctantly agreed, Ross got up and started to walk out. But just before he reached the door he turned and pointed his finger. "I want you to remember one thing, though," he said. "I'm still a cop and you're still a crook. If, during this time that I'm watching you, you engage in any illegal activity, even park too close to a hydrant, I'm going to pull you in and I'm going to sit on you hard. Understand?"

William G. Mohr was the complete opposite of Alfie Gargulio. Small, weasellike, with gray hair, gray eyes and gray skin, he dressed in clothes that even the Salvation Army would turn down. He was a tough man to get to, which made Ross feel that he didn't have to spend much time watching him. When Ross approached the wire gate that lead to his house a Doberman Pinscher, frothing at the mouth, sprang from behind the bush and because it couldn't get at him, attacked the gate. But even if he slipped the dog a sleepinducing hypo it wouldn't have done any good because the gate was securely locked and Ross could see the circuits of an elaborate alarm system attached to the hinges.

The first four times Ross walked in the front door of Mohr's two room office, Mohr slipped out through a rear door. The fifth time Ross gave a hippie-looking kid $10 for walking in through the front door while Ross waited outside the exit. When Mohr came steaming out he grabbed him and pushed him back inside. The real estate man whined that he was going to call the cops and as Ross threw him back into his chair he said, "Forget it, buddy. I am the cops."

Mohr didn't say a word or even look straight at him while Ross explained just who he was and what he wanted to do. But when Ross was finished he smiled and seemed pleased, thankful for police protection, shrewd enough to realize that it would probably save his life. And it wouldn't cost him a thing. On his way out Ross accidentally touched the back of Mohr's hand and as soon as he got home he scrubbed himself until it hurt.

Gargulio had not lied about his sex life. The very first morning Ross followed him he stopped for a quickie three blocks from his house, barely missing the husband going to work, doing the job on the kitchen table with his pants and underwear dropped to his ankles. What his partner lacked in looks and figure she more than made up in passion. As Ross ducked under the window to return to his car he heard her moan, "Oh, Alfie, I just can't ever seem to get enough of you."

T HEN GARGULIO left his office at 11 o'clock and came skidding to a stop in front of a swank looking lingerie shop. Ross sauntered in after him and pretended to be looking at a quilted robe the kind Chinese peasants wear while the mobster bought a pair of black net stockings, a garter belt the same color with roses embroidered on them and a brassiere with holes for the nipples. And while Alfie waited for the sales lady to wrap up his purchase he discreetly sauntered to the part of the shop where the dressing rooms were and tried to get a peek at the customers who were trying things on behind the skimpy curtains. When he passed Ross on his way out he winked.

His next stop was the room at the Hotel Stanhope. Ross heard someone giggle delightedly. "Alfie, you're late," as he let himself in with his key. Ross only put his ear to the door twice, once on the way up the corridor and the second time on his way back. He heard giggling sounds on the way up and the girl saying. "Oh, Alfie, you shouldn't do that," on the way back. But she wasn't protesting. Ross watched the room from a bend in the corridor for close to three-quarters of an hour. She came out then, giggling, kissing Gargulio lightly at the door. She was about the most stunning 22- or 23-year old blonde he had ever seen, with long, straight shapely legs and boobs like the tops of newel posts. And she hadn't been gone more than six minutes before another one arrived, an almost exact duplicate except that she had red hair and her rump was beautiful enough to cast in bronze.

"The son-of-a-bitch," Ross mumbled to himself. "The dirty, lousy son-ofa-bitch."

Gargulio had a dinner date with a gorgeous Japanese woman that night which also ended up in the hotel room. Ross had eaten a candy bar while the two had dined on lobster. While he waited for the elevator he had an opportunity to grab another one from the nearby news arid candy stand. He listened in at Gargulio's door three times during the course of that evening but all he heard was gasping and heavy breathing all three times. His eyes smarted, his stomach growled, he felt as if he hadn't washed, shaved or brushed his teeth in a week, as he finally followed the gangster up to his apartment at 2 that morning, and tucked him in, if you want to put it that way. "Boy," he told himself as he raced home through the deserted streets, hoping that he had the makings of even a bread and butter sandwich in his refrigerator. "If I wanted to rub out this guy I'd know just how to go about it."

But it didn't happen that way, and despite every precaution again, Ross was witness. It happened on the fifth day Ross had followed the two men, leaving one when he was as sure as he could be that that one was safe and hurrying over to the other. He had followed Gargulio into a large, expensive department store. It was one of the two places that the mobster went every day to buy something for his noontime date, or dates — one afternoon Ross watched while three different girls entered or left the busy hotel room. He also bought lingerie in the department store though sometimes he stopped to pick up various bottles of perfume. It was in the perfume section that it happened.

Ross was not more than 15 feet away, at another counter pretending to look at little bars of soap in the color and shape of lemons. He saw what seemed a saleswoman approach Gargulio with a sample bottle of scent for him to sniff. He watched the two of them disappear behind a large pillar and waited for them to appear again on the over side. The very moment he realized he should be seeing them was when he knew that it had happened.

Ross pushed his way through the shoppers. On the other side of the pillar was the entrance to a booth. First Ross saw the legs with the fancy kind of shoes that Gargulio wore and when he looked further he saw the heavy chest with the knife sticking into it. Blood was gushing out of the wound but from the way the body lay Ross could tell that he was dead.

He was thinking fast now. She would either be out of the store by now or, anticipating that they would either watch the exits right away or remember a woman without a coat rushing out into the street, she would have gone upstairs where she had checked her things. Then she could come down, just another shopper with her purchases, and walk out without any difficulty.

Behind him Ross heard a scream, then another, then a whole chorus. The lunch room would be a likely place where a person might leave a coat and then pick it up. The restaurant, he noticed as he walked his way up the escalator, was on the fourth floor. No one with a familiar face was in the restaurant, either at the counter or at one of the tables, or waiting to be seated. He started toward the elevator and it was then that he saw her. She was buying some towels at a nearby counter, as coolly as if she had enjoyed the day and was ready to return to the nunnery. Ross was certain she was the one. He thought back to the old woman with the gray hair and then the girl with the sample bottle of perfume whom he had glimpsed for a split second. Yes, it was the same one.

He waited until she had finished her purchase and had walked away from the counter before he approached her. He showed her his badge and said that he would like to ask her a few questions. She was startled. "Questions?" she asked. "About what? I hope it won't take long I have to get back to work." She was a dark girl, very pretty, with a nice figure, and she spoke with a soft southern accent.

At first she refused to leave the building. "I thought you meant ask me a few questions here," she said, beginning to cry. "Why must I go with you to police headquarters? I didn't do anything. Are you sure you are the police. Are you sure you're not a... " and the tears were now rushing down her cheeks and shoppers were turning to stare at them. Ross took her over to one of the many police officers who had suddenly flooded the building, this one a lieutenant, showed him his badge and identification card and he vouched for him. With the lieutenant standing by watching he took her purse and examined it, first for weapons and then to look for identification. A driver's license, several letters and a Blue Cross card all gave her name as Delpha Gard. All of them were authentic, there was no doubt about it. Still Ross was certain that she was the killer.

ROSS PUT handcuffs on her before they left the store and by then she was really crying, her mascara was all smeared and her nose was running. When she got into the front seat her skirt shot way above her knees to show a lovely pair of legs for a second but she grabbed with both of her handcuffed hands and quickly pulled it back in place. Once during the ride she asked if Ross had any Kleenex and he took the handkerchief out of his breast pocket and gave it to her. She blew thickly into it and dabbed at her eye. When Ross told her about her right to remain silent and to be represented by a lawyer she began to cry again.

He took her up to the office he shared with Detective Sergeant Hall, who sometimes worked with him. He asked if she wanted coffee, or tea and she just shook her head. Hall came in just as he started talking to her and he indicated that he should join in. With Hall now as a witness he again told her about her rights, this time reading it from the printed cards that had been given to all officers.

"I have not done anything," she insisted, this time angrily instead of tearfully. "I demand that you let me go right now. If not I will call someone who will get me a lawyer and I will sue you and whoever you are working for for everything I can get, and I will also sue that you be removed from your job. You are not supposed to hold innocent people or bring them here to this filthy place. Even I know that."

Ross looked at Hall and Hall looked back at Ross.

"We are not holding you, Miss Gard," Ross answered. "We have merely brought you here to run your fingerprints and name through our information computer to see if you have a record. We also intend checking on your home address and place of employment. There have been a few murders and there is enough evidence that you're the one we're looking for to hold you for at least that long."

"What evidence?" she asked, exasperated.

"Me," Ross said. "I've seen you kill two of the men."

"You?" she answered. "How could you have when I don't know what you are talking about."

Hall looked at Ross and this time Ross didn't return the look. That was all the evidence there was —unless there were fingerprints on the knife that had killed Gargulio, and Ross doubted that there would be.

There was no record on Delpha Gard. The operator who answered when they called J. H. Meyer & Company, who manufactured and sold bathroom fixtures and mirrors said that there was a Miss Delpha Gard who worked for them as a pool stenographer and typist. No, Miss Gard was not there at the present time, she had gone out shopping and then to lunch and she had not yet returned. She had given them the telephone number for Meyer and they had doubled checked it in the telephone book. The woman she said she rented a room from answered the phone on the eighth ring, just as Miss Gard said she would, because she was a little deaf. Yes, a Miss Delpha Gard lived with her, who was this and could he please speak a little louder? Yes, she had dark hair, was about 25 years old and spoke with a southern accent. The police? What was a nice girl like that doing at a police station?

ROSS SCRATCHED his head then and motioned for Hall to meet him out in the corridor. "Geez," he said when they had closed the door. "I would have sworn that this is the one. I saw her. I know I saw her."

"You've got to come up with something tangible or let her go. They'll have your ass in a sling if you've been terrorizing innocent women, accusing them of having murdered somebody."

In the end, and despite the fact that he was certain, they let her go. She was angry, furious, and crying. She swore that she was going to speak with a lawyer and sue the city and state. She slammed the door after her and almost broke the glass in it. Ross called down to the desk and asked that she be tailed.

He and Hall sat in the office for a long while without speaking to one another. Ross had his feet up on his desk and Hall made believe that he was busy with some papers. Ross was the first to speak. He said, "Geez, I know that she was the one." Then things began happening in bunches. First Hall snapped his fingers and said, "You know, a couple of years ago I heard about this hood named Petey Gardino. He was involved with one of the gangs in the Nashville area. The reason I bring him up was that the mob killed him and a guy I met from the Tennessee State Police said that his daughter swore that she was going to kill every mobster she could find. It's funny. Gardino, Gard, you know what I mean?"

Ross dropped his feet to the floor. "Quick, you call J. H. Meyer again and I'll call the deaf landlady."

A man answered the J. H. Meyer number. No, there wasn't any Delpha Gard working for them, he never heard of anyone with that name. When Hall asked to speak with the telephone operator who had been on duty about 40 minutes before the man said, "What telephone operator?"

The dead landlady's telephone rang eight times, then another eight times, and a third eight times, and was never picked up. When he slammed the phone down onto the cradle it rang and he brought it back to his ear.

"Ross," he said.

"Ross, this is Patrolman Keith Boudreau. I was given the assignment of tailing a woman for you? Dark hair, good looking, about..."

"Yes, yes, what's the matter."

"Well, ugh. Mr. Ross. I don't know how it happened but suddenly I lost her. I saw her get into this cab and then when I looked into it when it stopped for a red light, it was empty."

Ross jammed the phone down and started to run out.

"Where you going?" Hall asked at the same time as the telephone rang for the last time.

"Mohr," Ross said as Hall picked it up and identified himself.

"Hey," Hall yelled as Ross was running through the door. "This is Mohr on the other end."

Ross grabbed the phone out of Hall's hand. "Ross," he said.

"Mr. Ross," Mohr said. "This is William C. Mohr. I'm calling because there's a young woman here who says she's working with you and..." Ross heard the shots, two of them, and he heard the last hit fall dead to the floor.

●●●

"Have you seen a little boy with a double-barreled slingshot?"

"It is Fucking Brilliant. Buy It Now."

– JUSTIN MARRIOTT,
Publisher

Battling Britons,
The Paperback Fanatic
The Sleazy Reader
Pulp Horror

Featuring more than 200 book covers, posters, original paintings, and model reference photos from Lesser's personal archives, illuminated by his own commentary. A unique insight into the man, his work, and the world of commercial illustration. Released in this deluxe hardcover edition.

The Art of Ron Lesser Vol. 1:
DEADLY DAMES
AND SEXY SIRENS

Edited by
Roland Deis, Bill Cunningham and J. Kingston Pierce

AVAILABLE WORLDWIDE VIA AMAZON OR DIRECT FROM
WWW.MENSPULPMAGS.COM

STORIES & ART FROM VINTAGE MEN'S ADVENTURE MAGAZINES

MEN'S ADVENTURE

ISSUE NO. 7   QUARTERLY

ZIP-GUN GIRL
MEN'S ADVENTURE BOOK BONUS

GANG GIRLS
AT THE MOVIES

CYCLE QUEENS
WOMEN ON WHEELS

GANG GIRLS!

EDITED BY ROBERT DEIS AND BILL CUNNINGHAM
GUEST EDITORS ANDREW NETTE & JULES BURT

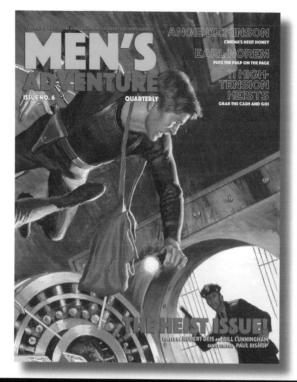

ON SALE NOW

MAQ
MEN'S ADVENTURE QUARTERLY

AVAILABLE WORLDWIDE ON AMAZON

AND AT THESE FINE INDEPENDENT BOOKSELLERS:

MENSPULPMAGS.COM
BUD PLANT
STUART NG BOOKS
MIKE CHOMKO BOOKS

FOR MEN ONLY

SEX DIARY OF A BASEBALL GROUPIE | **I FLEW ORPHANS OUT OF SHATTERED SAIGON**

OCTOBER $1.00 02401

Take A Sex I.Q. Test
HOW WOULD YOU RATE HANDLING EXTRAMARITAL SEX

SMASH BOOK BONUS
THE DAY CASTRO BEAT THE CIA'S MAFIA
Hit Men Hired By Washington To Rub Out Fidel

10 SUPER SEX TECHNIQUES THAT ESPECIALLY APPEAL TO EXPERIENCED WOMEN

AMERICA'S BRAVEST UNION LEADER-- ARNOLD MILLER

SEX SWAPPING, APARTMENT STYLE
Newest Wrinkle To Keep Out The Bedroom Blues

Going On A Vacation?
10 SUMMER SPEED TRAPS YOU SHOULD KNOW, AND DUCK!

MEMOIRS OF A HEAD-BASHING RAILROAD DETECTIVE

IT'S TIME TO ZAP THE GOVERNMENT SNOOPS

For More Of Rose's Racy Red Stockings In Full Color, Turn To Page 17

By Wayne C. Ulsh
From *FOR MEN ONLY*, October 1975
Artwork by Bruce Minney

This next story is interesting for several reasons aside from the fact that it's illuminated with another fantastic illustration by top men's adventure magazine artist Bruce Minney.

When it was published in 1975, reports that the U.S. Central Intelligence Agency had recruited the Mafia to try to assassinate Cuban Communist dictator Fidel Castro had been made by the pioneering investigative journalist Jack Anderson and discussed in Congressional hearings.

However, it wasn't until 2007 that the C.I.A./Mafia team up was publicly admitted by former C.I.A. Director Allen Dulles. And, it wasn't until the National Archives declassified previously secret files about the 1963 assassination of President John F. Kennedy that the attempted assassination collaboration between the agency and the Mafia was clearly confirmed by documents in "The JFK Files."

Thus, Wayne C. Ulsh was somewhat ahead of his time when he wrote "The Day Castro Beat the C.I.A.'s Mafia." It's a fictional story. But its plot is not as far out as some the C.I.A.'s real life plots to kill Castro.

In fact, in addition to sending hitmen to Cuba to try to shoot Castro, the C.I.A. came up with various wild schemes to snuff out El Jefe. They included exploding cigars, a fountain pen

INTRODUCTION BY BOB **DEIS**

that hid a syringe full of poison, lethal femme fatales, and infecting his favorite diving gear with tuberculosis. Castro survived all of the hundreds of attempts made to kill by the U.S. government, the Mob, and anti-Castro Cubans and sometimes joked about it. He died unscathed, of old age, in 2016.

I'm fascinated by Cuba and have read quite a bit about Castro, the Cuban Revolution and its aftermath. Several years ago, I co-edited a collection of MAM stories on those topics, titled *CUBA: SUGAR, SEX, AND SLAUGHTER—CUBA AND CASTRO IN MEN'S ADVENTURE MAGAZINES.* I also live near Key West, which has had close cultural and historical ties with Cuba for two centuries years and is home to many families of Cuban descent.

Wayne Ulsh

Wayne C. Ulsh of Discovery makes his living by putting his dreams and wildest thoughts down on paper.

He's a freelance writer, who sells most of his articles to men's magazines. He's written so many and had them published in so many magazines that chances are if you read men's magazines you've read something by Wayne.

He started his writing career as a reporter and sports editor for a Pennsylvania newspaper and later an industrial editor in New York.

But neither job satisfied his creative writing itch, so Wayne, his wife Carol and their son Christopher, 8, moved to Discovery. There Wayne writes and markets his articles. It's not an easy life but what is most important, Wayne says, is that his job makes him happy.

"I get ideas for my stories by just being observant about things around me and I'll sit and dream and think up situations."

While most of his articles are spiced with adventure and sex, Wayne wouldn't describe himself an "adventurous soul." "I'm not in the stories to any degree," he says.

Wayne had his first book "Rip-off" published last fall.

Wayne C. Ulsh

Author Wayne Ulsh

Those are some of reasons why I especially enjoyed Ulsh's story. Another is that it's damn well written.

Today, few people are aware of Wayne C. Ulsh. But during the 1960s and 1970s, he was a favorite writer of the editors of various men's bachelor magazines and MAMs.

Among his admirers is my online friend, James Reasoner. James is the award-winning author of hundreds of Western, historical, action/adventure and crime novels and short stories. He's also the founder of Rough Edges Press, an affiliate of Mike Bray's great Wolfpack Publishing company.

"I was a fan of Ulsh's work back in the '70s. when I was getting started as a writer," James told me. "I saw his stories in men's adventure magazines and they seemed like the closest to what I liked to read and write, so I tried to emulate them. MAMs were still on every magazine rack in every drugstore and grocery store, and I really wanted to write for them. I never cracked that market before the genre disappeared. But Ulsh seemed to be the type of pro I wanted to be, so he was an inspiration and influence."

Nowadays, you'll find a lot of info online about Reasoner and his work, but very little about Ulsh. Here's a brief overview of what I've been able to piece together...

Wayne C. (for Campbell) Ulsh was born in Altoona, Pennsylvania in 1935. After graduating from Penn State University, he started his writing career as a sports journalist. In the early '60s, he became a regular writer of short stories for a long list of men's bachelor magazines, including *ADAM, CAD, ESCAPADE,*

magazines you've read something by Wayne."

In that article, Ulsh said being a professional writer was not an easy life, but being a writer made him happy. "I get ideas for my stories by just being observant about things around me and I'll sit and dream and think up situations," he said.

He also said that while his stories are spiced with adventure and sex, he himself wasn't an "adventurous soul."

Ulsh did definitely have an adventurous imagination when it came to both the action and sex in his stories.

FLING, GENT, MR., JAGUAR, NUGGET, ROGUE, SWANK, and *TOPPER*. In the '70s he also became a favorite writer of the editors of the Magazine Management men's adventure mags *(ACTION FOR MEN, FOR MEN ONLY, MALE, MEN, STAG,* etc.).

He continued to write short fiction stories for men's mags and mags in other genres, like *EASYRIDERS*, in the '80s and early '90s. And, although short stories make up his main body of work, he did write two now hard-to-find crime novels published in the US—*RIP-OFF* (1975) and *MCDADE* (1981)—and a third novel that appears to have only been published in Europe in 1981, *SOLO DE FLIC* ("Lone Cop").

Ulsh and his wife Carol and son Christopher lived in Maryland from the mid-1970s until his death in 1994. In 1976, a local Maryland newspaper published a brief article about him that noted: "He's written so many [short stories] and had them published in so many magazines that chances are if you read men's

Compared to bachelor mags, MAMs had relatively elliptical, euphemism-filled sex scenes in most stories they published in the '50s and '60s. By the '70s, explicit sex scenes were common in both bachelor mags and MAMs.

Thus, the sex described in stories like "The Day Castro Beat the C.I.A.'s Mafia" is pretty graphic. I think Ulsh was adept at writing those parts of his stories, as well as the action/adventure elements. That's probably why he was so popular with men's mag editors—and with readers like me and James Reasoner.

It's too bad Ulsh died at age 58. Had he lived a couple more decades, he would have written many more cool stories and maybe more novels, and might be better remembered today. Hopefully, this story in the MAQ and other stories by Ulsh we include in future issues will spark renewed awareness of his work.

●●●

OPPOSITE: An *EASYRIDERS* anthology that includes a story by Wyane Ulsh, his novel *RIP-OFF* (1975), and his novel *MCDADE* (1981). BACKGROUND: Earl Norem artwork for the Wayne Ulsh story "The G.I. Who Stole Guns for the I.R.A." in *STAG*, April 1976.

Hit Men Hired By Washington To Rub Out Fidel

THE DAY CASTRO BEAT THE CIA's MAFIA

By WAYNE C. ULSH
ART BY BRUCE MINNEY

ARLINGTON, VIRGINIA, MARCH, 1961—
Cogan had Inez in for the night. He figured he wasn't going to sleep very well anyway. His plan—to assassinate Cuban prime minister Fidel Castro—would be a reality by this time tomorrow if everything went right. History was about to be made. So how the hell could he sleep?

Inez was a beauty, a native of Brazil who worked in the State Department as a linguist. She had black hair, the deepest brown eyes Cogan had ever looked into, and a slim, tawny body. She was on his bed, naked

RECENT NEWSPAPER REPORTS SUGGEST THAT, BECAUSE OF MAFIA-CIA CONNECTION ON POSSIBLE CASTRO "HIT," PRESIDENT KENNEDY WAS SUBSEQUENTLY ASSASSINATED.

from the waist up, a glass of wine in one hand. He was standing beside her, tall and lean in a dress shirt and slacks, smiling as he gazed at her breasts. Inez cupped them in her hands and said, "Come on, Johnny. Don't keep me waiting."

CASTRO

Cogan was drinking wine too. He put his glass down and unbuttoned his shirt. As he did, his phone rang. It was sitting on a bedstead, at arm's length. It rang, and rang again. Inez frowned and said, "Don't answer it, Johnny."

"You know better," Cogan said. He picked up the phone and said his name.

"Page," a man's voice replied.

Cogan frowned now. "Yes?"

"You'd better get in here. On the double."

"Yes, sir."

"On the double, John."

The phone went dead in Cogan's ear. He put it down and rebuttoned his shirt.

"Oh no," Inez said.

Cogan looked at her breasts again. They were light chocolate in color, and their nipples were dark, swollen nuts. "The boss," he said.

"You're worse than a policeman," Inez said.

"One of these days I'm going to get out, " Cogan said. "But not tonight." He crossed the room to his closet. He wrapped a tie around his neck and quickly knotted it. He slipped a holstered, snub-nosed .38 on his belt, then put a suit coat on.

"Should I wait?" Inez said.

Cogan looked at her longingly. But he said, "If this is what I think it is, it would be a long wait." Then he walked to the door and went out.

IT TOOK Cogan less than twenty minutes to get from his apartment to the Central Intelligence Agency's old headquarters in Washington, D.C. Carl Page was waiting for him in his office, which except for a desk lamp was dark. Page was in his fifties. He was a thin, intense man with a balding head and penetrating blue eyes. Cogan slipped into a chair opposite him, and Page said, "We've got a problem."

"With Operation Canefire?"

"Yes. With Canefire. In a word, John, they're on to us."

"The Cubans?"

"Yes. Castro's people."

"Says who?"

"Lopez."

Cogan lit a cigarette. "If Lopez says so, it's so," he said.

"I agree," Page said.

"How?" Cogan said.

"The girl," Page said. "Louisa. Beyond that, don't ask. Lopez's message was cryptic. And he used a new code. I get the feeling he was lucky to get it out at all."

"He probably was."

"All he gave us was this," Page said. "The Cubans blew Louisa's cover somehow. This afternoon, she disappeared. Permanently, I would imagine. But Lopez says they learned everything she knew about Canefire first. Now, here's what they're doing. They're planting a girl in her place. From Castro's secret police, maybe Army intelligence—DIER. We don't know. But she's definitely one of their agents. Okay. Now, we get to the worst of it. They're not going to just kill our Mafioso assassin. Hell, no. If they were, I wouldn't even have called you tonight. No, they're going to go through with the meet between him and Louisa's replacement. In fact, they're going to let the plan proceed right up to when Marzano's ready to hit Castro. Then they're going to grab him. They're going to take him alive. And then, John, they're going to make a propaganda plum of him."

"Propaganda?" Cogan said.

"Yes," Page said. "The worst possible thing that could happen. God. I can just see Castro on TV. Ranting and raving. He'll have Marzano standing there beside him. He'll denounce the United States as an international murderer. A country that employes mobsters, no less, to do the killing. He'll point to Marzano and say, 'Here's my proof. We caught this man in the act. Preparing to shoot me down on my own soil, in my beloved Cuba. His name is Marzano. He is not only a Yankee, but a member of their Mafia. A criminal, under contract to the CIA.'" Page pressed his fists to his eyes and shook his head. "That's the picture I keep getting," he said. "And I don't like it one bit. What's worse, a lot of people around this town won't like it either. The Agency will get a lot of heat. Me. And you too, John."

Cogan smoked and said nothing.

"I don't like heat," Page said. "So we're going to call Canefire off."

"We are?" Cogan said. He glanced at his watch. It was almost midnight. "Marzano's gone."

"I should have said *you're* going to call it off, John," Page said.

"Sure," Cogan said. He stubbed his cigarette out. "Operation Canefire's my baby. So why not?"

"It's not that. It's too late to make a simple phone call. Marzano's out of touch. The boat has no radio. Right? And no one in Cuba can do the job, can they?"

"No. Lopez could try. But he's nervous. Like you said. They're watching him. And they'll be watching this girl of theirs. If he goes anywhere near her or Marzano, he'll tip his hand. That's all Castro's boys would need. No, forget Lopez. We can't afford to lose him. There's Pablo, but without Lopez, we can't get to him. Marzano wouldn't listen to any Cubans anyway. Not him. Not when there's a job to be done. No, I'm the only person he'd listen to, who can stop him. I'll have to go down there."

"I came to the same conclusion," Page said. "There's an Air Force jet waiting for you at Andrews. And by the time you get to Florida, there'll be transportation to Cuba lined up. Plus everything else you'll need." Cogan stood up and started for the door.

"John?" Page said.

"Yes sir."

"Just... just get it done, John. Castro's scored on us, but without Marzano he can't make it hold up. So get that Mafioso back here."

"Sir," Cogan said. "I'm already on record on this. But Operation Canefire wasn't my idea. I was opposed to the *idea* from the start. I set it up on this end. I recruited Marzano and coordinated it with Lopez down there. Basically, it's my *plan*. But that's all. However this turns out, I want that clear."

"Get Marzano out of there, and you won't have to worry about that being clear," Page said. "Will you, John?"

"I guess not."

OFF THE COAST OF CUBA, later that night— The 90-mile trip down from The Keys hadn't taken long at all. Now, Vincent "Vinnie the Fist" Marzano knelt on the deck of a small fishing trawler as it bobbed in the Straits of Florida. Ahead of him, three miles off, was the coastline. Ten miles to the east lay Havana. Behind Marzano, at the trawler's wheel, was a Cuban exile he knew only as Jose. They waited together for a half hour, saying nothing to each other. The only thing they had in common, Marzano thought, was their current employer. All Jose cared about was returning to his native land some day. He wanted Fidel Castro dead, yes. But not for the same reason Marzano did. It was the same with the CIA man, Marzano thought. Cogan had handed him a pile of garbage about how the CIA and the Mafia had worked together for the good of the country before. During World War II, for example, the Mafia had helped protect United States ports from sabotage. The Organization had had a hand in the invasions of Sicily and Italy, too. Marzano had already known that and he'd thought, so what? Cogan had been trying to appeal to his patriotism. He didn't give a damn about the "good of the country." Or about the CIA's motives for wanting Castro dead either. Politics didn't interest him. Nor did it matter to him that the Mafia itself might stand to gain if Fidel was done away with. Marzano knew all about that too. Some good heroin and gambling connections had been lost to The Organization since Castro had taken over in Cuba. But the hell with that too. All that Marzano cared about was the hit. He was one of the best hit men anywhere. In his twenty-eight years, he'd killed sixteen men. Fidel Castro would be number seventeen, and that was what this was all about to him. Getting the job done, and getting it done right. That was why he was here. Because of that—and the money. Yeah, the money they were paying him was good, goddamn good. A quarter of a million bucks. Half up front and the other $125,000 when it was done.

Another boat came then, out from the shoreline. It was a rowboat, a Cuban bent at the oars, his back to Marzano and Jose. As it approached the trawler, Marzano said, "I'm going in *that*?"

"A small boat has the best chance of getting through," Jose said.

Marzano grunted, watching as the rowboat pulled alongside, bumping the trawler's bow. The Cuban at the oars looked up. He was a thick-bodied man with a heavy mustache. His eyes flashed as he smiled widely. "*Senor* Marzano?" he said. "Fidel's assassin? Welcome to Cuba. I am your official tour guide, Pablo."

He held his hand out, but Marzano ignored it. A goddamn comedian, he thought. He didn't like people who tried to be funny, especially at times like this.

"Come aboard," Pablo said.

Marzano jumped down into the rowboat, then quickly seated himself in the stern.

"No, no, *senor*," Pablo said. "Here. At the oars. Join me. There is one for you."

"Me?" Marzano said.

"*Si.* It will be much quicker, with both of us rowing. Don't you agree?"

Marzano had never rowed a boat in his life. But, grunting, he stepped to the middle of the rowboat, sat beside Pablo and took hold of an oar. Three goddamn miles, he thought. There wasn't anything funny about that either.

It was a long haul. But eventually Pablo and Marzano rowed the boat onto a dark stretch of beach. They pulled it up under some trees, and from there, Pablo led Marzano to a car. It was an old Ford, hidden beside an unpaved road. Marzano moved around to the passenger side.

"No, *senor*," Pablo said, pointing to the rear of the car. "In the trunk."

"The trunk?" Marzano said.

"*Senor*," Pablo said. "There are not many cars in Cuba, especially at night. If we are stopped, I have identification. A reason to be out. But what about you?"

MARZANO swore to himself, but walked to the back of the car. Pablo opened the trunk, and the Mafia hit man crawled in.

Pablo drove for twenty-five minutes before the Ford stopped. The trunk was opened, and Marzano saw that he was in an alley. There was a building on one side, a fence on the other. "Get out, please," Pablo told him. Marzano got out. "Go there, *senor*." Pablo pointed to a doorway in the building. The door was recessed, Marzano saw. He could stand there in shadows. He looked at Pablo. "I'll return in one hour, *senor*," the Cuban said. "Be there, in the doorway."

Marzano glanced at his wristwatch and nodded. He didn't like the way Pablo was spouting orders. The Cuban got back in his car and drove off. Marzano moved into the doorway and watched the Ford turn at the end of the alley and disappear. He stood there, alone then. It was quiet, and he could hear the faint sound of music coming from behind him, from somewhere in the building. Marzano knew where he was. In Havana, and behind a joint called "Pepe's." Pepe's was part bar and part whorehouse, one of the few gathering places left in Cuba for Americans and other foreigners who either didn't want to get out of the country or couldn't. Marzano didn't have to worry if he was seen there, Cogan had told him. Marzano wasn't worried. No one was going to see him besides the girl. Louisa.

She opened the door almost immediately. "*Senor* Marzano," she said.

He turned and looked at her. The face peering out at him was dark, young and pretty. Real pretty. *Oh yeah,* Marzano thought. "Louisa?" he said.

"*Si.*" It wasn't Louisa, of course. The girl's name was Dora, and she was a Cuban military intelligence agent. "Come in, *senor*," she said.

Marzano stepped inside, and Dora closed the door. They were in a dark hall. "Follow me," the girl said. As she turned away, Marzano let his eyes sweep down over her. He liked what he saw. Perky breasts under a blouse, full hips, long legs below her skirt. Her buttocks snapped from side to side as she moved along the hall to a flight of stairs. Nice, Marzano thought. He followed her up the stairs, watching her ass all the way. Real nice. He almost reached out for a pat. At the top of the stairs, there was another hallway. Dora walked down it, her hips still swaying.

Dora stopped before a door. She clattered a key in the lock and went inside. Marzano followed. The music was a little louder here, coming up through the floor. Dora turned on a light, just one. What Marzano saw was a single room, bare except for a dresser and a bed against one wall. A bright red bedspread reached to the floor. Dora walked to the bed, sat on it, smiled, and patted a spot next to her. "Have a seat, *Senor* Marzano," she said. "We'll have to conduct our business here."

"I've got something else in mind for there first," he said.

"What?"

"Pleasure," Marzano said. "Don't you want to thank me, Louisa? For coming here to rid your country of a scourge such as Castro? Hmmm? To give you back your freedom?"

Dora smiled. "*Si*," she said.

MARZANO AGREED with that. He often admired his strong Latin profile in mirrors. And his naked body too. He was a stud. He had the equipment, and the track record. He screwed as well as he killed. Still standing before Dora, he began to undress. He was wearing an old, doublebreasted suit.

The idea had been to make him look poor and shabby, much like the other foreigners who frequented Pepe's. But the suit had a dual purpose. Special pockets had been sewn inside the loosefitting coat. In them were the components for the rifle Marzano would use. So when he removed the coat, he laid it aside carefully. The rest of his clothes came off more quickly, however. He was glad to be out of them. He felt good naked, proud, powerful. He saw Dora's eyes on him, admiring his muscular build-and his equipment.

"Ooooh," she said. "So strong. So big, *senor*."

"Vinnie."

Marzano knelt, stripped Dora's clothes from her body, and gazed at her. She was all that he'd imagined. Rich, ripe, firm. He drew into his arms and rolled her onto her back. Above her, he rose to his knees and feasted. His mouth and hands tasted every part of her, partaking until she was quivering. Then he entered her, and he thought she would come apart. Pumping, Marzano grinned. It was always like this. With the men he killed and the broads he screwed. He tore them up. When his fleshy gun exploded inside Dora, she screamed. Delighted, Marzano wondered if Castro would scream when his turn came. He was anxious to get on with it now.

Marzano pulled out of Dora and sat up beside her on the bed. She put a hand on his leg and said, "Good, Vinnie? I wanted it to be good for you."

"It was good," Marzano said.

"Now we talk," Dora said. She sat up and rolled off the other side of the bed. In a moment, she was back, still naked, but carrying a bottle of rum, two glasses and a large map. She handed Marzano the bottle and glasses, sat on the bed Indian-style and opened up the map. "How much do you know?" she said. "I do not know which details Lopez could get out to you and which he could not."

"Details?" Marzano said, pouring the rum. "Hell, baby, all I know is that I'm going to hit Castro in a small town. From the top of a building. I *do* know how I'm going to get away afterwards. I mean, I'm no dummy. I made Cogan lay that out before I said okay."

"We could not give you more for security reasons," Dora said. "I'm sure you understand. Codes, couriers—we do not know from one minute to the next what is reliable these days. Look at the map, if you will, Vinnie."

Marzano looked. The map was of Cuba. Southeast of Havana, he saw two circles of red. Dora placed a finger on the one closer to the city and said, "This is the small town where you will do it. It is called Riaz." She slid her finger to the other circle. "This town is Christobal," she said. "Fidel is scheduled to make a speech there tomorrow at noon. Too bad he won't arrive." She smiled, then pointed to Riaz again. "Fidel and his party will drive down from Havana and enter Riaz just before 11:30 a.m. He will be in a jeep, seated in the back. Two soldiers will be in the jeep also, plus the driver. Two truckloads of soldiers will precede and follow the jeep. In addition, there will be a car of TV cameramen and reporters. The party will stop in Riaz's plaza. They plan to stay only ten minutes. No more, or they will be late for Fidel's speech in Christobal. There will be a ceremony in the plaza. It will be brief and informal. Security will be lax. Only a few hundred townspeople will attend. Everyone will be in Christobal. Thousands of sugar cane workers. A big event. If an assassin was to strike, it would be there. No? But there *will* be a ceremony in Riaz. Now, look here, Vinnie."

Dora moved the map and pointed to one of its corners. There, pasted in, was a hand-drawn inset. It showed Riaz's plaza, with squares penciled in around it to represent buildings. All of this was done in detail and marked with red X's. "Here," Dora said, "in the center of the plaza, a small platform has been erected. Fidel will leave his jeep and go there. Riaz's town officials will be waiting for him. They will shake hands and exchange gifts. Fidel will wave to the crowd and say a few words. Only a few, which will be difficult for Fidel. When he steps forward to speak, that might be your best time, Vinnie."

"Where's my building?" Marzano said.

"Here," Dora said. She pointed to one of the X's. "It is a church. From the steeple, you will have a lovely view of the plaza. A ringside seat for the ceremony."

Marzano grinned. "A church," he said. "A goddamn steeple. I like it. Yeah."

"The church is on the southwest corner of the plaza. From the steeple to the platform it is a distance of 100 yards."

"Beautiful," Marzano said.

"Pablo will have you there before dawn," Dora said. "You will not be bothered up there. Fidel's soldiers will not check the buildings in Riaz ahead of time. They have no reason to suspect anything." She paused.

"Now, you say you know about how you will escape afterwards."

"All accept where the floor is," Marzano said. "Where I'll hide out."

"*Si*," Dora said. "It is in the steeple, at the foot of the ladder that takes you to the top. The floor is raised there, with two steps leading up to it. The steps have been rebuilt to swing out from the floor in one section."

"Okay," Marzano said. "I think I got it all now. Let me take it from there. I hit Fidel. Three shots, to be sure. I pick up the shell casings and climb down the ladder. I pull out the steps and crawl under the floor." "The steps lock from the inside," Dora said.

"Okay. I lock them and lay there. Waiting for Castro's soldiers."

"*Si*. They won't come fast. There are buildings on all four corners of the plaza." Dora pointed to the map. "But even if they should come to the church first, you will have time. It should take you no more than ten seconds to get under the floor."

"Yeah," Marzano said. "Okay. When they come, they search the church, including the steeple. But they find nothing. They take off. They look around all day, maybe longer. But I wait. No problem. I've got food and water behind those steps, all the comforts of home. After a while, Fidel's boys give it up in Riaz. They figure the assassin is long gone. They pull out. Then, at night, my boy Pablo returns. He parks his car out front. He comes inside the church to say a prayer. For Castro's soul maybe." Marzano laughed. "If the church is empty, he comes up to the steeple and raps on the Floor. I come out, and down we go to the car." Looking at Dora, Marzano said, "How am I doing?"

"Good, Vinnie. Except Pablo will drive the car around *behind* the church before coming up for you. You will go out the back together instead of the front."

"Yeah, yeah," Marzano said. "Anyway, I get in— in the goddamn trunk—and he drives me back to that beach where we landed tonight. We go out in his rowboat, and Jose is waiting there with his fishing boat. And then, it's back to Florida and New York. Home, baby."

"*Si*," Dora said. "That is it. Any questions, Vinnie?"

"No."

"Any doubts?"

Marzano looked at the girl. "Doubts? Not about myself, baby. A lot depends on Pablo. Cogan tells me he's a good man."

"He is. The best."

"He's got a thing going with that car of his. Right?"

"*Si*. He's a state sugar cane inspector," Dora said. "He visits plantations and mills to check quality control. So no one looks at him or his car twice. And Riaz, like Christobal, is sugar cane country."

"Okay," Marzano said.

"Pablo will not let you down," Dora said. She was drinking her rum now, and smiled at him over the glass. "Has anyone let you down yet, Vinnie?"

Marzano sipped his rum, looked at Dora, and said, "Not you, Louisa. That's for goddamn sure."

She held her glass up. "To tomorrow then," she said. "To your success. To the death of Fidel. To the freedom of the Cuban people."

"I'll drink to that," Marzano said. They drank together. Then Marzano swept Dora into his arms again and said, "And now, Louisa, you can thank me again—for *all* the Cuban people this time."

"Your hour is nearly up..."

"I can read maps," Marzano said. "I have time. We'll use another hour of it. Here. You and me, baby."

FINALLY, Marzano got up, dressed, and went down the stairs to the hall at the back of the building. He could still hear the music. He went out into the alley. The Ford was sitting there, and Pablo was leaning against a fender, nervously smoking a cigarette.

"*Senor*," he said. "You are late."

Marzano shrugged. "Louisa, she's some hunk. You know?"

Pablo didn't seem to know. "Please get in the trunk, *senor*," he said. "Quickly."

"The trunk," Marzano said. He hated it. He climbed in, but he hated it. Pablo sealed him in again, ran to the front of the car, and started the motor. In the trunk, Marzano curled up in a ball. To keep his anger down, he thought of Louisa.

And Louisa—Dora—was busy upstairs now. When she heard the car start up in the alley below, she slipped from the bed. She dressed hurriedly. Then she dropped to her knees, reached under the bed, and slid out the battery-operated tape recorder that was hidden there. It was recording. She turned it off, stood, and carried it across the room. From a closet, she removed a carrying case and put the recorder into it. A tiny revolver was in one pocket. Then she returned to the bed, folded the map and crammed it into the case with the recorder.

She snapped off the light, walked to the door and opened it. Locking it behind her, she eased out into the hall and down the stairs to the rear door. Peeking out, she saw that the alley was empty. She stepped out and hurried away from the building. It was 4:30 a.m.

HAVANA...Cogan knew the city well, like the back of his own hand. He'd been here before, many times, before Castro. Havana had been a fun city then, wide open, warm, pulsing. But not now. The change saddened Cogan, and he felt old, He was only 33, but he'd seen a lot. Too much. He pushed those thoughts from his mind. The trip down had been a whirlwind. The supersonic jet, the high-speed car from Homestead AFB to the Florida beach, Jorge's souped-up power boat that had daringly deposited him in the shadow of Havana. And now, the streets of that city, dark and empty, with Pepe's not far. Cogan hurried, while trying to appear not to. Cubans rarely hurried. And that was what he was now, Cuban. Pancake makeup, a drooping mustache, baggy tropical suit, a Panama hat. At a distance, Carl Page wouldn't have known him.

Pepe's was still going strong. Nearly 4:30 in the morning, and it rocked with sound. There was hope yet, Cogan thought, and shouldered his way through the front door. A dozen men lounged at the bar and around tables. Most were foreigners, North and South Americans, but there were a few Cubans. Girls were sprinkled here and there. The place was dark, the cigarette smoke thick. Cogan moved to the bar. A girl was standing there, a black Cuban, big breasted in a shimmery satin dress. "*Hola,*" he said.

"*Companero,*" she said. She sized Cogan up, then smiled. Under his makeup, he was a good-looking man.

Cogan waves a 10-peso noted in the girl's face. "Louisa been in tonight?" he asked in Spanish.

The girl's smile faded. "Louisa? What's wrong with me, lover? My name is Celia."

"Another time, Celia. Louisa and I had a date tonight."

Celia looked hurt. "Well, she has not been here tonight. Not at all."

"Where's her room? Cogan said. "Where she entertains."

"I can't tell you ..."

Cogan pushed the 10-peso note under Celia's nose. "This is yours, sweetheart, if you tell me."

Celia stared at the note, shrugged took it and stuffed it between her breasts. "Out that door," she said, nodding toward the rear of the bar. "Through the storage room. There is a hall and a stairway. Take the stairs to the second Floor, third door on the right."

"Good," Cogan said. He held another 10-peso note in front of Celia's face. "Now, if Louisa's not there... Where?"

"She lives at 19 Santa Clara," Celia said. She took the note and pushed it in with the other one. "But she also goes to a barbershop..."

"A barbershop?"

"*Si.*" Celia grinned. "But not to get her hair cut. She sleeps with the barber I think. Upstairs, above the shop."

"Where...?"

"Four blocks down. On Aguerra..."

"Right," Cogan said. "I know the place." He patted the two peso notes between Celia's breasts and smiled. "Next time, sweetheart, the money will be for you— not information."

"Soon, I hope," Celia said.

But Cogan was already by her, going through the doorway she had pointed out, to the storage room. No one was there nor in the hallway behind it. He saw the stairs, and ran up them to the second floor. On the way, he pulled his .38 from its belt holster. He ran on to the third door. He didn't bother to knock, just hurtled against it, leading with a shoulder. The door cracked, splintered, and gave way. Cogan went in diving, sprawling on his stomach, gun out and ready. His eyes and ears searched the darkness, waiting. When nothing moved, he groped for a switch and lighted the room. One quick look around confirmed it. The phony Louisa, whoever she was, wasn't there. He hadn't expected her to be, not at this hour. But she had been. Yes. He saw two glasses. He picked one up and sniffed the swallow of rum left in it. Yes, the girl had been there, and so had Marzano. Right on schedule. The question was, where were they now? Marzano could be in, or on his way to, any one of a thousand small Cuban towns. But Castro's girl...He had to find her, Cogan thought. If he didn't, there was no chance he'd catch up to Marzano.

Cogan left the room, ran downstairs, back through the bar, and outside. Castro's girl might be using Louisa's address, he thought. Maybe. But the barbershop was closer than 19 Santa Clara. And he didn't believe for a second that "the barber" was either a barber or had been a lover for Louisa. No, he had a strong feeling that the barber was another of Castro's agents. He was the reason Louisa's cover had been blown. He'd gotten on the CIA's payroll somehow, gained Louisa's confidence, and helped her set up the assassination. Then, yesterday, with everything set, he'd put the grab on Louisa. He'd brought in the other girl, and briefed her for her meet with Marzano. That had to be it, Cogan thought. Clever. Only, somehow, Lopez had been plugged in to the barber and picked up on the whole thing. If only he could go to Lopez, Cogan thought. He wondered if Lopez was still alive.

Cogan broke into a run. He took the four blocks with long, silent strides. Aguerra was a side street. When he came to it, he stopped and peered around the corner. Across the street, halfway down, he saw two things. One was a barber pole. The other was a girl. She was standing in darkness in the doorway of the shop behind the pole. But he saw her. She looked young, dark and pretty. And she was holding a case of some sort in one hand.

That's her, Cogan told himself. *Waiting for the barber…*

Cogan used the same approach he had with the door. He turned the corner and headed for the shop, sprinting. It was thirty yards away. He had a third of the distance behind him before the girl looked up and saw him. She just stared for a second. Then she dropped the case. Her freed hand plunged into her jacket pocket. Before she could bring it out again, Cogan had his .38 in his hand. Slowing, he aimed it at the girl. "Don't do it!" he yelled in Spanish.

But she did it. She pulled her hand from the pocket, with the gun, and Cogan shot her. He snapped off five rounds, not trusting the snub-nosed accuracy of the .38. The girl took two faltering steps forward to the sidewalk, then collapsed. The gun slipped from her hand, and she tumbled onto her face. Cogan ran on across the street to her. He leaned down, and saw that she was dead. Then he stepped over her and into the doorway. He picked up the case, looked at it, and recognized what was inside. Holstering his gun, he glanced up and down Aguerra. Still no barber in sight. No one. Carrying the case, Cogan recrossed the street, slipped around the corner and hurried back toward Pepe's. He was nearly there before he saw what he was looking for: A walkway between two buildings, dark, yet with some light from the street.

Cogan sidled into the walkway. Well back between the buildings, he hunkered down and pulled the tape recorder from the case. As he did, the map fell out. He played the tape and studied the map at the same time. Both were damn interesting and damn informative.

RIAZ, 8 a.m.—Marzano was in the church steeple. He'd been there several hours, and everything was fine. A ledge lined the inside of the steeple, around the bell, and he was able to sit or kneel there without being seen from the ground below. Not that there were many people around to see him. A few peasants were drifting in and out of the church, but that was about it. So far, the plaza was quiet. An old woman, a couple of kids, stray dogs—that was it. Marzano had a clear view of the platform that had been erected. He had fitted together the components of his rifle–wire-frame stock, magazine, barrel, scope–and had it ready to fire.

RIAZ, 11 a.m.—Cogan whipped the reins he was holding against the flanks of the two yoked oxen. Behind them, in the oxcart, he swore. It was hot inside his peasant garb and under his floppy straw hat, and he was running short on time. Oxen were not only the dumbest animals in the world, but the slowest. The town was just ahead now, however, and he could see the church steeple.

Cogan had had quite a morning. After listening to the tape, he had stuck It into a coat pocket and walked on to Pepe's. A taxi had been sitting there, its driver asleep at the wheel. Cogan had jerked him onto the sidewalk and knocked him unconscious just as he'd woken up. Then he'd stolen the taxi and driven it out of Havana, fast. An hour after sunup, he'd been a mile north of Riaz. He'd dumped the taxi there and approached the town on foot. Worried about his "city" clothes, he'd moved into the fields beside the road and walked there. It was *zafra*, the cane cutting season, and workers were hacking, bundling and piling cane into ox-driven carts. He had avoided the workers, but the carts had given him an idea: Maybe he could use one to get Marzano out of Riaz.

If he got to Marzano. Cogan had been concerned about that. Once the barber found the girl dead in Havana, whoever was running the show for the Cubans might decide to change their plans. They might figure the thing to do was grab Marzano early, while he was still around to grab. They wouldn't have the propaganda plum they'd hoped for, but at least they'd have one would-be Mafia assassin. But then, a half mile north of Riaz, Cogan had stumbled across something that had erased that concern.

He'd seen activity around a large stone house by the road. Army trucks out front, soldiers and militiamen in fatigues milling about. Curious, Cogan had crept through the fields to the rear and side of the house. He'd run out of cover and stretched out thirty yards from the house. He'd tried, but had been unable to see what—if anything—was happening inside. He'd lain there, watching for a few minutes. Then, just as he'd decided to move on, there'd been an explosion of laughter, and half a dozen uniformed men had come out of the front door. They'd strolled about aimlessly, talking and smoking, and Cogan had noticed that one of them was the center of attention. The others would stop frequently, step back, stare at him, pointing, commenting and nodding with approval. Cogan had looked closer and seen why.

The object of all their attention had been—Fidel Castro.

Impossible.

Just as Cogan had been convincing himself that it was possible, "Fidel Castro" had put his hands to his face and removed his beard.

An uproar of laughter from the others. It wasn't Castro. It was a double. A lookalike. The beard, the fatigues, the soft Army cap. The double and the others had gone back into the house then, and Cogan had quickly put it together. They *weren't* going to change their plans. It was just that their plans had never included allowing Fidel to take a chance at getting his head blown off. No, he—the real Castro—and his retinue would come down from Havana, but stop at this point. The double would take Castro's place, and he and the soldiers would proceed into Riaz. He would take part in the ceremony there, and the soldiers would close in on the church steeple. They'd play it out right down to the wire. When the double stepped forward to make his remarks, and Marzano got ready to fire, the soldiers would spring the trap. Into the steeple, and all over the Mafia hitman. With TV cameramen and reporters on their heels. The double might get blown up, but the Cubans would have their propaganda plum, gun in hand. Castro, having been routed around Riaz and on south to Christobal, would get the good word there. Marzano might even be hauled down there and put on display with him.

What a goddamn coup!

Cogan had crawled away from the house, moved back into the fields, and made his way on to Riaz. One thing, he'd thought: He had more time to play with now. Riaz had been only half awake. Staying off the plaza itself, Cogan had seen the platform and the church. Peasants—peasants who hadn't looked like peasants to Cogan—had been coming and going around the church. He had a knack for recognizing his own kind. And these clowns—whether military intelligence or secret police—had been real amateurs. Marzano was up there in the steeple, and they'd obviously been keeping an eye on him. Stumblebums, but they would still have to be dealt with.

COGAN HAD walked out of Riaz and into the cane fields again. He'd had to look for a while, but finally, about a mile from the town, he'd come across a solitary peasant. The Cuban had been at work, loading cut stalks of sugar cane onto an oxcart, then binding them with two lengths of rope. Cogan had followed him as he'd driven the cart to a railroad spur a half mile further from the town. He'd watched there while a crane had lifted the load of cane from the cart to a railroad coal car. Then Cogan had followed the peasant back to the field for another load of cane. The cart idea had occurred to Cogan before. But now he'd developed it into a full-fledged escape plan for Marzano and himself.

That rail spur, he'd known, would join a track that would lead to a sugar mill. From the mill, other tracks would go to the docks in Havana. And beyond Havana lay the Straits of Florida.

Cogan had waited until the peasant had restacked his cart. Then, creeping out from where he'd been watching in the uncut cane, he moved in behind the peasant and knocked him out with a single slash to the back of the neck. Quickly, he'd dragged the Cuban into the cane and changed clothes with him. He'd stuffed the reel of tape under the waistband of the peasant's sun-bleached pants and put his revolver in a pocket of the loose-fitting shirt. Then, his face hidden below the wide-brimmed straw hat, he had returned to the cart. Using the peasant's knife, Cogan had pulled some of the cane from the cart and hacked the middles out of the stalks. Then he'd shoved the ends into the front and back of the pile, leaving a pocket in the center.

Be a Detective
Make Secret Investigations

Earn Big Money. Work home or travel. Fascinating work. Experience Unnecessary. **DETECTIVE** Particulars FREE. Write to **GEO.** F.R. **WAGNER,** 125 W. 86th St., N.Y.

MANY PEOPLE REPORT TO
BE TALLER

Yes, many short people have written to us that they had INCREASED their HEIGHT satisfactorily as a result of using our unique body routine methods. No Pills, drugs or mechanical apparatus required.

If you are short and have ever had a desire to BE TALLER, let us help you try to achieve INCREASED HEIGHT.

Send for FREE trial lessons which actually get you started in your attempts to BE-COMING TALLER.

You will also receive complete details and excerpts from testimonials written by satisfied customers. Please enclose 25c to cover cost of postage and handling.

THE NU-HITE SYSTEM, Dept. 42
Box 10, East New York Sta.   Brooklyn 7, N. Y.

DOMINATING WOMEN PHOTOS AND STORIES
NOW AVAILABLE

These adult items are a must for collectors. Send just 15 cents for latest profusely illustrated captivating bulletin that is bound to please or mail 50 cents for five different bulletins on a satisfaction guaranteed or money back basis. Send orders to:

NUTRIX CO., 35 MONTGOMERY ST.
Dept. DM', Jersey City 2, N. J.

A pocket to be filled by Vincent "Vinnie the Fist" Marzano. Cogan had tied up the cane then and crawled up on the cart behind the oxen. After some false starts, he'd gotten them turned around, and headed for Riaz.

But all that had taken time—a great deal of time.

And now, with Riaz in sight, Cogan hoped he would have enough of it. He spurred the oxen on. They entered the town and he took the cart down a dusty side street, moving in behind the church. Beyond it, in the plaza, he could see banners, fluttering in the bright sunshine. Pictures of Castro were tacked up everywhere. A small crowd was gathering, and the atmosphere was festive. More peasants were on the street leading to the church, some in carts like Cogan's, but none of them paid any attention to him. He kept his head down, his hat low over his eyes.

At 11: 15, Cogan had his cart opposite the church's rear door. A single peasant was standing there. Arms folded, he leaned against the church's adobe wall. Cogan prodded the oxen on to the side of the church. There, he halted the team and jumped down. He walked around to the front of the church. Two more of Castro's agents were lounging there, flanking the front door. Cogan nodded and walked between them into the church, hat in hand. They glanced at him, but that was all. The church was empty. Cogan knelt, crossed himself, then walked down the aisle to the altar. He skirted it, moving to the rear door. He opened it and peered out. The "peasant" was still standing there. He looked over, and Cogan hooked a finger at him. "*Companero*," he said. "Come here. Quick." Then Cogan stepped back and pressed himself to the wall at one side of the door. The "peasant" came through, head and shoulders first, and Cogan gave him the same shot to the neck that he had the peasant in the field. The Cuban hit the floor with a thud, and Cogan hauled him into a small room. Patting him down, Cogan found an automatic pistol. He stuck it under his shirt and returned to the main part of the church. It was 11:20, and the pews were still empty. The faithful were outside, waiting for Fidel.

Cogan hurried up the aisle to the stairs that led to the second floor. He took them two at a time and crossed the front of the church to the steeple. It was walled off, and there was a door. Cogan stopped there momentarily. With his disguise, he was afraid Marzano wouldn't know him. He'd stick his head inside, and the Mafia hitman would blow it off. Cogan didn't have time to debate his approach. He opened the door, kept his head back, and yelled, "Marzano! Canefire! It's Cogan!"

No reply. The bastard was up there, wasn't he?

CAUTIOUSLY, Cogan leaned in. He saw ropes hanging, a wooden ladder, light streaming down from above. He looked up and saw the muzzle of a rifle looking back at him. Above it was Marzano, kneeling beside the bell, his face hard, body tense. He looked confused.

"Don't shoot that damn thing," Cogan said. "It's me, Cogan."

Marzano just stared, disbelief in his eyes.

"Take a close look," Cogan said. "Listen to my voice. It's Cogan."

Marzano's disbelief began to fade. But he kept his rifle aimed at Cogan. "What the hell are you doing here?" he said.

"Operation Canefire's off," Cogan said. He started up the ladder.

"Easy," Marzano said.

"It's me, damn it," Cogan said. "You want me to recite details about how I came up to Jersey to recruit you? The restaurant on the Garden State Parkway? What we ate?"

"Okay, okay," Marzano said. He was still watching Cogan closely, but he was sure now. He swung the rifle aside.

Cogan scurried on up the ladder and crouched next to Marzano on the ledge. "Whattaya mean, Canefire's off'?" Marzano said.

"I don't have time to explain it all now," Cogan said. He pulled the reel of tape from under his shirt and held it up in front of Marzano. "The Cubans are on to us. Louisa—who you had such a good time with last night—wasn't Louisa. She was an agent for Castro. She recorded everything you said. It's all here, enough to fry you. But that's not all. Some more of Castro's boys are downstairs right now. And when he gets here, his soldiers are going to join them. You're set up here, Marzano. They know all about you."

"I don't... "

"Believe me, Marzano. Why else would I be here?"

"Yeah," Marzano said. "All right. But how... ?"

"Never mind that now. The thing now is to get out of here."

Marzano pushed up and looked out over the steeple railing. "Now?" he said. "Look, they're coming. Another five minutes, Cogan, and I'll have Castro on ice."

"And then we can shoot our way out, huh?" Cogan said. He peered out too. It was so. North of town, the party was coming. Two trucks, a carload of press people, and a jeep.

"Sorry, Marzano, but that isn't Castro."

"Whattaya mean?"

"It's a double. They're not taking any chances, friend."

Marzano stared at Cogan. "Shit," he said.

"My sentiments exactly. Now let's get out of here."

Marzano was still peeking out, longingly, looking reluctant. Cogan had to grab his arm and shake him. "Come on, goddamn it. Another minute, and we'll have soldiers all over the place. Take that weapon apart and let's shag ass."

"I might need this," Marzano said.

Cogan pulled out the automatic and handed it to him. "Use this if you have to. But keep it out of sight."

Marzano got with it. He quickly disassembled the rifle and stuck the parts into his coat. Cogan climbed down the ladder. Marzano followed him, and they left the steeple, crossed the second floor and went down the steps. The church was still empty. Cogan led Marzano through it to the rear door. There, they stopped. Marzano said, "You mind tellin' me...?"

"I've got an oxcart outside," Cogan said.

"A what?"

"You heard me. They're as common as cars are in the U.S. There's a load of cane in it. With space for you to crawl in. I'm going to bring the thing around to the door here and pull off some cane. When I signal you, you come out and get in."

"Goddamn," Marzano said. "And then what?"

"I'll let you know when the time comes," Cogan said. He moved to the door and looked out. The street was quiet now, just one or two stragglers hurrying to the plaza. Cogan stepped outside, walked to the side of the church, and crawled up behind the oxen. He turned them around and guided them to the rear of the church, swinging the cart about so that it was away from the street. Then he jumped down, strolled to the back of the cart, loosened the rope there, and pulled off the shortened stalks. With one arm, he kept the man-sized hole he created from collapsing. He nodded toward the door, and Marzano came out doubled up and burrowed into the cart. Cogan stuffed the stalks in behind him. He was prepared to make a show of readjusting the ropes, but it wasn't necessary. No one was on the street to see him now. So he merely tightened the one at the back of the cart, returned to his seat behind the oxen, and whipped them away from the church onto the street. Heading out of the town, he had to fight an impulse to look back. They were there now, in the plaza, the phony Castro and his party. He could hear the cheering. He could imagine the soldiers drifting toward the church, looking up the street, seeing the cane-laden cart going, when it should have been coming. He waited for their shouts. Or shots. But he heard neither. Slowly, painfully so, Cogan took the cart on out of Riaz. When he was into the fields again, he allowed himself a look back. It was 11:30 now, past 11:30. They had to be wondering back there, he thought. They just had to be.

BUT NOTHING happened on the way to the rail spur. The loading there went smoothly too. The stack of cane—with Marzano inside—was lifted into a coal car. Cogan helped, then watched, afraid that the extra weight would cause the cane to slip from the ropes. Or make the ropes snap. But the bundle went aboard intact. Cogan pulled his empty cart away from the crane and hid it as well as possible in a field of cane nearby. He walked back to the spur then. The coal car Marzano was in was the third one in a line of four. The first one was coupled to a locomotive, an old coal burner. The engineer was in the cab, dozing. Cogan circled the locomotive, strolled along the train until he came to the last car, saw that it was fully loaded, and climbed in. He crawled to Marzano's stack of cane, made sure air was getting in, then found a hiding place and waited. He knew they would sit there until more cane farmers came with more carts. And that would probably be after the ceremony had ended in Riaz. The soldiers might come too, Cogan thought. But they didn't. An hour later, all four coal cars were loaded. The train began to roll. Snugged down in the cane, Cogan relaxed a little. But only a little. The main track lay ahead, and then the mill. The cane would be unloaded there, and any goddamn thing could happen

Cogan started to sweat it.

As it turned out, he had reason to. The sugar mill was north of Riaz, about halfway to Havana. In the rail yard behind the mill, Cogan's luck began to trickle away. When the train squealed to a stop, he looked out and saw—in addition to another crane operator and a helper—two Cuban militiamen. They were

standing by the locomotive and had rifles slung over their shoulders. They appeared to be just hanging around, though. They waved to the engineer, and when he climbed down they lit cigarettes and talked together. The militiamen paid no particular attention to the train. Cogan stayed where he was until the crane began transferring cane from the coal cars to a line of flatcars. They sat on an adjacent track, on the side opposite from the militiamen. But the crane rode on an overhead rail, between the two tracks, and from the cab, the operator had a good view. So Cogan could only get himself out—and was taking a chance doing that. While the crane operator and his helper were busy with the front coal car, Cogan slipped over the side of his car. He crawled under the closest flatcar and lay there while the unloading continued. He kept hoping that the militiamen would leave, but they didn't. Then he decided it would be best if they stayed put. Once Marzano was on a flatcar, and it started on its way to the mill, he would climb up and get the Mafia hit man out. They would jump down, search for another train bound for the Havana docks with processed sugar, and hop on. They would be on their way again then, on the last leg to escape.

But it didn't go that way.

The crane came to the third coal car. Two stacks of cane were lifted off, and then it was time for Marzano's. The helper fastened hooks to the two ropes. The crane lifted, swinging the stack out between the coal car and the flatcar Cogan was under. And then what he'd feared would happen at Riaz happened here. The weight was too much for the ropes. The cane sagged out of one of them, then dropped from the other and spilled on to the ground. Marzano tumbled out too. The helper saw him, and so did the crane operator. He yelled to the two militiamen, who unslung their rifles and started around the front of the locomotive. Marzano sat up and whipped out the automatic Cogan had given him. He aimed it at the helper, who was still standing atop the coal car, and shot him three times. The helper dropped into the cane, a dead man. Then Marzano scrambled under the flatcar in front of Cogan. "Militiamen!" Cogan said to him, and gestured toward the front of the other line of cars. "Take the first one!" He had his .38 out.

As the two militiamen cleared the locomotive and started down between the tracks, Marzano emptied the automatic at the one in the lead. The militiaman dropped to one knee and shouldered his rifle. He got off one shot before Cogan began firing the .38. Cogan's first round missed, but the next two hit the militiaman, one in his neck. He coughed up blood, but worked the bolt action on his rifle and winged another shot toward the flatcar. This one pinged off a wheel near Marzano, and he yelled, "Get the sonofabitch!" Gripping his right hand with his left, Cogan squeezed off the last three rounds in the .38. All three slammed into the militiaman's chest, and he toppled forward on his face.

Cogan tapped Marzano on the back and said, "Okay. Let's go."

"Not yet," Marzano said. He rolled over and jabbed a finger upward, toward the crane operator. "We gotta get that one too."

"Forget it," Cogan said. "That cab he's in is made of solid steel. It'll protect him."

"Maybe," Marzano said. "Maybe not. You got more rounds for your piece?"

"Yeah."

"Well, load it and let's find out." "The only way we'll know for sure is if one of us goes up there."

"I'll go, if you won't," Marzano said.

"No, you won't," Cogan said. "That'll eat up time, and time's all we got going for us."

"But he'll see where we go."

"If I'm right, not for long," Cogan said. "Now come on, goddamn it!"

Cogan crawled out from under the far side of the car, Marzano after him. They ran across several tracks, then around more train loads of cane. At the edge of the yard, tracks wound around the side of the mill. Yeah, Cogan thought, he'd figured that. The outgoing trains would be in front of the mill. Using a row of empty boxcars for cover, Cogan led Marzano to the side of the mill. There, they could no longer see the crane—or be seen from it. They kept going. In front of the mill, was another rail yard. More boxcars were lined up, some being filled with bags of processed sugar. Cogan looked for a moving train and saw one. It was at the far end of the yard, rolling slowly, but gathering speed.

"There!" Cogan yelled, and pointed.

Behind him, Marzano was already winded. "Jesus," he puffed.

"Come on!"

It was a long, hard run. Two hundred yards, and then some. The train nearly eluded them, going faster and faster. Cogan sprinted, losing his straw hat. Marzano fell further and further back. Finally, Cogan reached the last boxcar—there was no caboose—and pulled even with it. Still running, he managed to slide its door open. Sugar was piled high inside, but there was room. He grabbed hold and swung himself up and in. Then, on his knees, he looked back at Marzano. The Mafia hit man was faltering. Take away his artillery, and he was nothing. In lousy shape. "Come on, you horse's ass!" Cogan shouted. "You want to be on TV with Castro? You want to rot in one of his jails? You want to die here? Run, Marzano, run!"

Marzano made a final effort. The surge brought him up to the boxcar door. Eyes desperate, he stretched an arm out. Leaning from the car, Cogan reached, grabbed, linked hands, and hauled Marzano aboard. He slid the door shut, and then both men Flopped down on their backs, sucking in air.

"Your ass is safe now, Marzano," Cogan said.

"For...how...long?" Marzano gasped. "They'll ... stop ... all ... the ... trains ... They'll ... stop ... this ... one ... and … search ... it ..."

"We'll get off first," Cogan said.

AND THAT was exactly what they did. The Army caught up with the train five miles short of Havana. And while it was slowing around the city and a half mile east of it to a deserted beach. They were where Cogan had been brought to shore the night before by Jorge and his power boat. There, under a line of palm trees, they sat down. Jorge had agreed to return at midnight.

"Looks like we're gonna make it," Marzano said. "Huh?"

"Yeah," Cogan said. "Unless my man gets caught. They do patrol these waters."

"He'll make it," Marzano said. "He's got to. I got things to do back in the States."

"I'll bet."

"I do, man. Contracts." Marzano grinned. "And broads. How about you, Cogan?"

Cogan thought of Inez. "Yeah, me too."

"This was a mistake," Marzano said. "Coming down here. From now on, I work only for The Organization. Not the goddamn government. The Organization wouldn't have screwed up this thing the way you guys did, Cogan. I'll tell you that." He paused, then cocked his head thoughtfully. "Still, you know, it might not be a total loss. I mean, I'll have something to tell my grandkids, you know? About how I almost hit Fidel Castro. Had him in my goddamn sights, damn near. Yeah. Or... Well, can you imagine what the press would do with my story? A bigassed city paper like the *Times* maybe. The CIA in bed with the Mafia, plotting murder. Man, that would sell copies, wouldn't it? Marzano laughed. "Yeah. Hell, I might even do me a book about all this some day."

Cogan stared at Marzano. "You wouldn't," he said. "You agreed to keep your yap shut, Marzano. Remember?"

Marzano stared back. "Hey, CIA man," he said. "That was before you government guys screwed up. You violated the contract, man. It's null and void."

"The CIA didn't really mess this up, " Cogan said. "It's just one of those things."

"Yeah," Marzano said. "Well, the way I see it, I'm out 125 grand. And I'm gonna see to it that I make that up. That's one of them things too, Cogan."

Cogan was silent for a moment. Then he said, "Don't be stupid, Marzano."

"Stupid?"

"You've devoted your life to killing people. Well, I've devoted mine to my country. To looking out for its interests. I love America, Marzano. I love the CIA too."

"So...?"

"So." Cogan said. He reached behind his back. Under his shirt, taped to his spine, was a strip of .38 slugs. He removed one, pulled out his revolver, and thumbed it into the cylinder.

"What're you doing?" Marzano said.

"Hey..." Marzano raised his hands. "Look, Cogan.

Easy. All that about the press. Writing a book. Hey, that was just talk. I can keep my mouth shut. I know how to do that. Believe me..."

"I can't take the chance, Marzano."

Marzano started to get up. Fear widened his eyes. He wagged his hands. Please, Cogan. I'll do it. Not a word. I promise. I swear. Hey, in my work, secrecy's what it's all about. Huh... ?"

"In my work too," Cogan said. Then he pulled the trigger of the .38. The nearby surf muffled the sound of the exploding bullet. But it made a big roar in Vincent "Vinnie the Fist" Marzano's head, as it turned his brain into pulp. When Jorge and his power boat arrived on schedule, John Cogan took Marzano's body out to sea and dumped it.

AUTHOR'S NOTE: John Cogan told his story from his home in a small Georgia town. He lives there alone, "in retirement," as he puts it. But he chuckles dryly when he tells you that. He admits to being troubled. "Once I thought I'd take this story to the grave with me," he says. "I killed a man to keep it secret. But now it's all coming out, or will soon. So I guess I want it to come out correctly." He smokes and sips on a drink, and seems to think about that. "On the other hand, maybe it doesn't matter anymore. It all seemed so important then, what we were trying to do. But now..." He shakes his head. "The world's changed. I have to wonder, if we'd succeeded, would it have made any difference. I don't know..." Then Cogan laughs. "Hell," he says, "some people won't believe this anyway. The Agency will deny it." He stares into space. "Sometimes, I wonder myself if it really happened."

●●●

Quit Dreaming, and Get on the Beam!

People who get things done are people who get out and do things
Better step on it—the sands of life are running through the hands of time.

BE LONELY NO MORE! OPEN DESTINY'S DOOR!

$2.00 brings CUPID'S DESTINY, World's Greatest Social Publication, including coast-to-coast and international listings with names and addresses, men or women. Captivating descriptions; sparkling pictures; widows, widowers, bachelors, beautiful girls desiring early marriage. Includes also the addresses of correspondence clubs in U.S.A., Canada, and other countries. (Year, quarterly, $5.00).

There is always a chance that in the current issue you may find the one you've been looking for — the very person who has been looking for someone just like you. It is within the realm of possibility that while you are answering this ad your future wife or husband may be answering the same ad. Such speculation shouldn't overtax your imagination.

DESTINY LEAGUE
P. O. Box 5637, Reno, Nevada

DESTINY LEAGUE K
P. O. Box 5637, Reno, Nevada

No need to write a letter. For **quick action**, simply fill in name and address and mail with $2.00 for latest issue (or $5.00 for full year subscription).

Name _____

Address _____

City _____ State _____

STORIES & ART FROM VINTAGE MEN'S ADVENTURE MAGAZINES

MAQ
MEN'S ADVENTURE QUARTERLY

"I've run out of superlatives to describe just how good MEN'S ADVENTURE QUARTERLY is. I give this issue and all the previous ones my highest recommendation."
– James Reasoner,
Award-winning novelist & founder of Rough Edges Press

"I was caught off-guard by the absolutely stunning quality of the magazine—from it's striking visual layout, to its informative editorial content, to the stories themselves. This is top notch specialty publishing at its finest."
– Paul Bishop,
Writer, pulp maven and host of the Sixgun Justice Podcast

"Bravo gentlemen, you're on a streak to the benefit of all pulp tans, old and new. Thank you so very, very much."
– Ron Fortier,
Legendary comics writer, novelist, and founder of Airship 27 books

READ, HOT, AND DANGEROUS!

PULP 2.0

AVAILABLE ON AMAZON WORLDWIDE AND FROM THE MENSPULPMAGS.COM BOOKSTORE

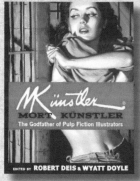   

   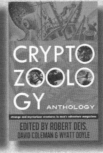 

THE MEN'S ADVENTURE LIBRARY

TEN YEARS OF TWO-FISTED ADVENTURE.

MensPulpMags.com # new texture